CRAZY APOLOGETIC CANADIANS

CATHRYN FOX

COPYRIGHT

Discover other titles by Cathryn Fox at www.cathrynfox.com. Please sign up for Cathryn's Newsletter for freebies, ebooks, news and contests: https://app.mailerlite.com/webforms/landing/c1f8n1
ISBN: 978-1-989374-78-8
ISBN Print: 978-1-989374-77-1

CANADIAN TERMINOLOGY.

Beaver: Sovereign animal and also a term for lady parts.

Yeah, no: No.

Yeah, no, for sure: Yes.

Yeah, no, for sure we're not doing that: Not doing that.

Oh, yeah, no for sure you do: Yes, you do.

Zamboni: Vehicle that smooth and cleans ice in a rink.

Scooch. Squeeze by you an inch.

Sorry: Sorry.

Toonie: Two-dollar coin.

Loony: One-dollar coin.

Canadian Bacon: Back bacon. (In Canada, we just call it bacon.)

Beaver Tail: Delicious pastry.

Eh?: Express solidarity, reassurance, or confirmation.

Oot and aboot: Out and about.

Tim Horton's: Our fast food donuts and coffee.

Toque: Wool knit cap.

Out for a rip: Going for a drive, snowmobile or any excursion.

COLIN

C anada.

Poutine and politeness. Back bacon and beavers. Loonies and toonies.

Bloody hell, a toonie is a two-dollar coin, and they can't even spell it properly? It should be *two*nie, not toonie. Don't even get me started on the country's obsession with hockey. The only game worth playing is football. Every good Brit knows that.

But you're not in Britain anymore, are you, Colin?

A laugh—more like a groan—crawls out of my throat as I glance around the airport, at the crowd of people walking around in slow-motion. Who leisurely strolls through an airport? Canadians, that's who. Don't they have a plane to catch? Somewhere to be?

As I maneuver around them, it suddenly occurs to me I'm the brainless muppet amongst this relaxed lot—the loony twoonie—no matter how one chooses to spell it. I'm definitely out of my mind, considering I agreed to fly across the pond, leaving my castle behind—sure, it's big and damp, but it's the only home I've ever known—to spend a few days in rural Nova Scotia, aka the armpit of the western world.

I hurry down the terminal, my thoughts distracted, and collide with some woman speed-walking past me. She drops whatever it is she had in her arms, and latches onto the sleeve of my suit jacket. The grasp pulls me off balance, and I stagger backward, breaking the tight hold. I dip my head and find a petite woman staring up at me, her blue eyes wide as she holds her hands up palms out.

"Sorry," she says quickly.

Wait, wasn't I the one who bumped into her? "What are you sorry for?"

She angles her head, her gaze moving over my face. "You're British."

I frown. "You're sorry I'm British?"

"No, no!" Her long dark hair bounces on her shoulders as she repeatedly shakes her head. "For colliding with you, and... tugging on your jacket. It was a knee jerk reaction."

"Touching strangers in airports is a knee jerk reaction for you, is it now?" I glance out the rotating doors leading outside and take in the streaks of purple and pink bruising the night sky above the large concrete parking garage. "Do you only grope in airports, or can I expect to be accosted once I step outside, as well?"

She frowns at me, and I get it. I'm grumpy as hell. It's been a long day, and I missed my connecting flight, and now I've arrived at my destination much later than planned. My driver would have given up on me hours ago. Rightfully so. No one in their right mind would continue to wait for a no-show. I'm not about to call Bryant now, the guy who owns the bed and breakfast where I'll be staying, and have him come back to the city at this point. From what I understand, it's a good three-hour drive.

"I thought you were going to fall. Sorry I touched you," she apologizes again as she picks up a sign she'd dropped and scampers off. Alrighty then. Her legs aren't overly long, but she moves like lightning, the only person in the airport in any kind of hurry. She must not be a local, and I should probably tear my gaze from her cute arse, which happens to be nicely framed into a pair of frayed shorts, and put her out of my mind.

I straighten my shoulders, in need of a pint before I figure how and where I'm going to find another driver at this hour. I walk through the airport terminal looking for a pub, but a small store with gobs of Halifax, Nova Scotia merchandise catches my eye and reminds me I'm supposed to bring something back for my cousin's daughter. Might as well get it over with, because the sooner I'm out of this place, the better.

I drag my suitcase along and adjust my leather bag over my shoulder as I step into Hudson News. With no idea what to buy an eight-year-old girl, I walk up to a rack full of plush toys. As I debate between a beaver and a moose, someone crouches down in front of me, her body brushing mine, right around the vicinity of my...dangly bits.

"Can I just scooch..."

I glance down, and realize it's the groper again as she bends and reaches for something off the bottom shelf.

"'Scooch?'"

She straightens, a plush lamb in her hand, and her smile falters when her gaze lands on me. "Oh, you again."

"Nice to see you, too," I respond.

One manicured brow lifts, as the strap on her tank top slips a bit, exposing a hint of a lacy bra. "Is it?"

"Is it what?" I ask as I snatch up a beaver.

"Nice to see me again?"

Okay, I get it, she's being cheeky. "How could it not be? It's been what...all of five minutes." I step around her, my body between hers and the checkout. "If you could just scooch," I say using her slang. "I'd like to pay for my beaver."

She makes a sound, and I turn back to catch a grin flirting with the corners of her mouth. While I'm trying to be less grumpy, considering she's the one who apologized when I bumped into her, I get the sense that whatever it was I said, she's finding a different kind of humor in it. "Something funny?"

She steps back and waves her hand. "Nope. You go right ahead of me. I would never stand in the way of a man trying to pay for his beaver."

I clutch the toy in my hand as I stand over her and glower. Does she really think I play with beavers? "It's not for me."

She holds her hands up, palms out again. "No explanation needed, my friend." I eye her, and she nibbles her bottom lip. What is the matter with her and why is it killing her to keep a straight face? "What a man does with his beaver is none of my business." She frowns, taps her chin and scans the store. I follow her gaze until it lands back on me. "Got wood?" I angle my head, note the way her body is almost quaking. "Beavers like wood, you know."

The girl behind the counter lowers her head and snickers, and that's when I realize I'm the butt of some joke. I just don't know what it is. Here I thought Canadians were nice folk, but really, they're just a bunch of wankers. I won't make that mistake again.

I toss my beaver onto the counter. "It's not for me, and it's not a real beaver," I state. "It doesn't need wood."

"No, of course not." Another snicker before she pulls herself together. "Who's it for?"

Why has this conversation not ended already? Canadians talk too much. Or maybe it's just this girl who likes to blabber on. "If you must know, it's for my cousin's daughter."

"She's going to love it. My friend's daughter collects lambs. They moved to Toronto a while back." She frowns like she's missing them and then shakes the lamb in her hand. "What do you think we should call this one?"

"Lamb," I say and check my watch.

"Aren't you going to name your beaver?"

"No." I grab my luggage ready to leave, but turn back to her. "Does this place have a pub?"

"There's a lounge right over there," she answers in a piss poor British accent as she extends her arm to point down the long hallway. "You'll be able to find yourself a right and proper pint."

I stare at her and she grins at me. "Thanks, eh," I respond, using Canadian slang I heard on the plane, and hoping I'm using it in the right context, although from her grin, I'm guessing I'm not. I take a step toward the exit, but pause. "And I'm sorry for bumping into you earlier." Cripes, I've been in Canada for all of ten minutes and I've already started apologizing. Before I can stop myself, I ask, "What's your name?" I'm not sure why I suddenly have the urge to know. It's not like I'm going to broadcast this comedy of errors all over social media. That's my younger brother Nate's specialty.

"Violet. Yours?"

Violet, pretty and delicate, just like her. Although I'm not so sure she's all that delicate. I think in this case, looks can be deceiving.

"Colin."

"Colon? Like..." She cringes as she points her finger over her shoulder, and down toward her bum.

What is she getting on about? "Colin," I repeat.

"Oh, okay." She exchanges a look with the clerk, and they both stifle a laugh. Wait, does she think I'm saying colon, as in my bum parts? She's the one with the ridiculous accent, not me.

Before I can ask, she turns back to the clerk, and I let it go. I'm far too tired for this and if she thinks my name is Colon, then so be it. It's not like I'm ever going to see her again. I glance at my watch. She's right about one thing, though. I am going to need a right and proper pint before I try to make alternate arrangements.

I'd rent a car and drive myself to the middle of nowhere, but Canadians drive on the wrong side of the road—or rather the right side of the road—which is wrong. I think it's best to get a driver until I'm used to it. With my luck, I'd probably hit a daft beaver trying to cross the road. I'm pretty sure killing or maiming the country's sovereign rodent would send my arse straight to jail. Then again, they do eat beavers' tails. At least that's what the girl seated beside me on the flight over here told me. *You have to try one.* Sure, right after I climb the famous lighthouse at Peggy's Cove and hurl myself into the cold Atlantic. Yes, I've been doing my research on this intolerable province. Now I fully understand Mum's threat to send us to Nova Scotia to live when we misbehaved, although that was more my brother's specialty than mine.

I head down the long terminal and glance outside as the bruised sky fades to black. The great white north. What was I thinking? I shake my head. It's not like I had any choice in the matter. Nope. Grandfather tasked me with the job of coming here to secure land for an international boarding school he wants to build. We have perfectly good schools in the UK, built and owned by my grandfather's great grandfathers. Why he needs another one, or one here, is beyond me. Nevertheless, I couldn't very well say no. I'm one of the lawyers who oversees land deals and amendments, but the timing couldn't be worse.

Or maybe it is good timing. I might be missing the cricket match, but at least I won't have to put up with Mum trying to shove some debutante down my throat. I'll marry when the time is right—never—and with the right and proper girl of my choosing. She doesn't exist. Even if she did, I wouldn't know it. I'm not even sure what love is, or if I have it in me to fall for a woman. I'm pretty sure I don't. Don't get me wrong, I love my family, but that's different. I didn't—couldn't figure out how to—love the girl I thought I was going to marry a couple years ago, and when I heard her on the phone having a conversation about me, and our future...I ended things between us then and there.

I take a seat at the bar, and the first thing I do is order a pint. The second thing I do is shoot off a text to Bryant, to let him know I've arrived and ask if he knows of any drivers. He texts back quickly.

Bryant: *Are you at the airport?*

Me: *Just grabbing a right and proper pint.*

I laugh as I send the text. Violet's bad accent reverberates in my brain. Is that how she thinks we sound, and why the hell am I thinking about her anyway? The barman brings my drink and I sip the watered-down ale while I wait for Bryant to text back. Three dots appear and then disappear. Maybe he's pissed that he made the trek to the airport for nothing. The missed flight was out of my hand, but if he's a man like me, and doesn't like his time wasted, I can understand him being upset. I stare at my phone a little longer, and shrug when no message comes through. I'm about to ask the barman if he can help a guy out, when my phone pings.

Bryant: *I'm here.*

Me: *At the airport?*

Bryant: *Look up.*

I look up, and stare at the bottles of high-end alcohol behind the bar. My phone pings again, and I check it again.

Bryant: *Turn to your right.*

I do as he asks and when I spot Violet in the doorway, holding up a sign with Mr. Parker on it, I nearly fall off my stool.

You have got to be bloody joking!

2

VIOLET

Well, well, well. What are the odds that the grumpy Brit—who I've also dubbed as Mr. Brit with a stick up his bum—is the man I was supposed to pick up hours earlier.

"I thought you missed your connection," I say as he walks toward me, pulling along a designer suitcase that likely costs more than I make in a year. I hold my phone up and shake it, not that he can see his text from earlier, and not that I'm displaying it.

"It's you...you're Bryant?" he asks.

"Why didn't you tell me you caught another flight?"

As we stand there hogging the entranceway, he says, "I thought you were a man."

A group of women in purple hats head our way and I back up into the terminal, giving them a wide berth. Colin follows and I say, "I was planning to come back first thing tomorrow to get you."

"I don't even know why you're still here waiting." He stares at me, dumbfounded. "Why would you do that?"

"You really should have texted that you caught another flight."

We stare at each other, both having our own conversations with one another, and getting nowhere. He finally shakes his head, a deep line in his forehead, and I'm guessing the tumblers just aren't falling into place.

"You're Bryant?"

I snort. "You should at least try to hide your enthusiasm."

"I'm not—"

"I know. I know. You're shocked and not at all happy about any of this. It's easy to tell by that throbbing vein in your forehead."

"I do not have a..." He straightens to his full height and adjusts his dark leather bag over one shoulder, and it's right then that I notice how broad it is. Kidding. I noticed it the first time he bumped into me—and I groped him. "I'm surprised is all." Those salted caramel eyes of his narrow in on me. "Why are you still here?"

"Oh, I have a friend coming in from Toronto." I wiggle my fingers. "Two birds, one stone." He stares at me like I might have two heads instead of two birds. "You know, achieve two things at the same time."

"I know what it means. I'm not daft."

Okay, this conversation is getting us nowhere. I hold my hand out for a shake. "Nice to meet you, Colin Parker. I didn't realize it was you earlier. I only knew you as Mr. Parker. Violet Bryant, the groper, at your service."

His shoulders sag a bit, a new kind of weariness about him as his big hand closes over mine for a very efficient shake. "I think we might have gotten off on the wrong foot."

"The first two times sure, but the third time's the charm, right?" I give him a wink and check my watch. "Come on, my friend should be at the luggage carousel by now."

I reach for his bag to help him—he must be exhausted—but his big palm quickly closes over mine to stop me. Holy moly. Okay, it's been a long time since I've felt a man's touch, and there is no way my girly parts should be standing—fine, fine, jumping—to attention.

"I've got this," he says, his voice an octave deeper.

I pull my hand away, and in an effort to cover my body's ridiculous reaction, I joke, "Do you have the crown jewels in there or something? Smuggled them to Canada, eh?"

He stares at me, like I'm a puzzle he can't figure out, but I'm anything but complicated. I'm an open book, an easy read. I don't mean I'm easy, you know sexually, just...well... What the hell am I doing? Why am I thinking about sex with this guy, a man who is hell bent on shutting down our beloved seasonal theme park and putting up some pretentious boarding school for the elite.

Those privileged students won't fit into the easy going, laid-back town of Annapolis any more than Colin Parker will. I'm just worried his reception will be met with pitchforks and torches. Although we're no longer living in the nineteenth century, not since last week anyway, when we got our first Tim Horton's coffee shop—ten miles out of town. Oh well, beggars can't be choosers, and I did a lot of begging on the townsfolks behalf.

His head lifts, his body a little stiffer. Hard to believe, I know. Clearly offended by my crown jewels question—hey, I wasn't talking about *his* jewels—he runs his hand down his perfectly smooth tie and says, "No, I did not smuggle anything into Canada."

I grin. I'll have to remember that he takes everything literally. "I was just kidding. Can I help you with your shoulder bag then?"

"I've got everything."

Yeah, you do.

Whoa where did that thought come from and why did the voice in my brain sound like Joey from Friends?

"Suit yourself." I turn and speed walk toward the gates, and he kicks his legs out, easily keeping pace beside me. Everyone might be slow moving, but I have a few more steps to get in to make my daily goal. It's not an obsession, not like everyone back home thinks. Not really. Maybe a little.

I spot Emily snatching up her bag and call out to her. She hauls her suitcase from the belt and waves at me, and I don't miss the way her attention suddenly jerks to the man standing close. He really is hard to miss. From the corner of my eye, I let my gaze travel from the top of Colin's head right down to the tip of his leather shoes.

Tall. Check.

Dark hair. Check.

Chiseled jaw. Check.

Smoking hot. Check.

Mr. All Kinds of Wrong for Me. Check.

Not that I'm looking for Mr. Right. I'm not. I'm quite happy running my little bed and breakfast, and working at the park my grandfather envisioned, designed and helped build—the same park this man is about to tear down. But the park is run by the non-profit Hanson society now, and while I'm on the board, I have little to no say in what happens to the business. I do know it's been hemorrhaging money, and I invested my entire inheritance to keep it running. If I go any deeper in debt, I'll have to rent out my entire house and sleep in the corn stalks in my back yard.

Emily comes over and I take her bag from her shoulder and put it over mine. I'm about to hug her when Colin's fingers brush my bare shoulder and goddammit, I think I might have just climaxed a little. He takes the bag from me, and tosses it over his deliciously broad shoulder.

Deliciously broad shoulder?

Who are you, Violet Bryant?

"Oh my, what a gentleman," Emily says instantly going from zero, (not flirting) to sixty (flirty) in two seconds. I try not to snort. Should I remind her that she's married? Nah. If she wants to get her flirt on with Colin, who am I to stop her? It's not like I'm jealous or want to flirt with him myself. The guy probably doesn't even know the meaning of the word anyway.

"I was raised to be a gentleman," he says, and on the flirtation scale between one and sixty, his comes in...minus ten. I was right, he doesn't know the meaning of the word and the man is wound so tight, he probably squeaks when he has sex.

Stop thinking about sex already!

Emily's curious, yet slightly disappointed gaze, shifts to mine, and I jerk my thumb out. "Emily, this is Mr. Parker. As in Colin Parker, from the Waltonstound foundation."

"Oh," she says, her smile dissolving faster than that new vitamin supplement I'd swallowed at breakfast. I make a fist and pound my chest. I think it's still stuck.

"Nice to meet you, Emily."

"Be nice," I murmur under my breath. I'm just as upset as everyone else that this guy is here to tear up our town, but it's not his fault. I can't shoot the messenger. Ogle and admire him yes, shoot him, no.

"Nice to meet you too," she grumbles.

I switch subjects. "How was Toronto?"

As I guide her outside to the parking garage, she talks a mile a minute, telling us about her visit to her cousin Tanya's place after Tanya was rushed to the hospital. Apparently, Tanya was insistent that she was having an appendicitis attack, but it turned out she just had a bad case of gas. Too many cruciferous vegetables, a new diet she'd been on, according to Emily.

I steal a fast glance at Colin. His handsome face twists, like he's mortified that Emily is talking about one's bowels in public, and I bite back a laugh. We might move slowly in Nova Scotia, but we talk fast, openly, and non-stop. I guess this must all be a lot for him and for a moment I feel a hint of pity.

We reach my car, and Colin insists on loading the trunk, although he's calling it a boot, and it's so small I'm not sure it can be described as either. Emily switches topics, giving every detail of a delicious meal she had at some fancy downtown Toronto restaurant.

"You better take the front seat," Emily says to Colin as she pushes a piece of gum from a foil package and holds it out to us. We both shake our heads no.

"You can take the front. Sounds like you two have a lot of catching up to do, and I'd like to check my emails," he replies.

"Suit yourself." Emily flips the seat forward, and gestures for him to climb into the back. He puts one leg onto the floor of the back seat, pushes forward and grunts. I'm about to circle the car, but notice he's not moving, or grunting. I'm not even sure he's breathing. Great, I think we've killed him. We certainly have the motive. As I glance around, and contemplate on how to hide, or even move, the body, a loud groan reverberates through the near empty parking garage.

"Violet."

"Yeah."

"I'm...stuck."

I admire his perfect ass, wedged between the back seat and the frame of my car. "Um, do you want me to push?"

"I think maybe you should pull."

I take in the angle of his body and consider the logistics. "What do you want me to pull?" Emily chuckles beside me and I nudge her with my elbow. "Stop it."

"Ow," she complains.

I glare at her. "You're not helping."

She snaps her gum, enjoying this entirely too much. "What am I supposed to do?"

"I don't know. Go around the other side and push on his head."

"I thought that's what he wanted you to pull."

"Ohmigod!" She grins, clearly proud of her quick-witted sexual innuendo. "Do you want to walk home?"

The car rocks as he tries to free himself, and I pray to God he hasn't heard Emily, or think in any way that I want to pull his...anything.

Emily drops her gum back into her purse. "Fine."

She circles the car, and I step up to him. "I'm going to put my hands on your hips and pull, okay?"

"Yes, I believe that will work."

Pity once again hits me. The man is obviously embarrassed. The British are so stiff—do not think about head and stiff.

Dammit, I'm thinking about it.

Let me try that again. The British are stoic and reserved, and this must be mortifying. Then again, maybe he's none of those things. People have misconceptions about Canadians too. Yeah, okay, it's true. We're ridiculously nice and overly apologetic. Sue me.

As he struggles, I take a fast second and consider drawing this out, letting him wallow in his embarrassment. I mean he is here to destroy our town, but because I only have one mean bone in my body—you did just hear me say we were ridiculously nice right—and I might need to use it later, I put my hand on his sides, and brace my pelvis against his rear.

Oh my.

I glance over my shoulder and pray no one is watching. The last thing I want to be accused of is bum-fucking some Brit in the back of my car. I'm not looking to cause an international incident here. I suppose I could just tell them I'm trying to remove a stick that's lodged deep. That's more believable, anyway.

He mumbles something under his breath, and I'm certain it's gibberish about three times the charm, because yeah, this is the third time I've groped him and the first, or possibly the third, time I've enjoyed it.

I'm about to pull but stop. "You're not going to leave me a bad review, are you? Bad reviews are bad for business. I can't have that, Colin."

"Get me out of here and we'll call it even. Oh, shite, what are you doing?"

I loosen my grip on his hips. "I'm not doing anything?"

"Not you, Emily. Stop. You're going to compress my spine. Shite, that hurts. Ow, bugger off will you." He curses some more, his ass brushing up against my pelvis. I'm not sure whether to laugh or cry. Maybe I should get a selfie.

"I thought I was supposed to push on your head, and Violet was supposed to pull," Emily says.

"No, I didn't...Blasted, have you gone mad? None of this is helping. In fact, you're giving me a migraine."

Emily huffs. "You don't have to be so hard to get along with."

"I am not..." his voice falls off and he takes a deep breath. I love Emily, but sometimes we all have to take a moment around her. "Violet, can you pull?"

I dig my fingers into his hard, muscular sides, and with all my strength I yank on him, and after a few good pulls, I manage to dislodge him. We both tumble backwards, until I'm flat on my back and he's sitting in my lap.

He quickly jumps up, turns, and pulls me to my feet. Worry dances in his eyes as he gives me a once over. "Are you okay?"

"I'm fine. I'm tougher than I look." I brush my hands over my ass to clean the debris.

"Stronger too," he says, respect and appreciation in his voice.

My chin lifts an inch at the compliment, his hand still lingering on my arm, and the warmth of his fingers seep under my skin, travelling all the way through my body until it reaches my girly parts. Emily snaps her gum, bringing me back to the present.

"We...uh, we should get out of here," I say. "I think you should take the front this time."

He nods and we all climb into the car. He falls silent for the most part, checking and answering emails on his phone, as Emily continues to tell us about her trip. Many hours later after I drop her off at her place, I ease my car into my drive-way. The porch light illuminates the cracked stone in the walkway, and I gesture to the front stoop of the old farm-house as I reach for my door handle.

"Door's open. You can go right on in. I'll get the luggage."

"You leave your doors open?" he asks, and follows me to the trunk. I open it, and he brushes my hand away to pull out his luggage.

"This is Annapolis. No one locks their doors."

"You're not afraid of break ins?"

I snort. "Yeah, no."

He stands there staring at me. "Yes, or no. I don't understand."

I stare back. "What's that now?"

"You said, yeah, no. Which is it?"

He gathers up his luggage and I laugh as I head up the walkway. "Oh, right. That means no. Sorry."

"You don't have to apologize."

"Habit." I push open the door, and flick on the lights. He stands there for a long moment, looking around. "Let's get you settled. You must be tired."

"I'm a bit knackered," he responds, and I angle my head. I guess that's how the British say tired. It's going to take me getting used to his slang as much as it's going to take him getting used to mine, not that he'll be here all that long.

"Follow me." I walk toward upstairs, and after I take the first couple steps, a loud bang, followed by a menagerie of funny curse words, vibrates through me. I spin, and find him holding his head and glowering at the low stairwell header.

"Are you okay?"

He crouches. "Why is everything so small in this country?"

"It's not. You're just big." That's not entirely true. Some of the headers in my house are low, especially for someone of his stature.

"How many guests have conked themselves out?"

"None. Most duck."

"You could have warned me."

"Yeah…" Ah, there's that one mean bone. Not really. I'm just so darn tired, and maybe a bit distracted by his presence that the low header slipped my mind.

He angles his head, and as his caramel eyes narrow, I resist the urge to tell him a bump on the head is mild compared to the wrath the townsfolk plan to bring tomorrow once they find out he's here. The sale of the park, and how to stop it, has been the talk of the town for months.

Making light of the situation, I say, "You should have let Emily compress your spine. You could have been a couple inches shorter, and easily fit under this header." From my perch on the third step, I tap the header.

"If we'd listened to Emily, you'd be pulling my…" His words fall off, and my heart lurches.

Ohmigod, he *did* hear Emily, and her ridiculous sexual suggestion. I really hope he doesn't think I want that. I have no desire to push or pull his anything…

At least not before I shave my legs!

3

COLIN

Bloody hell! What is that god-awful sound?

I roll over in bed, surprised at how comfortably I slept last night, and check the clock. Shite. I jackknife up, and rub the sleep from my eyes. It's nearing eight a.m. I never sleep this late at home. I guess the travel exhausted me more than I realized, and while I would have liked to have started this day earlier, I doubt the town council convenes before noon around these sleepy parts.

"Maa..."

My gaze goes to the window, to the cheery yellow curtains with the cheery white daisies. Bloody fucking hell. As the fabric billows in the warm morning breeze, I catalogue my room. Last night I was too tired to notice anything, and this morning I'm noticing that everything about the space is quaint. Country. Downright Podunk. The sooner I get out of this Norman Rockwell town, the better. I push to my feet and the wood floor creaks as I step to the window and pull the curtain back to discover an overgrown garden that travels all the way to the end of the earth and back again.

Wait, is that...

I lean forward and narrow my eyes to take in the cute bum aimed my way. Does that bum belong to Violet? Maybe I should go find out and see about breakfast while I'm at it. I'm hoping for a right and proper English breakfast, with sausage, eggs, and maybe a crumpet or two, but something tells me that might be too much to ask for.

I turn toward the door, and I'm about to explore, but since I'm dressed only in my boxers, I stop to pull on the trousers that I draped over the chair before bed. I work on buttoning up my shirt as I head downstairs, being careful not to crack my skull wide open. Violet should have her guests sign a waiver before she gets sued. Then again, she said I was the only wanker to ever bang his head, and Canadians aren't all that litigious, or nice, which I'm learning the hard way. Still, you'd think there'd be better building codes for a commercial business. Maybe I should look into that for her, and maybe I banged my head harder than I realized, because I'm not about to go meddling in Violet's affairs, or Violet's...anything.

And that includes her knickers.

Where the hell did that thought come from?

A warm floral breeze washes over me and instantly sets off a sneezing fit. Great, I'm allergic to Canada. Am I really that surprised?

"Maa..."

I circle the house, walk past a small shed, the door slightly open, and follow the annoying sound. Moving gingerly, as this overgrown weed bed that can only loosely be described as a garden has no rhyme or reason and I don't want to crush any of the vegetation, I walk around a row of cornstalks and come to an abrupt stop. I stand there, and stare at a set of rectangular eyes, blinking innocently up at me.

"So it's you making all that noise, is it?"

"Maa…"

What is that stench? "Do you think you can take me to Violet?"

"Maa."

"That's a no?"

Great now I'm engaging in banter with a goat. I lift my head and glance around, but can't see much over the corn stalks.

"Maa…"

I give a wave of my hand. "Fine, piss off then. I'll find her myself."

I sneeze again, about eighteen times straight, and the goat jumps, startled by the outburst. I make a move to step around it, when something rustles from behind. Assuming it's Violet, I'm about to turn, but before I can, I'm rammed in the back with a stick, or something equally as hard, and I stumble forward.

Bollocks, I'm under attack!

My hands flail and I grasp for something to hold on to, but no flimsy corn stalk is going to keep me upright. I yelp as my skull hits the solid dirt ground with an unforgiving thud, and my brain pings around my noggin like a runaway pinball. My fingers curl into the damp soil as I take one breath, then another and struggle to refill my collapsed lungs.

What the hell was that?

My body stiffens, about to jump up and fight back, when nothing but silence surrounds me, and a fly. I take a swing at the annoying bastard, and miss as I slowly open one eye, and then another, until I'm once again staring directly into a set of rectangular eyes. The goat cocks its head to the side, studying me like I'm a bug under a microscope.

"Maa…" he says, his head lifting, obviously communicating with something behind me.

I glance over my shoulder to see goat number two. Is the little bastard smirking at me? "Listen bud, I didn't mean to scare your friend here."

"Maa…"

"Okay, I get it. You were just protecting him, but I come in peace. If you could just back off."

Colin, you're negotiating with a goat.

But these are not just your regular run of the mill goats. These are Canadian goats and they're mad. It takes a threatening step toward me.

"Uh, easy there, fella," I say quietly, using my best soothing voice, one reserved for the courtroom when things get heated. Seriously though, those horns on his head can do real damage, and I'd be wise to be careful. The goat I scared with my sneeze moves closer, and nips at my open shirt like he's about to make a meal out of it.

"Back off, buddy."

The goat takes a step back and I breathe a sigh of relief. My neck strains as I slowly try to pick myself up without startling either beast.

The goat barks, or cries, or whatever the hell that sound is, and I once again get a mouthful of that god-awful stench. It settles on the back of my tongue and tests my gag reflexes. "A tic tac wouldn't kill you, mate." Cripes, these animals smell like hot garbage left on the sidewalk too long, and I need to get the heck out of here. I go up on my hands and knees, mimicking a four-legged farm animal, and quickly realize my mistake. Goat number two comes at me again—from behind —and I fly forward. This time I land in something warm and soft. Something that smells like a big steaming pile of...

Oh shite!

"What did I ever do to you?" I yell, and roll to the side. Tears sting my eyes, compliments of the foul odors assaulting my senses. The goat lets loose that sound again and eyes me like he's ready to charge a matador's cape. Any second now I expect him to rake one foot through the ground. I take a fast breath and consider my options. Draw on my excellent negotiation skills, or bugger off.

Move, Colin!

I jump to my feet and run, the pungent tang of dung clouds the air and clings to my clothes like a dryer sheet. I hurry through the corn field and nearly trip on a wayward vine as it lunges for me, obviously in cahoots with the goats. I steal a glance behind me to find one of the goats hot on my heels. Is this really happening? I take a turn, hoping to lose him in the high stalks, but if he has any sense of smell at all—I know nothing about Canadian goats other than they're assholes, obviously—I'm a goner.

I cut through a tall stem and come to an abrupt halt when I see a lovely bum stuck in the air. "Violet," I say, breathless and probably not just from my run in with the goat.

She glances over her shoulder, and her eyes go wide as she takes in my open shirt and mud coated chest. "Whoa, are you okay?"

"No," I blurt out and jerk my thumb over my shoulder. "A horny goat...he's after me."

Horny goat?

Great choice of words Colin. I point to my head. "I mean he has horns." Wait, is she laughing at me? "It's not funny."

"No, you're right. It's not funny at all." Her gaze drops from mine and rakes down the length of my soiled clothes. Once she's done her inspection, she asks, "Did you sleep well?"

"Did you not hear me?" I jerk my thumb over my shoulder.

"Oh, Waffles and Popcorn are harmless."

Waffles and Popcorn?

"I beg to differ."

She's grinning again, and I can't help but think how cute she is. "Breakfast then?" She brushes her hands together, and tugs off a pair of soiled gloves. "I think you're going to enjoy our traditional Annapolis breakfast."

"I will if it includes goat." She laughs at that and my dick twitches at the sound. "What kind of names are Waffles and Popcorn, anyway?"

"They were named by the kids in Mrs. Edmonds' primary class." She gives me a playful wink. "Waffles is the horny one."

I shake my head at her. "Were the kids hungry or something when they named them?"

"I don't know but you must be. Why don't you go get a shower and I'll get breakfast ready." A long strand of her hair falls from her forehead and she blows it from her face. I watch it billow and fall back over her eyes. "Colin?"

"Shower, breakfast, right."

She plugs her nose. "Come on, I'll walk you back so you don't run into any of my horny goats."

"There are more?"

"No, just the two." She snickers as she moves ahead of me, and I try not to stare at her cute bum as she walks. Once we're inside, she gestures toward the stairs. "Don't forget to duck."

"I'm not daft," I mumble. Yeah, maybe I am. I'd have to be to agree to this trip. "I'll be down in a jiffy." I duck my head and hurry upstairs. One good thing about this bed and breakfast is I have my own loo. I'm not much into sharing. Not that there are any other guests here to annoy me, and would sharing with Violet be a hardship?

What the hell am I saying?

I step into the small loo, strip down and turn on the water. I hold my hand under the tap before I redirect the flow to the shower. It rains down on me, slowly. Christ, I can piss faster than this. Briefly closing my eyes, I take a couple of deep breaths, hoping when I open them again, I'll be home and this nightmare will be behind me.

You'll be gone soon enough. Just get the paperwork done, and back to your beloved Britain.

Back to mother's matchmaking.

Bollocks.

I'm not quite as speedy cleaning up as I thought I'd be, considering the non-existent water pressure, but hurry into a clean suit when I'm done. Double timing it, and wondering why I can't smell bacon, I hurry back downstairs and come to an abrupt halt when I spot Violet humming to herself in the kitchen. I stand in the archway, and despite the overalls she's wearing, the image before me still teases my dick. A sound I have no control over rumbles in my throat and she turns, a smile on her face.

"Everything up to your standards?"

Has she been reading my mind?

"Ah, what?"

"The bathroom, shower, your bed?"

"Oh yeah, sure." I run my hand through my damp hair. "You could use with a bit more water pressure."

She slaps her hand to her forehead. "I'm so sorry."

There she goes with the sorry again.

"For what?"

She jerks her thumb out and points at the wall. "I put on a load earlier."

"A load of what?" I examine her wall as I try to decipher her Canadianisms.

"Of laundry." She laughs. "The laundry room is behind that wall. How do they say, I put the laundry on where you come from?"

"I put the laundry on."

She rolls her eyes so hard it nearly gives me a headache. "It messes with the water pressure," she explains.

"I have that same problem back home."

"I'll be more careful next time, and when this load is done, I'll put your soiled clothes through a cycle." She waves her hand toward the table, and I turn, and stare at the single bowl, spoon, and box with big bold letters letting me know it's Tim Horton's Timbit cereal.

"What's this now?"

"It's breakfast."

"That is not breakfast."

She opens the box, and pours the dark nuggets that resemble rabbit turds into a bowl. "It's delicious." Tossing a handful into her mouth, she munches, and a groan of pleasure reaches my ear. "They've only been out for a few weeks." She tosses a few more into her mouth. "My God, how did I live without these?" She holds the box out. "Here try. Once you taste these, the second half of your life begins."

I do a quick scan of the ingredients. "I'm not eating this."

Her brow arches, and I can't tell if she's messing with me or not. "Why not?"

"It's ghastly, and the number one ingredient is sugar."

"Yet you eat haggis..."

"What?"

"Nothing."

"That is not any kind of breakfast I know."

"Hey." She shrugs nonchalantly. "When in Rome."

"I'm not in Rome. I'm not even sure I'm in Canada."

She laughs and puts one hand on her hip. "Where do you think you are?"

"The Twilight Zone."

"Fine then. It's a hard no for you. Go ahead then, miss out on the best breakfast ever. I can make something—"

"Never mind. It's getting late. The town hall convenes today, and I have a meeting with the mayor at some point today, to get the paperwork started." With the mayor's busy schedule, my assistant was only able to nail down a day, not a time, to meet. "I'll grab something out. Can you recommend a good restaurant?" She opens her mouth and I cut her off. "You do have a restaurant, yes?"

"Yeah, no, for sure we do."

I shake my head as it spins in my brain. "That means yes, right?"

"Right. We have one cafe, it's called the Annapolis Café— clever, I know. I highly recommend it. But seriously. You paid for a bed *and* breakfast, so I can make you something." She opens her fridge, and bends forward to examine the contents. Is the dryer weather here shrinking my pants, right around the vicinity of my crotch?

"I don't want to put you through the trouble." I pull my cell from my pocket. "I need to get an Uber." She shuts the door and snickers.

"That's funny?"

"No, actually, it's hilarious."

I sigh and my shoulders sag. "You don't have Ubers, do you?"

"No." She snatches her keys off the table. "The restaurant is within walking distance, so is the town hall. But I'm headed that way, so I'll drive you. That way I can help you familiarize yourself with the town and the people who run it."

I'd like to say no. Hell, I'd like to go straight back to the airport and go home, not just because I have no desire to familiarize myself with this town or the people, but because I might need a reprieve from this gorgeous chatty woman, who annoys me as much as she arouses me.

"Fine."

I snatch up my briefcase and we head outside. I wait for her to lock up. She doesn't. I examine the small car I'm about to stuff myself into when an elderly lady with a cat on a leash glares at me.

Violet waves as she throws her purse into the car. "Good morning, Clara."

"Morning, Violet," she calls out as her cat hisses at me. Hello to you too, feline.

"This is Colin Parker, from the Waltonstound Foundation. Colin, this is Clara Henderson."

"Hello," I say, and she snarls at me before she scurries off. Alrighty then.

Violet tosses me an apologetic look. "Just be thankful she wasn't carrying a pitchfork. Can't say as you'll get as nice a greeting at town hall later."

"A horny goat, zero water pressure, a ghastly breakfast, and now I have an angry mob to look forward to."

"I guess things are looking up, eh?"

"Oh yes, totally looking up." I tug on my seatbelt. "Although I don't expect a mob. No one knows I'm coming. Other than the mayor, of course. My assistant sent a letter asking for the paperwork to be in order."

She looks a bit skeptical as she backs out of the driveway so fast, I'm sure I'll end up with whiplash before the day is over. I grab the handle above the window and hold on.

"What?" I ask.

"The townsfolk might not know about this meeting, but they will know about the next one. You probably won't be so lucky."

"Lucky, yes, that's what I've been so far." She grins and I continue with, "Don't worry, there won't be a next time. I'll get what I need done today and I'll be out of your hair by the weekend."

Once again that skepticism is back on her face. Does she know something I don't? "You're used to getting things done in a timely manner, aren't you?"

"Yes."

"Just remember, this is a slow-moving town, with slow moving people."

"I don't think Waffles got the memo. He's fast and stealthy."

She laughs out loud, and shakes her head. Seriously though, does she know something I don't? I let it go as she drives me down the one-road town and she points out the landmarks.

We go a little further, and slow when a construction worker holds up a stop sign.

"They're putting in a new merry-go-round, and a new exit to the highway."

I glance ahead. "Do you mean a roundabout?"

"Potato, patato. Wait, roundabouts were first built in Britain, weren't they? I remember it from a show I watched. So, I guess you're to blame for all this mess."

Does she ever stop talking, and how am I to blame? A song comes on that she loves and she turns up the radio and sings along. It's horrid, but better than her incessant chatting. I think. I sit back as the sign turns, and she waves to the men working as she continues down the road. A café comes into view, and she pulls into a parking spot.

"We're here."

"Much appreciated," I say. "I can find my own way back to the bed and breakfast after my meeting." I give her a curt nod. "I'll see you then."

"You'll be seeing me before that," she mumbles.

"What?"

"Nothing."

I don't question her, instead, I exit the vehicle. She also jumps out, but heads around the back of the building. The bell overhead jingles and all eyes turn my way as I step inside. Did the temperature just drop a million degrees? I grab a stool at the counter and study the menu that doubles as a placemat. I glance around, but the one server is chatting it up with a customer at a table. What does a guy have to do to get a cup of tea around here?

Snapping gum announces the arrival of another server, and I glance up. With her hair now pinned high on her head, and looking more gorgeous than ever as she ties an apron around her waist, and pulls a pad from her pocket, Violet asks, "What can I get for you?"

I shake my head. "Bloody hell."

I tap my pen on my chin as Colin stares at me with those light brown eyes of his. Damned if that doesn't make me want to drive straight to Pearl's ice cream shop and order a salted caramel sundae with all the sprinkles. Placing my pen on his paper menu, I drag it my way and read it upside down.

"Bloody hell," I murmur as I search the breakfast options. "Nope, I don't think bloody hell is on the menu. I could probably make you a bloody Mary though, but it might be a bit early for alcohol. We could skip the vodka and just go with the tomato juice." I eye him, his expression far from amused. "Do you need another minute, or would you like a recommendation?" He angles his head and stares at me like I'm a smart ass, and I might very well be.

"How many jobs do you have, anyway?"

"Oh, I just fill in here every now and then." I lean in conspiratorially. "You see Frank is in the city." I jut my hip out, and point to it. "Replacement surgery." I turn the mug over in front of him and arch my brow as I hold up the coffee pot.

"Do you have tea?"

"I could probably find a bag, but it might be as old as you. We don't have too many tea drinkers here in Annapolis." I shake the pot. "Yes or no."

"Fine."

I fill him up. He takes a big swig, and of course he's going to drink it black. A man like him has no time for cream. His lips twist as he sets it down.

"Good, eh?"

"Yes, if you enjoy dishwater," he says halfheartedly.

"Drink a lot of dishwater, do you?"

He doesn't respond, instead he grunts under his breath and asks, "Okay, what do you recommend?" I glance over his head, and unease moves through me as I spot the early morning construction crew making their way inside. Gossip spreads faster than a dandelion seed during a good windstorm in Annapolis and Colin's presence is not a welcome one. I probably shouldn't let him out of my sight for long. Who knows what one of those clowns might have up their sleeve, and I really don't want to see the man hurt. Much.

"Violet?"

"Right." I turn back to the menu. "I'm assuming a right and proper British meal includes bacon, eggs, and some kind of toast?"

"Crumpets, but hash browns will do."

I wink at him. "Ah, a sneaky way to get fries for breakfast. I dig it."

He stares at me, zero humor in his gaze, but holy, being the sole focus of this man's attention is a little unnerving. I bet he always gets his way in the boardroom...and the bedroom. Not that I want to find out. I mean, I've yet to shave my legs.

"A hash brown is not a French fry," he informs me.

My God how many times have I had this debate. "Look, you can cut it up differently and give it a fancy name, but really it's still a breakfast French fry. Don't worry. I'm not judging. I eat ghastly cereal, remember?"

"Of course, I remember. It was only five minutes ago." He checks his watch, and I once again remind myself he's over the top literal. "Eggs over easy, please."

I ring the bell on the ledge behind me. "Bill, one coronary please."

"Well, well, what do we have here?" Jacob says as he takes the stool beside Colin, his clothes smelling like hot tar as he takes his hard hat off and sets it on the counter.

"Jacob," I warn, and he gestures with a nod that he heard me. Not that he's going to listen. "Colin, this is Jacob Winters. He's a heavy equipment operator. Jacob, this is Colin, he—"

"I know who he is." I stiffen as I pour Jacob a cup of coffee, and he opens a creamer and pours it in. I cast a quick glance at Colin. He's not at all intimidated by Jacob. Either he's as dense as the hash brown he's about to eat, or he can hold his own. He's big enough, tall, strong enough, but I don't take him for a backyard brawler.

"Do you enjoy that?" Colin asks and I hold my breath. What is he doing? Why is he engaging? Maybe he really is daft.

Jacob stops stirring his coffee. "Do I enjoy what?" His voice is deep, accusatory, and it's easy to tell he's looking to pick a fight.

"Working heavy equipment. It's quite the skill." Colin takes a sip of his coffee, and this time he doesn't cringe quite as much. What is it with the British and their tea, anyway? "I watched you earlier. I've always had a great respect for those who can handle such rigs and make it look easy." He cocks his head, a rumble in his chest. "You'd have to be a twat not to realize the talent it takes."

"A twat?" I grip the counter. Does Jacob think he's calling him a twat, and who uses the word twat, anyway? I'm about to intervene when a smile quirks Jacob's mouth and he sits up a bit straighter, prouder. "It's a whole lot different than the toys we used to drag around in the dirt when we were kids." He nudges Colin with his elbow and laughs.

"I'd imagine it is."

For a second I think Colin is playing him, working to get on his good side, but no, he's not. He's actually being completely genuine. I never thought the grumpy Brit could charm a guy like Jacob without even realizing it. It gives me an idea on how to make his stay, as well as the transfer of land, go through a little smoother.

As much as I hate the idea of losing the park, I take care of the books. The declining number of visitors have been a constant headache for me. I'm being pulled in two different directions. While I don't want to lose it, the society wants it gone and off their hands, which means the townsfolk will soon enough have to come to terms with the idea of an elite boarding school. But one obstacle at a time, right?

"My boy," Jacob says, pride in his eyes. "He loves the dump trucks."

"Sounds like he's going to follow in his father's footsteps. What an honor that must be." I shake my head as I watch Colin say all the right things to Jacob. The bell behind me rings, and I turn to find Colin's order.

I slide it to him. "Jacob, you and the boys ready to order?"

He frowns, like he'd forgotten why he was sitting next to Colin. "Ah yeah." Pushing to his feet, he snatches up his hard hat, crosses the room and slides into the booth.

"Enjoy," I say to Colin. "This is on me, since I didn't make you breakfast today."

"You don't have to do that."

I just smile at him and make my way over to Jacob and the guys. They put their orders in and I warn them all to play nice with Colin. After I call out their orders to Bill, I refresh Colin's coffee.

"Do you want me to drive you to town hall after you're finished?"

"It's just a short jaunt. I can find my way."

"That was nice, what you said to Jacob."

He stares at me with that dumbfounded look on his face that I might just find adorable. "What did I say?"

"About his son following in his footsteps." He frowns and stares at his coffee and I sense I hit on something a little personal. "Was it something I said?"

He squares his broad shoulders, a stiffness back in his body. "No, it's what sons do."

"I don't know about that. I think a person should make their own way in life if that's what they want."

"Maybe things are done differently here."

I'm about to tell him what I really think, but stop myself. It's far too early for philosophical debates. I mean, I might need eight more cups of coffee before arguing my point. My beaver jokes did go over his head.

"Okay," I say, and point to the window. "The town hall is right there. See that big apple?"

"Why is there a gigantic apple on the front lawn?"

"We're the apple capital."

"Is that a self-proclaimed title, or does the town have proof to back that up?"

"It's the symbol of the town. A roadside attraction. What do they have in your town? A huge yardstick?"

He frowns. "Why on earth would we have a yardstick?"

Oh, he does not want to know.

He pulls his wallet out and I hold my hand up to stop him. "It's on me, remember?" I say.

He shakes his head. "I do not have short term memory loss, do you?"

"No." My gaze goes to the bills he lays on the counter and his eyes meet mine. Something in the way he looks at me hits like a bolt of lightning, and I nearly stagger backward.

"For the great service," he says.

"Be honest, it was mediocre at best." His brow raises, but he doesn't disagree, as he wipes his mouth with a napkin. "You be careful out there," I tell him when he stands.

He smooths a hand down his tie. "I realize no one wants me here, but I'm capable of taking care of myself, Violet."

"Weren't you taken down by Waffles this morning?" I snort under my breath.

He opens his mouth like he's about to say something, but starts a sneezing fit. I jump back, and grab him a handful of tissues. "Are you okay?"

"Allergic to Canada," he says, so deadpan, I can't help but laugh.

"No one's allergic to Canada. It's the best place in the world to live."

"I never had allergies before I came here."

I note the redness around his nose, and his watery eyes. "You might want to stop at the pharmacy and get some allergy pills." I jerk my thumb toward the wall. "It's right next door."

"Thanks."

He puts his wallet in his back pocket as he walks out, and I stare after him, taking in his broad shoulders and cute backside. The bell behind me pulls me back and I turn to grab the orders up. I spend the next few hours working, and worrying about Colin getting himself into trouble. When the clock hits twelve, I take off my apron, blow Bill a kiss and walk out into the sunshine.

On the sidewalk, I run into Grace Harper and her minature poodle. "Violet," she says, her white brows bunched together. "That man has been sitting on the steps of the town hall for hours now." I shade the sun from my eyes and spot Colin. He's patient and persistent, I'll give him that.

"He's waiting for the council to convene."

She presses her fingers tightly together, not an inch of space between them. "I was this close to calling the police on him." She glares at Colin. "I don't like the looks of him. I can tell he's up to no good. He's got trouble written all over him."

Yes, yes he does.

"He's here from the foundation. He's a lawyer, handling the paperwork."

She snarls, and her dog barks in response. "I knew there was a reason I didn't like him. Walking around town and sitting on those steps like he owns Annapolis Park."

Technically, he does. Or is about to anyway.

"Let's not be too hard on him." When she narrows her eyes, her gaze raking over my face like I might also be up to no good, I switch the subject. "Hey, what are you doing next Friday night?"

She snatches up Molly, and pets her head to soothe her. "Watching my shows."

"I'm thinking about a kitchen party. To give Colin a right and proper Annapolis welcome." Why do I always use a British accent when I say, 'right and proper'? Judging from the look on Grace's face, I'm still not pulling it off.

"He's not welcome here, Violet. You of all people know that."

My heart pinches. I get it. They want—expect—me to drive him out of town, and while it's my job to listen to them, the writing is on the wall. The park is failing. The townsfolk don't want to hear that though. Heck, I don't want to hear that.

"Come on, now. We're better than that." I throw my arms up. "Let's show him a little of that Canadian hospitality we're known for."

She makes a fist. "I'll show him something."

I bite back a smirk. "I'll see you next week."

I spot councilors Wanda and Cameron, and our Constable Ben Davis headed in toward the back. I suck in a tight breath. They're not going to like the surprise on the front steps waiting for them. Maybe I should get caramel sundaes for everyone.

I hurry my steps and go around back. I think I need to give everyone a heads up before Colin springs his surprise visit on them—although they know his visit is inevitable. The smell of old books and leather hits me when I enter and I hurry to the main meeting room, where I find the others waiting for me.

"Violet," they all say as they pull out their agendas.

"Before we get started, we have an issue that we must deal with first."

Cameron eyes me. "An issue."

I turn to Cameron, the town's attorney. "Did you happen to get the paperwork for the amendment to the land bylaws in order?"

"Why would I do that?"

"Wanda?" I say, hoping the city finance director will side with me on this.
me on this.

She sits back and folds her arms in defiance. The way our town works is that as mayor, I have full power over council decisions, but I have to live in this town. I don't want these people hating me, and yeah, this is going to be harder than I thought. No, that's not true. I was pretty sure Colin was in store for one hell of a battle. I'm just glad no one knew about this meeting. The next one, oh yeah, that's going to be broadcast all over the place and the goat incident is going to seem like a day at the beach after the townsfolk get through with him.

"Because..." I say as I walk from the meeting room to the front of the building. I turn the lock and swing the large doors open. Colin stands, and his eyes narrow as he zeroes in on me. I can almost hear his brain spinning.

He shakes his head. "You have got to be kidding me."

I hold my hand out. "Welcome to Annapolis. I'm Mayor Violet Bryant."

5

COLIN

As she drives me through town after a very uneventful meeting where nothing went right—I think she tried to warn me about that earlier—I turn to her and note the strain on her face, the weariness around her eyes as she negotiates the narrow country roads.

"Are there any other hats you wear that I should know about?" I query.

She glances up, and to the left, like she's searching the recesses of her mind. "I can't think of any right now," she says. "If I do, I'll let you know."

She takes a hard left, moving into the wrong lane—or the right lane if we were back home—to pass a big tractor. She honks and the driver waves. "That's Peter. He has a huge apple farm, and recently had gallbladder surgery," she says, and I'm guessing everyone knows everyone, and is into everyone's business around these parts.

She takes a hard turn to get us back in our lane once she passes the tractor, and I grab the bar above the window to hang on.

"Gallbladder, huh? Is that your way of telling me you're the town's doctor..." She slows as she goes over the railroad tracks. "A train conductor, perhaps?"

She laughs at that. "No, I'm not a doctor and a conductor does sound fun. Maybe I'll look into that. Oh, wait, I am a captain. I know my way around a lobster boat. Maybe I'll take you out to see the whales sometime."

"Yes, with all your spare time we should fit that in. How did you become mayor, anyway?"

"Dad was mayor, and after he...Let's just say everyone thought I'd be the best person to fill his shoes."

Without realizing what I'm doing, I reach across the seat and put my hand on her arm, giving it a little squeeze. "I'm sorry, Violet. I didn't know."

She turns to me, warmth in her eyes as she gives me a small appreciative smile, and while this woman is independent and capable, something tells me she gives too much and gets too little. Dammit if that doesn't bother me, make me want to step up to help.

"Thank you," she says quietly.

Not wanting to press, but wanting to know more about her, I ask, "Is your mum..."

"Yes, she lives just down the road from me. She works at the new Tim Horton's. She doesn't have to work." She shrugs one shoulder. "It just helps her keep busy you know, after Dad." I nod, and she continues with, "Are your parents..." My entire body tightens, cold moving through me, and she reads my reaction all wrong. "Sorry, Colin..."

"No, no. they're both alive and I have a younger brother too. Nate." He's fun loving like Violet. He's also reckless, and totally rebellious. Something tells me Violet once had that same carefree nature, but now she's loaded with responsibility. I'm about to ask what she was like as a kid, but bite my tongue to stop myself.

Not the business you're here to attend, Colin.

"He's kind of an arse," I say, my heart squeezing tight as I remember a few of Nate's childhood antics, and the time he thought he could jump the river on his bike. Twat. I do love the lad. "You'd like him."

"You're saying I like arses." She flicks on her signal. "Wait, I guess I must. I like you."

A little rush goes through me as she tosses me a playful grin. I stare at her, happy that she likes me when really, it shouldn't matter. "Yeah, I am a bit of an arse, aren't I?"

She crinkles her cute nose at me. "You've kind of been grumpy."

"I'm sorry." Bollocks, there I go apologizing again. "I'll try to be less grumpy."

"Maybe if I make you crumpets tomorrow, your day will be off to a better start." She aims an apologetic frown my way. "Sorry things didn't go your way with the council." Her lips form a tight line, her shoulders sagging slightly. "They don't want to sell the park, and are going to do anything to stall the transaction. They want it back in my family." I didn't realize until the meeting—if I can even call it that—that the park had belonged to her family. "They consider you the enemy. There's nothing I can do about that."

"You're getting a lot of pressure, aren't you?" I know all about pressure. I'm getting a ton of it from back home too. But this is a different kind of pressure, and it all falls on her shoulders. The townsfolks are afraid of change, and change can be scary. Once the plans for the school are approved, it will bring new life into the town. New jobs and new students mean more money spent in Annapolis. That's better for everyone, right?

"Yeah. I'm the mayor, and I have to listen to what my constituents want." As she turns the wheel with a tight grip, her knuckles whiten.

"Sorry about that."

"Not your fault." She cocks her head. "Well yeah, I guess it kind of is."

I laugh at that, and it eases some of the tension inside me. I go quiet for a moment, and consider what this must be like for her, to be losing a piece of her family's history. My heart pinches tight. She must have a lot of fond memories of the place, with her late father and grandfather.

"I didn't realize when we met that it was your grandfather who built the park, Violet. This can't be easy for you."

"It's not," she says quietly. "I'm sorry for not coming right out and telling you I was mayor. I thought you would have put it together, to be honest."

"I should have. My assistant informed me the emails for Bryant, the 'guy' who owned the bed and breakfast, was also the same email for the mayor. I think I was just too tired from the flight to put it together, or—"

"Daft," she says, and I laugh.

"You're right, and you don't have to apologize. I should be the one apologizing to you. I'm causing you a lot of trouble."

"For the record, I'm not the one stalling the sale. I asked Cameron to get the paperwork together before you got here."

I nod, appreciating that. "Do you enjoy the job?"

She crinkles her nose. "Sometimes. I do want what's best for this town. I'll do what I can to help speed things up for you, so the paperwork is ready for the next meeting, which of course, is in two weeks."

I push back into the very uncomfortable seat, and try to adjust my knees around my ears. Christ could this car be any smaller. "You can't push up the meeting? It has to be in two weeks?"

"No one is going to push it up to make things easier for you, Colin. You're just going to have to wait."

"Lucky me."

"Is it so bad?"

"Yes, it's—" She blinks at me with those pretty blue eyes of hers, and I register the hint of vulnerability about her. My heart softens. "I have to get home." I thought I'd be in and out, and back home in my own bed by Monday morning. Now I'm stuck in Podunk with Violet for a couple more weeks, at least.

Is it that bad, Colin?

"What's at home?" she asks.

"Everything."

"Fine, what does home have that we don't have here?"

"Crumpets." I sulk like a petulant child, and when she grins, I realize how ridiculous I sound. Nevertheless, I add, "And tea."

She nods, in total understanding, then inches her chin up. "You're missing your *right and proper* afternoon high tea?"

"It's good though, eh," I say in my worst Canadian accent and we both just sit there smirking at each other, a new friendship blossoming right before my eyes. I like her. She likes me too. She said so. Although I don't know why, but she told me so, and why the hell do I sound like a schoolboy with a crush. "Doesn't this car have air conditioning?" I loosen my tie.

"Yes, it's called a window." She presses a button and my window lowers. "Air conditioner broke a while back, but I kind of like the fresh air better anyway." I put my hand out the window, like I used to when I was a kid. It was never out for long. My father always yelled at me to get it back inside before I lost it.

"Have you ever heard of anyone losing their hand from doing this?" I ask as I oscillate my arm, letting the air run over and under it.

"What?"

"Nothing," I say quickly. What on earth am I doing? Canada is messing with my allergies and my brain. I sneeze into the crook of my elbow.

"Bless you, and I get it. It's okay to want to go home." There's a real sadness about her as she speaks. "It's a small town. Most want out first chance. You don't have to justify anything to me."

As I digest and dissect her words, I can't help but wonder what it is about this place that keeps her here. From what I've seen, the population is much older. Although I haven't seen too much of it yet.

She plasters on a smile. "We're here," she says and pulls onto a long-paved road. I glance at picnic tables spread out on the lush, green grass. The towering apple trees, some of them older than time, provide lots of shade.

"The grounds are lovely. A perfect place for students to study, or stretch their legs and get a breath of air."

"Did you go to a boarding school?"

"I did."

She parks in the near empty lot. "Did you miss home?"

"At first, sure. But I made friends and my studies and extracurricular activities kept me busy. It was nice when my brother came along."

She turns the car off, and shoves the keys into the front pocket of her overalls. "Wait, how old were you when you went?"

"Seven."

Her mouth gapes open, totally exaggerated. "You have got to be kidding me."

"Why would I kid about something like that?"

"You were just a baby, Colin," she explains, her voice softening. "I couldn't imagine sending my baby off to school at seven."

"You have a baby?"

She grins. "No, of course not. I just mean if I did, but I don't, and I'm not sure I ever will."

"Why not? You'd be great with kids."

"How do you know that?"

"You got a lamb for your friend's daughter."

"You got a beaver," she counters.

"I'm not the one saying I'm not sure I'll ever have kids."

"You want kids?"

"I'm not saying that, either." My God, this woman can talk me in circles. Getting the conversation back on track, I say, "I was seven. Hardly a baby, Violet. I turned out just fine."

One brow raises like she's going to challenge me on that, but instead she says, "Your brother was seven too?"

"Of course. Why are you so surprised?"

"I can't imagine growing up away from my family. I guess things are done differently where you come from. You're close to your brother, though?"

"As close as two arseholes can be." I open my door, and say. "He'd really like you."

She gives me a playful wink. "What's not to like?"

What's not to like indeed?

We both climb from the car and I remove my suit jacket and drape it over the seat. "I'm not sure he'd like it here, though. Not enough to get him into trouble." I glance at the wood cut-out of a lion, the face missing, allowing children to poke their heads through for a picture moment.

"Want to try?" Violet asks, as she darts behind the cut-out and stares at me through the hole. She gives me a cheeky grin, and bats her lashes.

"I'm good, thanks."

She shrugs. "Your loss. Come on."

We head inside the main building, an open-air lobby where customers get their entrance bracelets, and she stops to talk to the young man behind the counter. He says something that makes her laugh, and I stand there as she flirts back. Why wouldn't she? She's a beautiful young, unmarried woman who should be out having fun and meeting guys. A woman like Violet could have any man she wanted. Myself excluded. While I appreciate her beauty, I'm not about to get involved with her. I'm here to sign a deal, and she's not part of it.

Why is she still single?

Not your business, Colin.

Why do I have to keep reminding myself of that?

She gives a wave and gestures with a nod for me to follow her. "I'll catch up with you later, Caleb."

"Later, Violet," he says, and I ignore the odd jolt of jealousy as he picks up his phone and begins to scroll. As we walk through the lobby and enter the park, Violet reaches down and unzips the pantlegs on her overalls, turning them into shorts. Efficient. I like that.

I put my hands in my pockets. "You two are very friendly."

She grins at me. "Caleb and I go way back."

"I was right when I said you were good with kids."

"How's that?"

"I saw how good you were with Caleb back there." I'm kidding, I think. I'm definitely not jealous.

She bursts out laughing and pokes me in the chest. "You are an arse."

"Already established," I say, and capture her finger. I hold it in my hands, and lightly brush my thumb over her soft skin. Her breathing changes and so does mine, as heat sparks between us, driving the temperature up around us.

What the hell are you doing, Colin?

Warmth invades her pretty eyes, as she stares up at me. My gaze drops to take in her mouth as her lips part and swipes her tongue over her bottom lip. Is she preparing it for me?

"Colin," she says quietly, softly...the way she'd likely say it in bed, if she were under me.

"Yeah."

A train makes a sound in the distance, and she snaps up to her full height, tugging her hand back. "I just thought of something."

I stare at her, and resist the urge to adjust my shrinking pants. When she continues to stare back, like her brain isn't firing properly—mine isn't either—I ask, "Are you going to enlighten me?"

"I *am* a train conductor."

I angle my head and frown at her. "You are?"

She points and I turn as the park's train chugs along.

"When things are busy..." She frowns and looks at the rows of ropes that coordinate lines...not a single sole waiting for entrance into the park. "I help out here. I've pretty much run every ride, including that train, and worked in every shop. Mr. Barker even taught me how to whittle a whistle."

"I'm sure that's a skill that comes in handy around these parts."

"Yeah, I use it in the garden. It scares away horny goats."

"Funny girl." She laughs and tosses the bottom half of her pantlegs over a rail and hands me a brochure. I'm presented with a map of the park as I peel it open.

"Bloody marvelous," I say, mostly to myself.

"It really is." She holds her arms out and spins around. "Welcome to Annapolis Park, Colin."

The enticing scent of popcorn reaches my nostrils, and I note the buildings around me. Perhaps we won't have to tear them all down. Some could be repurposed. Maybe the town won't hate me as much if I keep a few of their well-crafted buildings. Distant laughter fills the park and I turn toward the sound.

Violet puts her hands on her hips and asks, "Are you afraid of heights?"

"No."

She grins and skips along. I grow warm under my collar and force myself not to stare at her cute backside as I follow her until we come to a rope bridge. She wags playful brows at me. "Want to try?"

"I hardly think I'm dressed for climbing, and isn't that for children?"

"It's for everyone, and you only stop being playful if you stop playing." Her gaze moves down my body, and she taps her chin. "We could check the lost and found to see if we can find you shorts?"

"I'm not wearing anyone's lost shorts." The thoughts of putting someone's soiled clothes next to my bits brings on a cringe.

"Okay." She points upward. "I'm going to climb that. You can wait here, or you can go explore without me."

"I'll wait for you."

She dashes off, and her ponytail bounces as she starts up the rope ladder. She gets on the bridge, and starts swaying it back and forth and some young boy who's halfway through starts laughing and doing the same. They sway above me, and I shake my head at her childlike enthusiasm. It begins to rub off on me, and for a second I think about joining her. Then I remember my purpose and pull myself together. More kids join her as she has the time of her life, acting like a damn fool.

She's laughing and out of breath when she finally climbs down the other side. "Are you done?" I ask. "Can we continue with the tour?" I flip open the map. "I'd like to see this building here."

"It's a gorgeous old building. It's been here forever. I don't know if my grandfather built it, or it was here long before my grandfather started the park."

"It looks like the park was built around the structure. It would be great for the headmaster's residence." Although my grandfather will likely want it demolished, as it sits right at the top of the majestic hill overlooking the park and distant orchard where he wants to build the school, and with this stone structure still standing, it'd be impossible to build the massive school he has in mind without tearing it down.

"We can go there if you want. The pedal boats, the roller coaster and log ride are on the way." Her eyes are bright, full of wonderment as she smacks her lips. "And we have to get a candy apple. Dominic makes the best candy apples." I'm about to protest, and she tugs on my tie.

"I thought you were going to try to be less grumpy."

She's right, and maybe it wouldn't hurt to check out the craftsmanship. Being here clearly makes her happy, which gives me a measure of guilt. It's my family's foundation that will be taking this all out from underneath her.

"What is this about a log ride? Is it like a Canadian lumberjack thing? You know like walking on logs in a river?"

She stares at me like I might be from outer space. "Have you never played at a park before?"

"No."

Her eyes are wide, shocked. "What did you do for fun as a kid?"

"I played cricket?"

She snickers. "I never played, but there's a stick involved, right?"

"A bat. What is it with you and sticks, anyway?"

"Nothing, come on."

We make our way along a paved walkway, and I survey the grounds and equipment, considering what must go, and what must stay. We reach a ride with logs that go down a waterslide and Violet runs to the entrance.

"That looks dangerous," I tell her.

"It's not dangerous. It's fun." I give her a skeptical look, and she says, "I promise, if you loosen up, you'll have fun."

"I am loose." She raises her brows in challenge, and I continue with, "Fine, and if I don't have fun?"

"Not an option."

I arch a brow and she takes my hand and tugs. "You take the front."

"Why? Is that where you get the wettest?"

She whacks me and it reverberates all the way to my dangly bits. "I'll be getting wet, too."

Bollocks, that's not what I need to be thinking about right now, or later tonight when I'm in bed alone. Which is exactly what I'm going to do. What was that I said about her enthusiasm rubbing off? Yeah, that's what I'll be doing. Rubbing one off.

"Are you coming?" she asks.

Bloody hell.

VIOLET

s I lick my candy apple and Colin takes a big bite out of his, I ask, "Were you scared?"

"Scared of what?" he grumps.

"The log ride. You screamed like a girl."

He looks mortified as he glares at me. "I did not scream like a girl. I did not scream at all."

"Your mouth was open, your lips turned up." Wait, was it possible that he was smiling? "Did it hurt?"

"Did what hurt?"

"The smiling."

"I wasn't—"

"It was either one or the other, Colin."

"Do you always talk so much? You know you don't have to fill every silent moment with chatter."

I grin at him, but inside I know he was smiling on that ride whether he wants to admit it or not. "What was your favorite part of today?"

He goes thoughtful as he chews. "Not facing a mob at town hall."

"Oh, it's coming. Unless, of course, you can summon a bit of charm and get the townsfolk on your side."

"I have charm."

"Oh, yeah, no for sure you do."

He angles his head, his hair still damp from the log ride and tries to puzzle that out. I grin and say, "What was your favorite part of the park?" As he considers it, I take a big bite of my juicy apple.

"Not the roller coaster. Who makes roller coasters out of wood anyway? Can you even call it a roller coaster? If you ask me, the only thing keeping it together is the termites holding hands."

I nearly choke on my apple as I burst out laughing, but he's being totally serious which makes it even funnier. "It's old, I know," I say when I can finally pull myself together. "Maintenance has been a killer."

I bump into him as I walk, my legs still wobbly from riding the rickety roller coasters. "I'm sorry," he murmurs.

"We just can't afford the upkeep anymore. I understand that. It doesn't make it any easier though."

He goes quiet, thoughtful. "What's your favorite part of the park?"

I bump him again. "Come on. I'll show you."

I pick up my speed and we circle the small lake until we reach the treehouse. I glance way up, and test the rope steps. I start up and glance at Colin still on the ground. He tugs on his collar as his gaze leaves my backside and slides to mine. Was he just checking me out?

"Coming?" I ask.

"Yeah." His voice is rough, tortured, and a thrill skips through my body, hitting every erogenous zone along the way. He might be a grumpy Brit, but he has the ability to set me on fire without even trying. Cripes, when he held my finger, I thought I was going to spontaneously combust. The last time my body reacted so feverishly to a man was...never.

I hurry upward, and step inside the empty treehouse. A sense of calm comes over me. I lean over the rail and take in the entire park from my aerial view. Colin moves in beside me, his big body overwhelming me in ridiculous ways.

I sigh. "I love it up here."

"It's a great view of the park."

I pucker my lips. "Do you think it will have to be torn down?"

"Probably." I frown as he backpedals. "I don't know, we'll have to see what the plans look like first."

"Did you have a treehouse growing up?" I ask him.

"No, but I once climbed into a large packing box."

I snort. "What?"

He holds his hands out and starts forming a square. "Mum had a delivery and Nate and I played in the box."

"Yeah, box, treehouse. Same thing." Breathing in the fresh country air and holding it in my lungs, I go back to taking in the view. I exhale slowly. "This is where I used to hang out a lot as a kid."

"It has fond memories for you."

I nod, even though he's making a statement, not asking a question. "I had a lot of firsts in this treehouse."

"Such as."

"Had my first cigarette. Yeah, it was nasty. Had my first drink of alcohol, and my first kiss. I was fourteen and madly in love with Brandon. He lives in Toronto now." I spin, and lean against the wooden rail. Memories bombard me. "When I was seventeen, well, you know…"

He stares at me for a minute, then his eyes widen. Ah, the lightbulb just went on. "You shagged up here?"

I laugh, not at all sure why I'm telling him any of this. "That's not how I'd put it."

"Well, it for sure has to go then. We can't have students sneaking up here to shag, now can we?"

I whack him and when my palm connects with his hard chest, I wish I hadn't. This time he grabs my whole hand and takes a step closer. His body crowds mine, and I momentarily forget how to breathe.

"Do you still shag in this treehouse, Violet?"

I laugh, and it comes out rough and needy and I don't even want to think about the riot going on between my legs. "I'm not seventeen anymore, Colin."

"That's a no?"

His eyes darken, and his head dips. Ohmigod, is he going to kiss me? I don't want that. Okay, let me rephrase that. I shouldn't want that.

"Violet, is that you?"

Air rushes from my lungs at the sound of Mr. Barker's voice calling up to me. I back away from Colin's body, his warmth, and his hands fall to his sides, his dark, hungry gaze still locked on me. What is going on between us?

"Mr. Barker," I say and lean over the side.

"What's this I hear of you coming to the park and not stopping to say hello?"

Candy apple still in hand, I make my way toward the ladder. "You were our next stop."

I hurry down and jump the last few steps to the ground. Colin follows me. "I was showing Colin around the park."

Mr. Barker grumbles under his breath. "Heard he was in town."

I give them an introduction and Mr. Barker only shakes Colin's hand because he's a man with manners.

"Violet speaks highly of you," Colin says. "I'm looking forward to her showing me the whistle you taught her to whittle."

"What do you know about whittling?" Mr. Barker bristles.

"Not a thing, which is why I'm looking forward to learning."

"Not much sense. It's a dying craft and once you shut this place down..." A frown tugs down his lips and nostalgia fills his eyes as he glances around. "A boarding school, huh?"

"That's the plan," Colin says.

Mr. Barker turns to me and puts his frail hand on my shoulder. He pats me. "No way is Violet going to let that happen. Isn't that right, Violet? Like her daddy, she'll take care of this town and do what's right."

My stomach tightens, and bile punches into my throat as guilt races through me. Without even realizing it, I take a small step toward Colin, and his palm lands on the small of my back.

"Mr. Barker," I begin, but I have no idea what it is I should say to him. He was involved in the building of the park and spent the last thirty years working in it. It's his home.

"I'm afraid it's out of Violet's hands at this point," Colin says, his thumb brushing my back in a soothing manner, a manner that lets me know he's got my back, which is so strange. I'm usually the one running around taking care of everyone else.

"We'll see about that, now won't we." Mr. Barker pounds his cane on the ground, and spins. "Don't be a stranger now, Violet, and if he really is into whittling you ought to show him your beaver."

Ohmigod. My candy apple falls from my hand and lands with a thud in the dirt as mortification races through me.

"You have a beaver?" Colin asks.

"Yes, I have a beaver," I blurt out. Good Lord, are we really having this conversation? I suppose I deserve it after teasing him at the airport. Well played, Karma. Well. Played.

"Okay, you don't have to bite my head off."

"Sorry..."

"You don't have to be sorry either. I'm just wondering about your beaver."

"Colin!" I practically yell. "A beaver is what some people call a woman's..." I stop talking and point to the apex of my legs.

His eyes go wide. "A beaver is..."

"A woman's naughty bits." Wait, I think the term naughty bits refers to male genitalia in Britain. Nevertheless, judging from the widening of his mouth, he gets it.

"When you were making fun of me paying for my beaver—"

"I'm sorry." I throw my arms out. "It was just...you left me an opening. How could I not?"

"Of course, you had to. I was a man buying a beaver." An adorable grin flirts with his lips—he's not even trying to hide it—and I'm glad he's finding humor in this. "You wouldn't even be able to call yourself a true Canadian if you didn't jump all over that."

"Right?" I say with a laugh.

"Wait." His smile falls, and mortification moves into his eyes. "Why does Mr. Barker want you to show me your...beaver."

I cover my face and groan as I will the ground to open up and swallow me. Where the hell is a good earthquake when you need one? Not that we have them in Canada all that often. Perhaps I should move.

"Is it spectacular?" he teases. "Hold up. Does that mean Mr. Barker's seen it?"

Kill me freaking now.

"That's not what he meant, and I don't just go around showing my beaver to anyone, I'll have you know." As he snickers, I let my hand fall from my face. I hold out one hand palm up, and slide the other palm over it. "But as soon as he said that, my mind just slid to sexually inappropriate."

One brow raises and goddammit, here I thought he couldn't be any cuter. "Does that happen a lot?"

"Not before I met you." Shit. Did I just admit I liked him? That he makes me think of sex?

"Oh, I see." He falls quiet, and takes a small, measured step back. All righty then. It's obviously not what he wants and maybe he wasn't being flirty earlier, maybe he wasn't going to kiss me. Maybe his mere presence and the lack of a man's touch is messing with my mind and body and conjuring up things that aren't real.

Needing to think about something else, I turn to watch Mr. Barker round the corner and disappear from my sight. As he hobbles off, I fold my hands over my chest. "That was not my favorite part of today."

Colin's arm goes around me, and he drags me to his body. "Yeah, me neither," he says quietly, all humor gone from his voice.

I glance up at him. "Thanks for coming to my rescue. I don't think he meant to be hard on me. He thinks with his heart, you know."

"I know."

"Let's get out of here." I start walking and his hand falls from my back. I instantly miss his warmth as we head back to the main building. I grab my pant legs from the rail I'd draped them over and give Caleb a wave as we walk through the open-air entranceway and head back to the car.

Colin opens his door, and takes another look around. "Thanks for showing me the park."

"Anytime."

"I should probably go get a car rental tomorrow if I'm going to be here for the next couple weeks. I can't expect you to chauffeur me around. You're busy enough as it is."

He slides into the passenger seat, and adjusts his body, tugging his shoulders together to fit. It's comical, really. "If this place wasn't closing down, you could have been a great side act. I'm sure everyone would pay to watch you get in and out of this car."

"I'm not sure others would find it as amusing as you. I certainly don't."

I start the car. "That's because you're not sitting where I am."

"Perhaps I should charge you for the show, then."

"Oh, I'd pay." Actually, I am paying. Being so close to him is taking one hell of a toll on my needy body.

"I just hope they rent bigger vehicles than the likes of this."

I back out of my spot, and head down the long winding path leading to the main road. "The closest car rental is an hour away. You can drive this if you want. I usually walk." I hold my hand up and show him my Fitbit. "I count steps."

"What do you need to count steps for? You're perfect."

My heart leaps in my chest. Colin thinks I'm perfect? Damn, I shouldn't like the idea of that so much. It's better when I thought he didn't want me. Getting involved with him isn't smart or wise, and I'm both. Mostly. Seriously though, he's here for two weeks, and like everyone else who has meant anything to me, he'll up and leave without a backward glance before I can even say goodbye.

"What was it you said before, about me charming the townsfolk?"

I cast him a fast glance. "If they like you, maybe it will stop them from stabbing you with their pitchforks."

"What do you have in mind?"

"A good old Nova Scotia kitchen party."

"What the hell is that?"

"Do Brits all swear as much as you?"

"Do you always answer a question with a question?"

"I don't know, do I?"

He shakes his head and gives a frustrated groan. Just then his phone pings, and that vein in his forehead begins throbbing. He's upset about something. I fall quiet as his fingers fly over his phone, and soon enough, I pull into my driveway. He sets his phone down, stares at the house for a second like he's working to pull himself together, then opens his door. His mood is a little dark, a little somber as I open the door and slide out.

He follows me out, and steps a bit closer, his warm scent teasing all my senses. He touches the strap on my overalls, and dips his head when he says, "Tell me, Violet. What does one have to do to see it?"

"See what?"

"Your beaver."

7

COLIN

Her eyes go wide as a scraping noise in the bushes beside the front stoop fills the silence of the night, and to be honest I'm not one-hundred percent sure what it is I'm doing. I should not be talking about her beaver, the one she carved or the one between her legs. Yet here I am standing close and loving the way her body is vibrating next to mine. Fuck, I want her. I'm sure the fresh Canadian air is messing with me somehow because I know better than to indulge in a hook-up while I'm here on business. It's not my style and I doubt it's hers either. Of course, I can't forget Mum is at home picking out a bride for me. Bollocks.

I step closer, our bodies a hair's breadth away as the floodlights on the side of the old farmhouse blink on. I wince as the brightness hits my eyes, and my body bumps hers. "Ah, I think I found it."

"Yeah, that's my beaver," she says and slowly slides away from me to turn and face her front garden. The warm white light falls over the three-foot wooden beaver displayed between two lilac bushes next to the house.

"It's spectacular." I grip the wooden rail. "Did you carve it?"

"Yeah, I did," she says her voice shaky and breathless. "With the help of Mr. Barker."

"You're a woman of many talents and surprises." Something moves in the underbrush again and I lean over the rail to get a closer look. She pulls me back and my body bumps her. She puts her hand on my chest, and as her warmth seeps under my skin, I resist the urge to close my palm over her small hand and hold it there.

"Careful, it could be a skunk." As if realizing she's still touching me, she quickly pulls her hand back, and shoves it into her pocket. "If you scare it, it will spray you. Trust me, I'm talking from experience here."

"Inside then, shall we?"

My stomach takes that moment to grumble, and she cringes. "I'm so sorry, Colin. You must be starving." She pushes open the door and steps inside.

I follow her in, and because it's habit, I slide the bolt into place. "You must be too. You only had sugary cereal for breakfast and then a candy apple at the park."

She drops her keys on the table near the door, and kicks off her shoes. "Sometimes I get so busy I forget to eat. I'll make us something."

"This is a bed and breakfast, not a bed and supper. You don't have to make me anything." She stifles a yawn, and my heart softens, everything inside me wanting to take care of her as she heads down the hall, her shoulders once again hanging out around her ears. I kick off my shoes too, which seems to be customary in Nova Scotia. "How about I make you something?"

"No, let me. I need to make up for breakfast." I follow her to the kitchen and she flicks the lights on. "It's not even September yet and it's already getting darker earlier. I hate that. Winters around these parts are so long."

"Nights are long back home too," I agree, but I sense she's telling me, the long winter nights can get lonely. Why again is it she's still single? I want to ask, but I shouldn't be getting personal. I stiffen and my gaze darts around the small kitchen. "Do you hear that?"

She grips the back of the chair and goes perfectly still. "Hear what?"

"A scratching sound."

"It could be mice." She does a quick scan of the floor and cocks her head, listening for the sound. "This is an old farmhouse, and they tend to find their way in when the weather gets cooler. Do you still hear it?"

"No."

With that, she goes to her fridge, pulls it open, and bends forward to root through the drawers. "I don't have much to work with."

Fuck me sideways.

If she was standing where I was, she'd see that she had a lot to work with and damned if I don't want to work it. Here I'm worried about delving into the personal by asking about her single status, while my brain is on a journey that involves the two of us shagging.

She glances at me over her shoulder but I'm too damn slow to react and she catches me drooling over her bum.

"Colin?"

"Yeah?" Shite, what did she just say to me? If I wasn't so focused on her body, and all the things I want to do to it, I would have heard. Hey, maybe I should sleep with her. That might clear my head. You know, like when a good thunderstorm rolls through and clears the air.

That's some great logical thinking there, mate.

Okay, so I need to keep my distance, and that's what I damn well plan to do.

"Do you want me to order in?"

"No, let me have a look." Really, I just want to get my head inside the fridge to cool myself down. I root around a bit and find eggs and vegetables from her garden. "How about an omelet?" I pull out the tray of eggs.

She nods eagerly. "Those are fresh. Just laid this morning."

"You have chickens?"

She jerks her thumb out, pointing at nothing in particular, and I get it's one of her cute habits. "At the end of the property."

"Are there any other animals I should be aware of. Anything that might jump out at me?"

She chuckles but it's mixed with a yawn. "I'll get the mice traps set up before bed."

"I can do that." I pull a chair out for her. "Sit."

"I can help."

"And you can sit." She looks like she's about to protest and I say, "You've been doing things for me all day. It's my turn to do for you." A warm flush climbs up her neck. Is she thinking about other things I can do for her in bed?

I clear my throat. "We get mice in the castle as well."

She sits up a bit straighter. "You live in a castle?" Her voice holds childlike wonderment and surprise.

"Yeah, it's old. Drafty. Damp, and it has mice."

She presses her hands together over her heart and blinks rapidly. "Wait, are you a prince?"

"I'm not a prince," I grouch. "Why does everyone think I'm a prince just because I live in a castle?"

"Because princes live in castles."

"Lots of people live in castles."

"Not where I come from."

"You should get yourself a cat."

"Do you have a cat?"

"No, allergic."

"And here I thought you were only allergic to Canada." She gives me a smirk and adds, "For the record, I don't *kill* the mice."

I search the cupboard for a frying pan, and she points. I pull it out, and start cracking eggs into a bowl I found. "Do you make friends with them? Keep them as pets?"

"I capture them humanely, and release them in the wild."

I snatch up a few bell peppers, an onion, and some mush-rooms. "Only for them to find a way to come back inside when it gets cold, right?"

"Something like that," she mumbles.

I chop up the vegetables. "You don't drive them out to the country and set them free."

She snorts. "You don't get more country than here, Colin." As I continue to work, she falls silent, lost in her own thoughts. A few minutes later she breaks the quiet and blurts out, "People suck."

"Yes, I agree."

I turn to her, and she stares at me for a second, her lips quirked. "You don't even want to know why I think they suck."

"Do we really need a reason?"

She laughs. "As a rule, I like people. I just don't like the ones who drive their pets way out here and release them. What the hell is wrong with them?"

"So goddamn much."

She throws her hands out. "You can't just leave a domesti-cated animal in the woods and expect it to survive."

"People suck."

Her chuckle curls around me, and she pushes forward, ready to stand. "Do you need any help? I'm not normally this useless."

"You're not being useless, you're relaxing."

"Same difference."

I eye her and as I try to puzzle out what she means, I say, "Omelets I can handle, and I'm pretty good with a barbecue, when given the chance."

"Do you have servants in this castle?" she asks, like the whole idea fascinates her.

I'm not entirely sure why I told her I lived in a castle. I don't normally talk about myself at all, or share private details. I can only blame it on the fresh Canadian air. "Yes, I do."

"That's amazing, Colin. I'm not much into Disney fairy tales, but I have watched Cinderella."

I chuckle at that. "Do you someday dream of being rescued by your very own prince?"

"Not even a little. To me, Annapolis is paradise. I have no desire to move or live in a gigantic castle. Although servants would be nice," she adds, almost under her breath.

"Living in a castle is not as amazing as it seems." Okay, now I sound like a real twat. This girl works hard and struggles every day and I'm complaining about my castle.

"How come? Are people always driving by and taking pictures? Is it a privacy thing? You come off as a private guy. Me, I'm just an open book." I turn to see her, and she has genuine curiosity in her eyes. Not pity or judgement, and I like that. I'm always judged, always being careful not to misstep otherwise my antics will be splashed all over the tabloids, like my brothers, bringing shame to our family name. Nate doesn't much care though, which makes me feel the need to walk an even straighter line to make up for it.

"Don't get me wrong, Violet. I love where I live, and I come from privilege—"

"I'm sorry, Colin." She plucks a paper napkin from the holder on her table and twists it. "I think I might have said something to make you feel embarrassed by that."

"No, you didn't." I dump the vegetables into the frying pan and stir them around.

"I would never purposely hurt anyone."

I glance over my shoulder and take in her big blue eyes. "I know."

"Tell me more about it." She waves her hands. "I picture big floor-to-ceiling fireplaces, always lit, in summer and winter. I imagine a lot of stone, and servants milling about in fancy outfits."

"Don't forget the singing mice and birds," I tell her. She throws her napkin at me and laughs. "It's a lot like that, though. It's big, and open, high ceilings where I never bang my head." She cringes. "It can be cold and damp."

"This place must feel like a cracker box to you."

My gaze moves over her small kitchen before I pour the eggs over the sweating vegetables. "It's actually cozy here." Home and hearth, a warm place for family to gather. While I have numerous fireplaces, the comfort one is supposed to experience with family has always been absent.

She smiles, liking my assessment.

"Cozy but girly," I tease.

Her chin lifts, and her chest juts out, all indignant like as she squares off against me. "Well, if you haven't noticed, I am a girl, Colin."

"Oh, I've noticed," I respond under my breath as I use a spatula to flip the omelet.

"I'm sure your place is all dark and masculine, and…broody."

"Broody?" I chuckle at that. Does she think I'm broody? "Maybe someday if you get across the pond, you could come visit me. See for yourself."

"Maybe," she says, but what she really means is not in this lifetime. Too bad. I wouldn't mind showing her around if she visited. Wouldn't mind offering my place up as a bed and breakfast, as long as it was my bed she was sleeping in.

"Do your parents and brother live in castles too?" I tighten at the mention of my parents, and my phone takes that moment to ping. "Someone has been trying to get hold of you."

"It's Mum." I pull two plates from the cupboard and set them on the counter, not wanting to discuss what Mum is up to back home.

"You're avoiding her?"

"Yes."

When I don't elaborate, she says, "Okeydokey, clearly not my business." I plate the omelets and carry them to the table. Violet inhales. "This smells delicious. Thank you so much, Colin. I really appreciate you cooking for me."

I slide in across from her, and our knees bump beneath the tiny bistro table.

She takes a bite and moans. My traitorous dick thickens. "She's at home trying to find me the perfect debutante," I blurt out before I can stop myself. What the hell am I doing? I don't know, but I do know that stress has been building for a long time now, and I just needed to get it out.

Her head inches back, surprise widening her pretty eyes. "She what?"

"I'm thirty-one, and I should have given them an heir years ago."

She gives a slow shake of her head, and cuts into her omelet with her fork. "Jeez, no pressure there."

"Yeah..."

"Colin?"

My head lifts to meet inquisitive blue eyes. "Yeah?"

"Does it get lonely? Living in that big old castle by yourself."

"Yes," I answer honestly. "Does living in the big old farmhouse get lonely at times for you too?"

"It does. I don't get many guests as summer comes to a close. I...like having you here."

"You must be damn lonely if you're enjoying my grumpy-ass company. Either that or we should have you checked for a brain tumor."

She grins at me. "You're not so bad, Colin."

"You're not the Bryant I was expecting, but you're not so bad either, Violet."

8

VIOLET

I went to bed smiling like a damn idiot and woke up much the same way. The grumpy Brit isn't so grumpy, and he's not such a bad guy either.

"...you're not so bad either, Violet."

That simple, innocent statement shouldn't make me so happy, but it does and that's that. The downstairs door creaks open and I sit up in my bed. Is someone coming or going? Colin is my only guest, so he must be going, but where is he sneaking off to at eight in the morning? Word of his arrival has no doubt spread, so perhaps a mob has descended, ready to drive away the enemy. Perhaps he's sneaking out to avoid imminent death. Either way, I'm going to need coffee for this.

There's a bit of a chill in the late August air as I climb from my bed and reach for my robe. I tug it on, and glance out the front window. The streets are free of pitchforks, so that's a good start to Colin's day. Off in the distance, I spot the dog walking club, aka, the triple G's. Golden Girls Gossip club. Oh, and of course Chester always tags along. Mr. Casanova himself doesn't have a pet, he just likes to keep up with the latest news while he flirts with the group of women—the widowed and the still married. No judgement here. I do, however, wish they'd keep their damn noses out of my personal life.

No, I do not have a boyfriend.

No, I don't need a man in my life.

Yes, I'm happy living alone.

The questions and the answers never change.

A movement below my window catches my eye and I press my face against the glass. Below me, Colin stretches out his arms and legs, like he's preparing for a morning run. Maybe I should sneak my Fitbit into the back pocket of his shorts.

He takes off running, and I stand there admiring the tight, hard view of his body. Despite his size, he moves with an ease few have. He's so fit, light on his feet, and I love the way his shorts hug his perfect backside. I stand there lost in my thoughts, until there's a strange taste in my mouth. I back up. "Eww..." I grab a tissue and wipe my damp window. I did not just lick the glass.

The triple G's and Chester continue down the road, and take an abrupt turn at my place. "Oh, boy."

I pray Colin put coffee on before he took off for his run, because I'm not sure I can handle what's about to hit me without caffeine. I take the stairs fast, dash into the kitchen and throw up a silent prayer. At least Colin is making himself useful around here.

Maybe he could make himself useful down here.

Whoa, who said that?

I glance down at my talking vagina, and point a stern finger. "We are not sleeping with our guest."

Pounding on my door reverberates through my body and pulls my thoughts back. I pour a fast cup of coffee, and a splash of milk and practically burn my mouth off as I suck it down. I take a few fast breaths, walk down the hall, and plaster on a smile as I pull my door open.

"Welcome triple..." Shit. Still not enough coffee, I guess. "Eugenie, Audrey, Irene, Chester. What can I do for you this early in the morning?"

"Chester saw it again," Eugenie says, her milky eyes wide.

Oh God, not this again.

"Are you sure it wasn't Douglas's new drone?" I question.

Eugenie shakes her head no. "He said he wasn't using his drone last night."

Of course, he said that. He'd rather deny it, then admit he uses it to peek into people's windows. Perv.

"I'm not sure alien invasions are my department. Have you talked to Constable Davis?"

"He sent us your way."

Thanks a lot, Ben. But I get it, he doesn't believe in flying space crafts any more than I do.

"You know the Greenwood military air force base is close. Perhaps they were doing some night flying."

"Haven't heard talk of them getting a new *round* airplane," Chester says, as he folds his arms. The women all nod in agreement, and Eugenie's yappy dog Pumpkin starts barking at something in my bushes. If there's a skunk hiding out in there, UFOs are going to be the least of our problems.

Eugenie picks her up. "What is it, girl?"

"She doesn't like your beaver. Never has," Chester says, staring at my carving.

Colin likes your beaver.

What was it he called it...spectacular?

A small chuckle catches in my throat.

"Something funny?" Irene asks.

"No, nothing at all." I look at my rustling bushes. Did I just hear a meow? I make a note to dig around later. So help me if someone dropped off their pet in the country... not that I can do anything about it, other than take the poor thing to the local vet with the hopes of someone adopting it. I could always keep it. To help with the mice. But I don't want to hurt any mice, and Colin is allergic. That shouldn't play into any decision I make though. I'll be dropping him back off at the airport before I know it, unless, of course, he decides to rent himself a vehicle.

Eugenie kisses her dog four hundred times on the lips, and Pumpkin sticks her tongue out to French her back and yeah, not even a whole pot of coffee is going to help me with any of this.

"There could be a skunk in there." I say and everyone picks up their pooches and inches back. I'll have to remember to pull the skunk card next time they bombard me at the crack of dawn.

"We should get out of here," Chester says, and holds his arms out, like he's protecting the others from a possible spray. Such a gentleman. Irene gives him a smile of thanks—a promise of things to come later—and I start to recite the alphabet, because I can't let my mind go to places that will scar me for life.

They back up, and Audrey snarls and scans the street. Her poufy wig is not quite sitting right. I resist the urge to reach out and straighten it for her. "Heard that fella from the foundation is here."

Here we go! The real reason behind the visit, although they have knocked on my door before about their sightings. "His name is Colin Parker. He arrived just the other night. He's a guest in our town, and I'd appreciate it if you extended your hospitality to him."

"Oh, sounds like you're sweet on him," Irene pipes in. I glance past her shoulder to spot Clara coming in fast with her leashed cat, which is probably ten times the weight of Pumpkin. But they all get along. If only adults played together so well.

"I am not sweet on him, whatever that is supposed to mean. He's staying at my bed and breakfast, that's all."

"You're young, he's young...one would assume."

"One should never assume."

"Does that mean you have a boyfriend now?"

Holy God, make it stop!

"You're not getting any younger, missy," Chester says.

"Why thank you." Just this morning when I glanced in the mirror I thought I was only twenty-six. I guess time flies when you're having fun. Although this is anything but fun, and it feels like an eternity has passed since this crew came banging on my door.

I'm seconds from slipping into my second childhood and throwing myself on the lawn for a good old fashioned temper tantrum, but I pull myself together at the sight of Colin running down the street. All eyes turn as I stare, and I pray to God drool doesn't dribble down my chin. His run slows to a jog when he sees us, and his eyes search out mine.

"We don't want him here," Eugenie says.

"He's trouble," Clara says as she steps into the fray and forms an impenetrable line with the others. I mean, it's not really impenetrable. A good wind could blow them over.

Colin slows to a walk, and starts our way. He swipes at the beads of perspiration on his forehead, and I never knew until this minute how deliciously alluring sweaty guys were.

Do not moan, Violet.

Do not under any circumstances moan!

Crap, I moaned.

"What was that?" Irene asks and spins on the tips of her toes, far too quickly for a woman her age.

I touch my throat as I clear it and swallow hard. "I think I just ate a bug."

"That's because you're standing there with your mouth open dear." Irene arches a white brow, and she might be more astute than I give her credit for. "You ought to close it."

"Right, I'm just ah, shocked and trying to process the UFO sighting." *Oh, God, don't encourage them, Violet.* But I needed a reason for my tongue to be hanging out.

"Yes, well. I'll be out looking again tonight. If I see it, I'll come right by."

"Or you could just phone," I suggest.

"Hey," Colin says as he approaches. "I didn't realize there was a meeting here this morning. I must have missed the memo."

"UFO sighting," I say and point upward.

"Ah, right. Get them a lot out here?"

"More than you know," Chester says. He turns back to me. "Keep an eye on those crops, missy."

"Crop circles, right," Colin says. "I didn't see any on my run, but I'll be sure to keep an eye out for them."

Chester eyes Colin, like he's trying to figure out if the man is sincere or mocking him.

"You've not had a right and proper introduction," I say, and hey, my accent is getting better. I take in the pained look on Colin's face. Or not.

I do a quick round of introductions, and when I get to Clara, she says, "We've already met."

"Right, okay. If there isn't anything else I can do for you, I'd like to go get ready for my day."

"My grandson will be in town this weekend," Irene says. "I'll bring him along to the party, and of course, my famous onion dip."

"Can't wait."

They scoot down the driveway and walk off. "Have a good run?" I ask.

"Uh, yeah...what's this about a UFO?"

I roll my eyes and explain who the three G's are, and that they need a new hobby. "Did you send out a memo about the kitchen party you were talking about? Is there a town phone line you all jump on or something?"

"It's not nineteen fifty and most of us have email. Although I didn't use the phone or computer. I told Clara, and she'll tell all the other influencers."

"Influencers?" He laughs hard at that. "Is that what you call them?"

"They do have a great deal of say around here, and their word matters, and the dog walking club, don't underestimate them."

"Trust me, I won't. Honestly, it's really not much different at home. You do or say one thing and the world knows about it. Our influencers come in the form of paparazzi and social media bloggers."

"Do the papers write about you?"

"I try not to give them a reason." He wipes his brow, and my gaze drops to take pleasure in the way his damp shirt clings to his chest muscles. Yummy.

"I bet they could write all kinds of juicy things about you."

"What?"

Crap. "Nothing."

"I should shower."

"Yeah." I don't move, I continue to stand there with a 'village idiot' grin on my face.

"Um, if you'll excuse me."

"Right." I move to the side as he steps past me, and I follow him inside, letting the screen door bang shut behind me.

Bang. Bang. Bangity bang...that is not at all anything I want to do with Colin.

"Your breakfast will be ready when you're done. Don't dally."

"Dally?" He glances at me over his shoulders, as he heads up the stairs and it's most difficult for me to keep my eyes off his backside. "When did you turn one hundred?"

"Excuse me."

"My grandmother uses the term dally."

"I do live in a town of elderly people." People I totally love. "Sounds like I'd like her."

He glances down, like he's lost in thought. "You would."

"Is she pressuring you into marriage too?"

He nods. "Yeah," he says quietly and heads up the stairs.

"Actually, you should take your time," I call after him.

He turns. "Which is it, Violet. Do you want me to be fast, or do you want me to be slow?"

"Slow, definitely slow."

Wait, am I still talking about him showering? Nope don't think I am, and I need to stop visualizing myself beneath him in bed, as he takes his good old time pleasuring every inch of me.

"I'm working on something down here, so take your time." I dart to the kitchen, open my laptop and go straight to Pinterest. I do a search for crumpets, and give a little hallelujah when I discover I have all the ingredients and they actually seem super easy and fast.

The shower turns on, and I hum to myself, keeping my mind occupied so I don't think about Colin beneath the warm spray, his hard body completely naked. I get to work on mixing the dry ingredients, and then pouring over the water. I reach for my water and yeast mixture, and I'm about to add it when a loud scream of fear reverberates through the entire house.

"There's a fucking alien in my bed!"

9

COLIN

I stand perfectly still as Violet's footsteps pound on the stairs. She pushes my door open and comes flying into the room. I slowly lift my hand, indicating that she shouldn't come any closer. Who knows what this alien is capable of. I spare Violet a fast glance, and spot flour on her cheeks. I have no idea what she was doing downstairs, but she couldn't look any more adorable if she tried. Although I can't think about that right now. Not when there's a hairless alien sitting on my bed looking at me like I'm the one from outer space.

"Colin," Violet says breathlessly. "It's not an alien."

"Of course, it is, look at it. Look at its long narrow head and web feet." The ugly alien climbs to all four feet, and walks toward me. I push back against the wall. "Christ, get me a broom or something."

Now that the beast has me cornered between the bed and the wall, it swipes at me, and tugs at my towel, which is the only thing covering my naked body after my shower. I try to swat its hand, or is that a paw, away but it extends long sharp nails and hisses at me.

"It's a cat, Colin," Violet blurts out. "A sphynx. One of those hairless breeds. It won't hurt you. It's just curious." She frowns as she looks to my left, an open window. "That would be a pretty big jump. Maybe it followed the mice in or something. I wonder if that's the cat I heard outside in the bushes."

"Maybe someone put him here so he'd either scare me or claw me to death."

"Who would do something like that?"

Every single person living in this town. "The broom, Violet," I say through clenched teeth.

She stiffens. "No, you're not hurting it. Talk to it nicely."

I stare at it, still not convinced that it is a cat. It's not like any furry feline I've ever seen. What are they doing to their cats in Canada?

"Say something soothing and nice."

"Get out of my bed, cat." As soon as the words leave my mouth the cat hisses at me and leaps onto my towel. I guess in a way he listened. Violet gasps, and I scramble to hold the cotton to my groin, as the knot unravels and the hairless feline drags it to the floor. It starts scratching at it and purring and I glance up to find Violet staring at my dangly bits, her mouth agape. I'm suddenly overtaken by a vicious sneezing fit, and all the dangly parts start jiggling. Now that's fucking attractive.

Bollocks.

I cover myself with my hands, and she makes an 'eep' sound, and turns around. Too late for that now, isn't it? I'm about to tell her if she got to see me naked, I should get to see her naked too, but stop when the alien cat looks at me again, like my pecker might make a very fine scratching post. I inch away, my back sliding along the wall.

"Did you take your allergy medication?"

This is what we're discussing? I'm standing here naked, in a face-off with a cat, and she's asking about my allergies.

"Yes," I grouch. "I think I'm allergic to this cat."

"No, they're hypoallergenic. No fur. At least I think they are." With that, she darts down the hall. She's leaving me in a time of crisis? Wait, maybe she's decided to get me the broom. She comes racing back, and hands me a towel. She turns around again, giving me privacy to cover myself.

"Thanks," I grumble.

"I didn't see anything," she says.

I drop the towel onto the bed. "Are you saying I don't have 'anything' between my legs?"

She chuckles slightly, and her back vibrates. "Okay, would you prefer it if I said, I'd seen...everything."

"And..."

"I'm sorry."

"Most women don't apologize after getting a glimpse of my bits, Violet."

"A lot of women check out your bits now, do they?"

I tug open the dresser and pull on a pair of boxers and trousers. "You might not go around showing your beaver to just anyone, but I don't mind giving the museum a tour of my bits," I joke.

She laughs hard at that, and a grin tugs at my mouth. "For the record, my apology is not directed at your bits. You're working with some spectacular equipment there." I called her beaver spectacular and find it highly amusing that she's using the same word. "I'm sorry that the cat stole your towel and frightened you."

I stand up a little straighter. "I wouldn't say he frightened me." Okay, maybe I did scream like a girl.

She lets it go, and says, "We need to take the cat to the vet. It's a gorgeous sphynx. I don't think someone would leave a cat like that on a country road. Maybe it's lost."

"You can turn around now, I'm decent."

She slowly turns and I pull on a T-shirt. "I guess all that talk of aliens really got to you, huh?" She takes tentative steps toward the window, and glances at the cat on the floor picking at my towel. "Hey there, kitty," she says, and it gives her a long purr. "I think he likes me. He doesn't have a collar, but he seems friendly enough."

"To you. He tried to eat my face."

"He only wanted your warm towel. Poor baby is probably cold."

"Then he should grow some hair."

She glares at me, her eyes narrow. "Be nice, and use your cat voice."

I glance around the bed. "I don't have a cat voice. Maybe we should call lands and forest or something. Get a trap."

She shakes her head slowly, and her soft curls bounce around her shoulders. "I got this. It's not my first time with lost or stray cats. Now talk nice and soft and slow."

"No."

"No?" she says with a laugh. "Hmm, what do you think we should call him until we can get into the vet?"

"Cat."

"Cat. Right. I don't know why I didn't think of that."

"Because you're not as clever as I am." Down on her knees, she inches closer, and whispers softly. Damn what would a guy like me have to do to get her to talk all sweet like that? "Wait, you can't touch it, Violet."

"Of course, I'm going to touch it. Hey, sweet kitty," she murmurs, and the alien cat rubs its head against her chest.

Smart bugger.

"You're just lost, aren't you, kitty?" It purrs some more and as she cradles it against her chest it angles its head to see me and if I was the cat whisperer, I'd hazard a guess that he was saying, 'look at how fast I got into her bosom, you wanker.'

She moves toward me and I jerk back. "Colin, he can sense fear. That will upset him. Come on now, pat him. Nice and slow."

"Pat him. He looks like a circumcised knob. I'm not touching a knob."

"Touch it."

"You touch it."

"I am touching it. Stop being a baby. He's distressed, and we need to help." I grumble, and she steps even closer. "Come on, listen, he's purring now."

"I'd be purring too if you were rubbing me like that." Why does my cock always find the worst time to thicken?

"Would you now?"

Shite, did I say that out loud?

Warmth seeps into her cheeks and turns them a pretty shade of pink. Is she thinking about rubbing me like that? Doubtful, but a guy can hope, right?

I shake my head. "I'm sorry, I didn't mean to say that."

"So it's not true?"

"Of course it's true. I'm a guy, what can I say?" I tentatively reach out and the cat purrs, until I get close, then it strikes out, and scratches my arm. I swear to God, he's smirking at me. Oh, he's going to get along just fine with the damn goats.

"Bastard," I blurt out and jerk back.

"Colin, be nice. He's a lost kitty."

"He just lured me in with his purrs so he could scratch me. He's smarter than he looks."

"Maybe he's afraid of men." She snuggles her face into him. "Are you afraid of big scary men, kitty?" It purrs and rubs against her.

Little bastard.

She slowly walks out of the room and I follow. Downstairs, she goes into the kitchen to get her purse and she crinkles her nose at me. "I was making you crumpets. I think this batch might be ruined, but I can try again when we get back from the vet."

My heart softens. "You don't have to do that."

"I thought a taste of home would be a nice way to start your day." She snuggles the cat. "But this..." She snatches up her phone and I open the front door for her. Outside, she walks to the passenger side of the car. "Can you hold him?"

"How about I drive, so you can hold it?"

"You think you're up for that?"

"I'd rather take my chances with a lamp pole than that thing." The cat hisses at me. "See?"

"You just called it a thing. He doesn't like that. You don't like that, do you, kitty?" She snuggles it again, and it once again smirks at me.

Oh, it's on, mate.

She slides into the passenger seat and I carefully close her door, not at all trying to get the cat's tail. That would just be cruel, but if the bastard stuck it out at the same time I shut the door, there's no way I could be held accountable. Okay, okay, I'd never hurt the cat, or any animal for that matter.

I circle the car, and open the driver's side. There's about two inches between the seat and the steering wheel. This is going to be fun. Before I even get in, I reach down and move the seat back as far as it can go, which isn't very far.

After much maneuvering and grunting I finally get in, my face practically smashed against the steering wheel. "If the air bag goes off, I'm as good as dead."

"It doesn't work. You're fine."

Oh Violet, nothing about this is fine.

"Where are we going?"

"The closest vet is in the next town over. You'll have to get on the highway."

"Perfect."

"Perfect?" she asks.

"Yes, I was hoping everyone in Canada would see me stuffed behind the wheel. Getting on the highway will really help with that."

She snickers and I back out of the driveway. Five minutes later, we're on the highway, and I avoid the glares of the people passing us and staring at me like I'm a circus sideshow. Alien cat is all wrapped up like a baby and snuggled into Violet when we arrive. His breathing is soft and easy, and his purr screams of contentment. Yeah, he really looks like he's in distress. I've seen sleeping koala bears with more anxiety than this guy.

I park, and circle the car to open her door for her. There aren't too many people in the waiting room when we enter, and Violet walks straight up to the counter to say hello to the receptionist. They obviously know each other well. Their voices lower and the woman sitting in the receptionist chair leans around Violet's body and glances at me. Way to not make it obvious that I'm the topic of conversation.

"Have a seat," she says, her voice back to normal volume. "Dr. Strang will be with you in a moment."

We walk past a woman with a big dog, with quills sticking out of its lips, and it growls at me.

"Stanley," the woman admonishes. Her look is apologetic when she meets my eyes. "Sorry, he usually likes everyone. Violet, how are you?"

"I'm good, Miranda. How are you and I hope poor Stanley is okay."

"He had a run in with a porcupine, again..." She shakes her head. "You'd think he'd learn after the first two times."

"Poor Stanley."

Yeah, poor dumb Stanley.

Stanley barks at me again. How are these animals able to read my mind?

We walk to the other side of the waiting room. "He's probably growling at the cat," Violet explains, but we both know he's not. I clearly have a knack of pissing off animals without even trying.

We sit, and Miranda and Stanley are called in. The dog greets the veterinary assistant with a happy tail. My phone pings and I pull it from my pocket. I stare at the message from Mum.

"Everything okay?"

"Brilliant," I lie. "Mum secretly snapped this picture at one of her latest garden parties." I hold the phone out and show Violet the picture of the girl in the summery blue gown.

She leans in for a better look. "She's gorgeous."

"Lovely indeed."

"A lovely princess for the prince."

I tuck my phone away. "I'm not a prince, but yes, if my Mum has her way, this woman could be my bride."

"Aren't you going to respond to your mum?"

"No."

"Maybe you could just stay in Canada," she jokes.

"I can't hide forever." I don't think.

"Can you just say no, Colin?"

I exhale and grip my hair. I want to say no, but tradition is so important and as the eldest son, I have obligations. They're still disappointed that I broke things off with Charlotte, and I grew up in a family where disappointment was worse than someone being angry. "It's not so easy."

"Rules are made to be broken, you know."

I eye her. She has no idea what it's like growing up under the watchful eye of the paparazzi. Sometimes I wish I didn't care so much, but obligation had been beaten into me since I was a small child. "Not in my world."

She shrugs. "I break rules all the time."

I see the way she is with others, always trying to please, always wearing the weight on her shoulders. "I doubt that." Maybe I'm wrong. Maybe she does mix in a little naughty pleasure and break a few rules, and maybe I want to be the guy to break them with her, have a little fun once in my life.

"You don't know my life."

"No, I don't. These rules." I stare at her hand as she pets the ugly cat. "Which have you broken?"

The door to the backroom opens. "Violet, we're ready for you."

I stand and we're both led to a room with an examination table and one chair. I continue to stand, and Violet takes the one chair as the vet comes in. He's an elderly man with white hair, who much like everyone else I've met, moves at a slow pace.

A smile lights up his face when he sees Violet and it's easy to tell how liked she is around these parts.

"Hello, Violet. So nice to see you."

"Hi, Dr. Strang." She hugs the cat a little tighter. "Nice to see you too. I just wish it was under different circumstances."

"What do we have here?" He reaches out and tugs the blanket away to expose a bundle of hairless wrinkles. "What a gorgeous sphynx."

I guess beauty really is in the eye of the beholder.

Violet strokes the cat's head. "I think he's lost."

The doctor steps a little closer and leans into the cat. I expect him to get a claw to the face. "Let me have a look at him."

"Be careful," I say quickly. "I don't think he likes men."

"Oh?" His brow raises, like he's a little offended by my statement. Canadians are a strange lot. Maybe I did offend him.

Violet hands the cat over and it snuggles into the doctor, purring like a proper asshole and making me look like a proper fool.

"I guess he just doesn't like you," the doctor says and Violet bites down on her bottom lip. Canadians really are a bunch of wankers.

"Hey there, little guy," the vet says as he places him on his examination table. He does a thorough check and when he puts the stethoscope next to the cat's heart—like he thinks he might actually have one—he frowns.

Violet's eyes meet mine and I spot worry there. Without thinking, I put my hand around her back and rub. "He's going to be okay," I assure her quietly, and pray I'm right. I don't like the worry or hurt in her eyes. She's a good person who wants to do right by everyone, which makes me want to do right by her.

The doctor removes the stethoscope from his ears. "Seems he has a heart murmur."

Violet jumps to her feet. "Is it bad?"

"I don't know his history, so we will have to do tests and some monitoring, and there's medication, but it's expensive..."

She stiffens in my arms. "Oh, I don't...I'm not sure..."

"That's fine," I pipe in. "Do whatever you have to."

"Colin," Violet says quietly.

"It's fine, Violet. I've got this. Whatever needs to be done, do it."

Her arm weaves around my back and she holds me close. "Thank you," she whispers up at me

God, those two simple words and the soft, appreciative way she delivered them tugs at my heart. I have no idea why I'd give her the damn world just to hear her say them again.

"We'll get started right away," the doctor says.

"You don't think he's lost?" I question. "You think someone discarded him off because he had a heart murmur?"

"I'm afraid we do see this kind of situation more than we'd like."

Anger flares through me. Who the hell does something like that? If I could get my hands on them...

A smile lights up the doctor's eyes. "Most animals aren't as lucky as this little guy. He found himself two caring paw-rents."

Paw-rents.

Ha. Ha. Clever. But wait, he just called us parents. My gaze jerks to Violet as a strange sensation grips me. Why the hell do I like the idea of her and I parenting something...even an alien cat. "Maybe we should call him Lucky," I suggest.

Her smalls smile wraps around my heart. "Lucky, yes, I like that."

"Or we could call him Marbles."

"Marbles?"

"You know, when you're an old cat lady and he gets out, you can run up and down the street screaming, 'help, I've lost my marbles.'"

She lets out a light, bubbly laugh and I'm happy to see the worry gone from her face. She goes up on her toes, puts her arms around me and presses her lips to mine for a brief, but mind-blowing kiss.

She goes back on her toes, and I blink repeatedly. "What... what was that for?' Her eyes widen, surprise and shock on her face, and she glances down. I touch her chin and bring her face back up. "Violet."

She shrugs. "I just got caught up in the moment. Thank you again for saving Lucky."

My insides are a hot mess, wanting more of where that came from. Wanting her lips on mine, as well as my lips all over her body. "I guess you're a cat mum now," I say for lack of anything else.

"And you're a cat dad."

"I'll be sure to put him in the will."

She laughs. "Is it that bad, Colin?"

Of course, it's not that bad, not when it makes her this happy. Clearly, I'm out of my mind.

I shake my head and say, "Maybe I'm the one who lost my marbles."

VIOLET

I end my call with Tucker and glance out the open window over my sink. As my gaze goes to the figure running down the road, sexy stripper music begins playing in my brain. And why am I suddenly summoning stripper music? Oh, probably because the hottest guy on the planet is running down the road in front of my house, sporting nothing but shorts and a hard body made for sin. I inch back so he can't see me gawking, and I grip the sink as he uses his discarded T-shirt to wipe sweat from his brow.

"Jesus wept, Moses crept, and Adam came on crutches." Lucky jumps on the counter and cocks his head, as if to ask what I just said. "Oh, that's just the way we curse around these parts, Lucky. I picked it up from my grandmother," I explain and run my hand over his hairless back. The front door opens and I quickly jump away from the window and busy myself by pouring two fresh cups of coffee.

Nothing going on here.

My heart matches his fast footsteps as Colin comes down the hall and I try to look breezy and relaxed, not at all aroused as he enters the kitchen, his shirt tossed over one shoulder. I curse my shaky hand as I hold a cup of coffee out to him and plaster on a smile. Cripes, from the way he's looking at me, I'm guessing I'm channeling the joker. I try to smile less, and take a sip of my coffee.

"Thanks." He swallows a generous amount and I admire the way his throat works as he swallows. Lucky jumps from the counter and curls around his feet, and yes, I'm actually jealous of my cat right now. "Are you okay?" he asks, his voice pulling me back.

I roll one shoulder. "Yeah, why?"

"You're flushed."

"Just unusually warm out today." I snatch my keys off the counter.

"It was hot on my run."

Hot, yes. So very, very hot.

"I...ah, have to go."

He frowns. "Another early shift?"

"No actually, Tucker Clements just called. I help him out every now and then. He's a bit under the weather today." He stares at me, clueless, which is so damn adorable. "It means he's sick."

"I know what it means, I'm not daft."

"Anyway, I'll be out in a boat."

He cocks his head in much the same way Lucky did only moments ago. "Is that one of those Canadian saying, like out and about, but it sounds like oat in a boat?"

I laugh. "No, well yes, it does sound like that, but I really am going out in a boat. I'm taking a group out on a whale watching tour to Brier Island. The house is yours for the day. Relax, enjoy, bond with Lucky."

He stands there, looking forlorn, and I shake my head as his sweet vulnerability curls around my soft heart. Christ, he wants to come—and I did suggest it the other day—but being around him, especially in close quarters, will be a special kind of torture.

Don't ask him, Violet.

Do not under any circumstances invite him onto the tour boat.

"Do you want to come?"

Crap.

His face lights up like a child's on Christmas morning, and dammit, seeing the stiff Brit smile messes with my brain and my body.

"That's a yes?" I ask.

He quickly wipes his smile away. "I'd like to see some whales. That would make for an interesting story back home, don't you think?"

He does not want to know what I think.

"Go shower, and be quick about it," I grouch as I wave a hand toward the stairs. Great his grumpiness is rubbing off. "I'm already running late."

"I can be fast."

"Oh God," I mumble under my breath as I envision the two of us indulging in a quickie in the shower.

"Then be fast."

As he darts up the stairs, I call out, "Did you eat?"

"Not yet."

The door slams upstairs and I stomp around and grab sunscreen, a hat, and go into Gramps' old trunk to find Colin a ballcap. Cripes, I hope he doesn't come down here in his three-piece suit. I don't think he packed too much, thinking he'd be in and out of town, but he needs shorts and a T-shirt, otherwise he's going to stand out like a herring caught in a lobster trap. I search the cupboards for quick snacks and find a box of granola bars to toss into the bag. We'll be able to eat on Brier Island, but he'll need something to hold him over until then. By the time I have everything ready, he comes downstairs in a pair of khaki shorts, and a nice T-shirt that shows off his lean, hard body.

"Nice," I murmur.

"What?"

"Oh, I'm just glad you're not in a suit."

"Why would I wear a suit out on a boat?"

"I just didn't know if you had any other clothes."

"I brought a few things. I wasn't sure what the temperature would be here."

"Bet you thought we all lived in igloos," I tease.

He rubs his arms. "This place does get chilly at night. But I'm smart enough to know you don't live in igloos."

I lift the reusable bag, and put it over my shoulder. "Some of us do."

"No, you don't."

"If I can prove it to you?"

"Are you saying you want to place a bet or something?"

"Maybe."

"I'm not a betting man, Violet."

"Oh, you like a sure thing, do you?"

I glance away. Crap, why did I say that? It sounded so sexual. At least to me. Colin might not take it that way at all, though. I slowly turn back to him. My gaze meets his, latches onto the tormented swirl of salted caramel as a storm brews in his eyes. Oh yeah, he's thinking the same thing I am...that I totally am a sure thing.

No, you're not, Violet. Do not get involved with a man who is taking your park, and will be trekking back to Britain in no time at all.

"So no bet then," I say.

"I'd be daft to bet against you when you sound so sure. But I'd like to see these igloos you're talking about."

I grin. "Good, come on then."

We head outside and he scrunches himself into my car. "The one thing I love about Annapolis is that you have the farms on the south mountain and the ocean right at your fingertips. It has it all."

I catch his eye and he looks like he begs to differ, but instead he shuts up and stares out the window as he tries to get comfortable. I sing along to the radio and remember the granola bars.

"Grab my bag from the back seat."

He reaches behind us, and the scent of his freshly showered skin reaches my nostrils. I breathe in deeply, and work to keep a moan at bay.

"There's a box of granola bars to hold us over until lunch." He pulls the box out and holds it up like it might be diseased. "What, you don't eat granola bars where you're from?"

"No."

"Try it, you'll love it."

With skepticism all over his face, he takes a foiled bar out and hands it to me. He sits there, like he's waiting for me to eat first. "I'm not trying to poison you."

I chew, and chew and chew, and he finally rips into his own and takes a bite. It's followed by a groan of disgust.

"Are you sure about that?" he asks.

"Sure about not trying to poison you?"

He picks the box up, and his face contorts as he reads it. "Violet, these expired years ago."

"Granola bars don't expire." I take another bite, and pretend it tastes good. It doesn't. "It's this or we starve."

He shakes his head. "Those are my only choices?"

I chew and swallow. "If you close your eyes, you'd think you were eating a crumpet."

He laughs, and glances at me like I'm crazy, and he's not wrong as he takes another bite.

"I promise a nice lunch."

He groans again and I stifle a chuckle as I drive to the docks. Seagulls squawk overhead as I park, and the smell of brine and fish fills the air as we exit my car. I shade the sun from my eyes and scan the line of people waiting to board the old boat and go on a whale watching tour.

I start toward it and turn to find Colin standing there, frowning. "You can't be serious."

"About what?"

"That's the boat we're going on?"

I laugh. "You were expecting a yacht or something?"

"Maybe not a yacht but that thing is small." He shakes his head. "Why is everything so small here?"

"Come on, you'll be fine." I capture his hand, and the second I do, a blast of heat goes through my body. I drag him along the wharf and pass the line of people all anxiously waiting, their cameras in their hands.

I jump on the boat, and gesture Colin to join me.

"I am not getting on that thing." He eyes me. "And really do you know how to ride it?"

"Why would I lie about that?"

"That's not an answer."

"Fine, I know how to *pilot* it." I glance around at the anxious crowd. "I worked on this boat when I was in high school. Now come on, let's go out for a rip."

He scratches his head. "Are you sure about this?"

"Positive, now get on."

He jumps on board, and lands with a thud. I toss him a hat and sunscreen, and put out a pair of steps to make boarding easier for the guests. I greet them as they step onto the boat, and I give instructions on where to sit.

Once everyone is on board, I call out to Gladys, who works the ticket booth, and she unties the boat. I step into the deck and start her up. I don't need to turn to know Colin is standing behind me, watching. His eyes drill into my back and cause a riot inside me.

"Believe me now," I say without looking at him.

His footsteps come closer, until he's a hair's breadth away from me. I carefully maneuver the old boat around the ones that are docked and go slow until we're in deeper waters. "You better hang on to something," I push on the throttle and the boat picks up speed. His big hand slides around my waist.

Okay, I didn't mean he had to hold on to me, and if I didn't like it so much, I'd tell him to let go. Instead, I stay silent, and we go deeper and deeper into the ocean.

"You really do know your way around a lobster boat, don't you?"

I grin at him, proud of my abilities. "Told you."

"Yeah, you did."

Someone shrieks, and I scan the water which I should have been scanning all along. Colin is a distraction I don't need.

"Right there, look," a guest yells out.

I slow the boat, and gently turn her to head toward the whale. More shrieks come from behind as I slow, and the whale jumps out of the water, putting on a show for us.

"That's Hildie," I say.

"Hildie?" His breath is warm on my neck as he asks that.

"Yeah, she loves to perform for the guests. She's so sweet."

"Did you name her?"

"I did."

"Do all the whales have names?"

God, why has his voice dropped an octave as his mouth gets closer and closer to my ear? Is the man trying to torture me?

"Yes, I like to give everyone names."

"When you met me, did you give me a name, before you knew mine?"

"Um...yeah, no." I sort of did, but I can't tell him I called him Mr. Brit with a stick up his bum.

"Why is it I don't believe you?"

"Fine, what did you call me?"

"The Groper."

A big laugh spills from my throat. "I thought I called myself that."

"But I was thinking it."

Without realizing what I'm doing, I lean against him, let the heat from his warm body seep under my skin. "Maybe we're not so different after all."

"Oh, we're different, Violet," he murmurs, his voice full of want and heat. "We're very different."

I spin around. "You say that like it's a bad thing."

Before he can answer, the boat rocks from the playful whale's jumps, and we bump into one another.

"Sorry," we both say at the same time, and a grin quirks his lips. I grin with him as sexual heat arches between us.

"Want to see?" I ask, my voice low and husky, even to my own ears.

His gaze drops to my mouth, and if I'm correct, I'm pretty sure he just growled, going all Roy Kent on me. "Yeah."

I swallow hard as my insides dance to the macarena. It takes every ounce of restraint I have not to tear my knickers off and jump him right here on the boat, for all the people and the whale to see. His eyes glaze with lust as he stares at my mouth, and I'm pretty sure we're not on the same page. Or rather, we are on the same page. But I wasn't asking him if he wanted to see me naked. Not with my words anyway.

"I'm talking about the whale. Did you want to go see the whale? You know so you have a good story for back home."

His head lifts quickly, his salted caramel eyes a shade darker as he gazes at me, like he can see right into my soul, see that I'm ridiculously attracted to him. "Right."

"What...what did you think I meant?"

"The whale," he blurts out. "I thought you meant the whale."

The boat stops rocking, and he stands there with his arm around me a moment longer. "You good?" I ask. "You got your sea legs?"

He inches back, and I take in his athletic thigh muscles. *Do not think about what they would feel like around your body, Violet. Under no circumstances should you do it.*

Dammit, I'm doing it, and I hate it. Clarification. I hate that I'm thinking about it. I don't hate the idea of it, and that my friends, wouldn't be good at all. Right?

Right, it wouldn't be good at all. It'd be great with a capital G.

I am so...DEAD.

11

COLIN

I stand back and watch the easy way Violet interacts with the guests as they laugh and take pictures of the playful whales. She's fun-loving, spirited, so unlike the women in my social circle—it's a bit contagious, if you really want to know—and she goes out of her way to put other people at ease, makes them feel comfortable. Then again, five seconds ago, I wasn't too comfortable around her. No, not comfortable at all. In fact, my khaki shorts grew so tight, it restricted my blood flow and made things quite uncomfortable. Probably my own fault, though. Yeah, definitely my own fault. What was I thinking, putting my arm around her and talking close to her ear so I could smell the sweet honey scent of her skin.

Get it together, Colin.

She casts me a fast glance and her smile is so full of joy it cuts through me, teases things inside me that I never knew existed. Things that make me think I might have the ability to fall for a woman, after all.

Okay, enough of that.

I might not be able to love, but I can't forget women want me because of who I am and what I can give them. With that thought racing in my brain, I work to keep my balance as I pull my phone from my pocket and take a couple of shots. I send them off to my crazy kid brother, just for fun. Whale watching, and indulging the day away, is definitely his kind of thing. I can see why, I guess. It is kind of fun. After everyone gets their photos, Violet makes her way back to the wheel, and I lean against the gaping cabin entrance and watch her.

"Want to try?" she asks from over her shoulder.

"Not really." I'd rather stand back and admire the view—of her bum.

She casts me a glance and laughs. "It's easier than it looks."

"Doubtful."

A moment of silence and she points. "Look," she says. "Over there."

I step closer, crowd her once again, and I'd have to be a dead man not to notice the quiver in her body. But I'll be a dead man if I do something about it. I am not here to get distracted. I have one job to do, and I need to focus on that, otherwise Grandfather might banish me to Nova Scotia forever. "What am I looking at?"

"Over there. Seal cove. Look at them all." She turns the wheel and heads toward the seals, and more laughter comes from the guests outside.

"You love this, don't you?"

Her smile is wide. "I do. I love being outside, on the boat, or at the park. I love seeing guests of all ages happy. It makes me happy."

I shake my head and chuckle.

"What?" she asks.

"You're just so...different."

Her smile falters for a second, and she turns her attention back to the wheel. Unable to help myself, I lean in and whisper, "I didn't say that was a bad thing, Violet."

"Oh, okay..." she says, her voice a bit huskier as the boat rocks and our bodies touch. She slows us down beside the seals. "Did you want a few pictures?" Our bodies brush again. "Pictures or it didn't happen," she blurts out, like she needs me out of the cabin before the sparks between us start a fire.

"Right."

I exit the cabin and join the others in taking pictures of the seals. After we get our fill, the boat starts again, and I take a seat, letting the cold spray cool down my overheated body. I'd be wise to keep my hands to myself where Violet is concerned, and that's exactly what I plan to do. Ten minutes later, she's pulling up beside a dock, and she tosses a rope to some man waiting for us.

"Welcome to Brier Island," he says in a deep, raspy voice and waves his big, meaty hand. I glance around the vast openness and catch a colorful bird in flight. It's brilliant. "If you all follow me, we have lunch ready, and then you can do some exploring."

The group of guests gather their things and follow the gentleman off, and I note that Violet is back on the boat. I turn to see what she's up to and her eyes go wide when she sees me.

"Aren't you joining in?" I ask.

"I don't normally." She gestures with a nod to the group. "But you go ahead."

Is she trying to pawn me off? "What do you normally do when you're here then?"

"I do my own thing, less touristy things."

"See now, viewing this island from a local's point of view sounds a lot better to me than a guided tour. I bet you know all the best kept secret places that tourists aren't taken to." A grin plays with her mouth. "I'm right, aren't I?"

"Maybe, but what makes you think I'm taking you? You're a tourist like the rest of them."

I put my hands in my pocket and rock on my feet. "I suppose." A refreshing breeze blows in off the water, and I suck it into my lungs. "I guess I could be considered a local now, though. Since my grandfather's foundation is buying up land."

One brow arches. "That's a stretch."

Just then my stomach grumbles, or rather churns, from the expired granola bar we'd eaten earlier.

She waves her hand. "You should go eat with the others."

"Where do you eat when you're here?" I ask.

"Here you accuse me of talking too much, asking too many questions."

"Not an answer."

"Fine, I'll show you, but if you leak it." She stops and slices her finger across her neck.

"Wow, aggressive."

That brings a big smile to her face. "Give me a sec."

She disappears into the boat, and my phone pings. I smile when I see the message from Nate.

Nate: Was that a whale?

Me: No, it was the Loch Ness Monster, you twat.

Nate: Canada must be rubbing off on you.

Me: What is that supposed to mean?

Nate: You're getting a sense of humor. You must totally hate yourself for that. I know you pride yourself on being a proper arse.

I can't help but laugh at that. My younger brother is brilliant at everything he does, everything he touches, but after he injured his knee at Uni and didn't make the cut for the premier league football team because of it, it's like he's given up trying…anything.

Me: You're the proper arse and if you're not careful, Grandfather will banish you to Nova Scotia too.

Nate: Dreadful.

Me: It's not so bad.

Nate: Oh, really. What's gotten into you, big brother?

I spot Violet moving around the boat and can't help think about what I want to get into.

Me: Nothing.

Nate: I thought you'd be home by now.

Me: Things aren't going as planned.

Nate: Good, the longer you're there, the better.

Me: What makes you say that?

Nate: The longer you stay single the better it is for me.

Violet walks up to me, a backpack over one shoulder, curiosity in her eyes as I text.

Me: Talk soon little brother.

I put my phone in my pocket. Nate is right, though. After Mum gets me down the aisle, she'll be turning her attention to Nate, and no way will he be allowed to get away with his antics then.

"Everything okay?" Violet asks.

"Nate," I say, like that explains everything.

"Getting himself into trouble again?" She starts walking and I follow her.

"Oh probably, and if he's not careful, he might find himself at your bed and breakfast."

"You say that like it's a bad thing."

"I didn't mean...I mean...it's not home."

"Home is where the crumpets are. I get it." Before I can say anything, she continues. "Come on." She starts toward a lighthouse, and I try to gather my thoughts as I follow her. "My friend keeps her Jeep here. She lets me borrow it whenever I like." We walk past a Jeep and she pats the roof. "Now," she says, "You're going to meet Roxane and Roxane is a hugger." I eye her. "Just warning you."

"Groper, like you. Got it."

She opens the door to the lighthouse, and I follow her in, surprised to see that it's been converted to a little café.

"Violet," Roxane says when her eyes land on me. She rushes to us and gives Violet a big hug. I stand back. Why do Canadians have to grope everyone? She turns her attention to me, and I stiffen, but she throws her arms around me anyway. I put one arm around her and pat her back. Violet bites back a chuckle.

"Who might this be?" Roxane asks as she gives me a once over.

I'm shocked she doesn't know. But maybe news doesn't travel so fast out here on the island.

"A friend," Violet says, sparing me the wrath that would no doubt come if she told her who I really was. "I thought we'd grab lunch to go, and eat at the beach."

"Oh, lovely," she says and claps her hands. "A picnic lunch for two coming right up." She darts behind the counter, and ten minutes later, Violet and I are in the Jeep and she's driving us to a place called Pond Cove Beach and Nature Preserve.

"I can't remember the last time I've been to a beach," I say, mostly to myself.

"You've never been to a beach until you've been to this one, Colin." I nod and take in the beauty of the island when a bunch of igloo-like tents come into view.

"Well, I'll be…"

She laughs. "Told you we have igloos. They're actually yurts in the shape of igloos. My friend who owns this Jeep runs an

Airbnb business here. Those yurts are quite popular. It's glamourous camping or as we call it, glamping."

"Clever, and I'm glad I didn't bet against you."

She drives a little further, and eases off the road and onto a small gravel area. The beach rises up before my eyes, and while we have beaches at home, they don't look like this. "It's brilliant."

"Yeah, gorgeous," she says, and I turn to her, take in the dreamy look in her eyes as she exhales slowly, her gaze leisurely taking in the waves and snow-white sand. "I'm so lucky to live here. I realize we don't have crumpets, but still…"

I shake my head at her as she gives me a cheeky grin and steps from the vehicle. I stretch and stare at the beauty around me. A warm breeze washes over me, the sound of the waves lapping against the sand, a soothing sound to my soul.

She starts walking to a hill overlooking the beach and I follow her. "Do you swim here or is the water too cold?"

"It's cold, but it's refreshing on a hot day. We can get in later if you like."

"I didn't bring a suit."

She glances at me over her shoulder. "You could go skinny dipping." I stiffen and step around a fallen tree branch. "You do know what skinny dipping is, right?"

"Of course, I do, and I am not skinny dipping. I am not interested in having my bum splashed all over the news."

"Why not? It's a great bum."

"What?"

"Nothing," she blurts out quickly, but I'm pretty sure she just told me I had a nice bum. "There's no one here to see, or take pictures."

"You're here to see, and how do I know you won't sneak a picture and sell it to the tabloids."

She chuckles. "Don't worry. Your crown jewels are safe with me."

"What is this fascination you have with the crown jewels?" I shoot back.

She laughs hard, and drops onto a sandy part of the ground. She taps the spot beside her and I sit beside her.

"Here's lunch."

She hands me a container and I open it to find a sandwich, a cookie and an apple. She opens her own and we both dig in, ravenous. We go quiet, lost in our own thoughts as seagulls soar overhead, quite interested in our lunch.

"I can see why you like living here," I say, and crack open my bottle of water. I take a long drink, and hand it to her. "Thirsty?"

"Sure." She takes the bottle and drinks after me, and I'm not sure why, but everything about it feels oddly...intimate. I recap it once she's done and she has a mischievous look on her face when she asks, "Want to see something?"

Hell yeah, I want to see anything she wants to show me.

"What do you have in mind?"

"It's not the crown jewels, but it's close."

"When you put it like that, how can I say no?"

We gather up our garbage and put it in her backpack. She's about to throw it over her shoulder but I take it from her and shoulder it myself. We take our shoes off before we walk along the sand and I can't remember the last time I felt sand between my toes.

I scan the shoreline, and when we come to a huge rockface, Violet asks, "You promise you won't tell?"

"I can keep a secret, Violet. Besides, who am I going to tell?" I examine the huge rock before me. "Are we climbing it?"

"We're going inside it." She rolls her shorts up higher, and walks into the water. I stand and watch her for a second until she disappears around the rock. "What the ever loving..." I follow behind, shivering as the icy cold from the water seeps into my skin. "Where are you?"

Her voice sounds distant, hollow almost, quiet as she says, "In here."

I walk a bit farther, until I find a cavernous opening in the rock, and I peer in to find Violet standing there. "This is magnificent," I say.

She presses her finger to her lips, and points up. "Bats."

I glance up and light filters into the cave, showcasing gorgeous stalactites. I admire the long icicle-shaped formations hanging from the ceiling. "Wow."

"Nice, huh?"

"Incredible."

She takes my hand in hers. "Follow me quietly." We walk along the rocky bottom, the ocean lapping behind us, until we come to a small pool of water. She slides in, up to her thighs, the water dampening the bottoms of her shorts. She grabs a fistful of water and splashes it onto her face, and her tongue snakes out to taste it.

"Salty," she says.

"Beautiful," I murmur, dying for a taste...of her.

"Right?"

"I have never seen anything quite like this before."

Quite like her before.

She winks at me. "Best kept secret."

Crikey, she's not the only one with a secret. My cock hardens, and as she crooks her finger to lure me in, I give myself a fast and hard lecture, reminding myself I am not here to shag the gorgeous woman who continually impresses me.

Unless, of course, she asks me to.

Bollocks.

12

VIOLET

I take a tray of finger sandwiches from the fridge and remove the plastic wrap before I set them on the kitchen table with all the other goodies. As I look around my house, all ready for the kitchen party, my heart beats a little faster in my chest as Lucky purrs and walks around the table. I still can't believe Colin paid all the vet fees last week, and we now co-paw-rent a cat. At least until Colin leaves. What will we do then? Will the cat stay or go? There is just so much to consider in a custody battle.

Voices from the road reach my ears as everyone makes their way to my place, and I untie my apron and smooth my hair back. Colin comes into the kitchen, and every freaking time he walks into a room, my stupid heart misses a beat. I take a fast breath—still shocked that I was close to ripping off my knickers on the boat and having my way with him. Maybe that's why he's been avoiding me. He knows it's a bad idea, too. Or he's simply not interested. Although I'm pretty sure he is. Then again, it could all be in my head and there's nothing at all going on between us.

I work to look and sound casual, even though the mere sight of him hits me like a triple shot of espresso—right between the legs. Honestly it's been insane having him here —in the most sexually torturous ways. Everything about him reminds me I'm a woman, who hasn't been touched in a very long time. He's been quiet after our adventures, staying away from me, mostly, as well as those wanting his head on a platter—which I'm hoping to change with tonight's party.

He spent the better part of the week on his computer, buried in his work. Honestly, he's lucky that he can work from anywhere. But the truth is, my entire house, as well as my body, has been filled with tension—of the sexual nature— every time I walk past him. Who am I kidding? I don't even need to walk past him, or have our bodies nearly brush on the small staircase, or the upstairs hall. Whenever I get home from work, every nerve ending sparks just knowing he's inside. So yeah, excruciating.

He looks over all the food and turns his attention to me. He angles his head, his eyes narrowing as his gaze moves over my face.

"What?" I ask and swipe at my cheeks, hoping he can't see through me and read my most inner thoughts, which happen to be dirty and delicious. "Do I have something on my face?"

"Yeah, worry."

"I'm not worried." Maybe I am, a little bit. I don't want the town to hate him, or blame me for not being able to stop it. "Tonight the town will fall for you as much as…" Shit, what am I saying. I'm not falling for this guy. He's proving to be likeable, especially after saving Lucky but falling for him is out of the question, because one, he's leaving soon, and two,

I'm smart enough not to get involved with a guy who can't wait to get out of this town.

He angles his head, his brow arched. "As much as who?"

Just then Lucky meows and curls around Colin's feet. "As much as Lucky."

Colin looks at the cat, with a mixture of fear and misery. "He's not falling for me, he's circling my legs and plotting the best way to trip me. He's been doing it all week and just this morning, he leapt out of nowhere when I was headed downstairs. I damn near broke my neck. I think he's trying to kill me." He picks up a potato chip, scoops up a bit of the dip I made earlier and takes a bite. "This is delicious."

"Secret family recipe."

The front door opens and in walks a few neighbors. "Doesn't anyone knock around here?"

"Not when there's a good old East coast kitchen party."

"Where the beer goes into a cooler, instead of the fridge." The look on his face suggests Canadians are wacko. He kicks at the big cooler full of beer, coolers and apple cider, but it doesn't budge.

"That's right." I open the cooler, reach in, shake the ice off a cold beer, and hand it to him.

"A right and proper ale, for the prince who lives in a castle."

"I'm no one's prince, Violet."

"That's true."

"Hey."

"But you will be soon, thanks to your mum."

As he grumbles I laugh and put my hand on his chest. His big warm palm closes over mine, and the heat of his touch seeps through my body and burns between my legs. The neighbors step into the kitchen and I snatch my hand back.

"Eugenie," I say and take the mini eclairs she brought and set them out for the guests. "You remember Colin."

"Of course, I remember Colin." She taps her head. "Nothing wrong with my memory, and no one is about to forget that he's here to destroy our town."

Ugh.

"Let's just all try to get along tonight, shall we?" I glance at Colin, and convey with my gaze that he has his work cut out for him. "Oh, did you hear that we rescued a cat?"

"Have you now?" Lucky purrs at Colin's feet, and I gesture for him to pick the cat up. Good Lord, from the look on his face you'd think I just asked him to lick a sewer pipe or something.

Don't think about licking...

He carefully bends and slides his hand under the cat. Lucky stares at him, and Colin stares back, like if he breaks eye contact, the feline will attack. It's almost comical.

"He's gorgeous," Eugenie says. "A cat this gorgeous must belong to someone."

I frown. "The vet says he has a heart murmur, so it's likely he was just set free."

"How horrible. Hello there, handsome," she says, going back to rubbing Lucky.

Colin pets Lucky's head and I'm tossing up a prayer that Lucky doesn't strike him.

Colin turns his focus to Eugenie. "I was thinking, if it was okay with you and the others, that I could walk him when you walk Pumpkin. I didn't want to do it too soon, I wanted him to settle into his new house, but now I think he might be ready to meet the others."

She narrows her eyes. "I'll have to talk to the others. We don't just let anyone walk with us." Yeah, they do. Anyone who can share gossip is always welcome.

"Thanks, I appreciate it, and did you hear Miranda's dog Stanley had *another* run in with a porcupine?"

Eugenie's eyes light, and she leans in, looking conspiratorial. "Oh, really? Do tell."

"Heard it when we were at the vet last week."

As he continues to tell her all he learned, I stand there grinning. Well done, Colin. Well done.

More people fill my farmhouse, and I search the crowd for my mother. She said she'd be here tonight, and I hope she comes. I'd really like her to meet Colin, although I'm not sure why. She's going to hate him every bit as much as the others.

I see a very familiar head above the crowd, and turn back to Colin. He's in deep conversation with Eugenie, holding his own, so I excuse myself and make my way into the other room to say hello to Caleb. He puts his arms around me and lifts me clear off the floor. Yes, it's true, we had a thing last summer when he was working at the park. It was short-lived, and we've stayed friends, and no, contrary to what Colin thinks, Caleb is not that much younger than me. He's twenty-three, finishing his last year of college, and yes, I'm getting the feeling that he'd like to go back to being a couple. I honestly have no desire. It somehow must be Colin's fault.

I don't need to turn to know Colin is in the room. I can feel his eyes burning in the back of my head. Caleb sets me on my feet and I turn to find Colin leaning against the archway, the beer bottle dangling by his side. My God, is he trying to look sexy, or does that just come naturally to him. My insides jump, and I'm not sure the lace bra beneath my cotton dress can do much to hide the hardening of my nipples. Did the temperature in the room jump a million degrees? I take a pull from my beer bottle to cool myself down.

"I hear you got a bald pussy." What the... I choke on my beer, and Emily starts patting my back, unable to stop laughing. "Are you okay?"

"Of course, I'm not okay. I just about choked to death."

"I told you a million times not to exaggerate."

I take a big breath, and cough a bit more. Colin looks like he's about to push off the archway and come to my aid when I finally get myself together. "Why would you say something like that when I'm mid swallow?"

"What did I say?" She shrugs. "Rumor has it you have a bald pussy. I was just confirming that."

"Stop playing innocent."

She puts one hand on her hip and pretty much aligns her nose with mine. "No, you stop."

I press my nose to hers. "Stop what?"

"Stop pretending you don't want him." She turns her head and blatantly stares at Colin. If he didn't know we are talking about him before, he sure as hell does now. "Hey maybe we can do a foursome."

"What?"

"You know, the four of us all double date." I don't miss the gleam in her eyes. Okay, I get it. She's trying to get a reaction out of me and I stupidly gave it to her. I also gave her an opening, and from her grin, it's clear she's going to jump all over it. She leans forward, her eyes wide. "What, did you think I meant?" She blinks innocently and gasps. "Wait, you thought I meant a foursome in bed." She shrugs and glances around the room. "I could talk to Trevor."

"Stop. No, that's not what I think you meant." I inch back, take a much-needed pull from my bottle, and sit on the edge of the sofa. "Emily, he's just a guest in my house and as mayor, I have to help him out. There is nothing more going on between us. Now or ever."

She finger-waves to her husband as he comes down the hall and stops to talk to Colin. Emily and Trevor are my closest friends, pretty much the only two of our generation not to up and leave Annapolis for bigger and better. Trevor stayed to take over the family farm, and Emily is a country girl at heart. I really hope they have kids and the new generation will see that paradise is right in our own back yard, not the bustling city streets.

Emily wags her brow at me, pulling my attention back. "I know, but you should be helping yourself out too."

"What is that supposed to mean?" I ask, but wish I hadn't, judging by the way she starts bobbing her head. A lecture is coming...and so is a headache.

"Girlfriend, if you really don't know what I mean, then it's been far too long since you've been laid, and stop playing with fumbling college boys. You need a man. A real man, and as much as I hate why Colin is here, I think he's probably killer in the sack." She starts gyrating her hips and I grab her hand to stop her.

"I hate him," I fib, my voice rising as more people enter the house and the noise level goes up. "He's here to tear down the park."

Her eyes widen in delight. "Hate sex. Ooh, even better."

"What do you know about hate sex?" I say loudly, right at the exact moment a hush comes over the crowd. Heat moves into my cheeks, and all eyes turn to me. Cripes, I'm in a room full of geriatrics, and now they're all waiting to hear what Emily has to say about hate sex.

"Who needs a drink?" I say. "And I made cucumber sandwiches, fresh cucumbers from my garden." I turn to Irene. "Your favorite. Come on, let's all go have a bite and I want you all to meet Lucky."

Before I can step away, Emily leans in and whispers. "I know lots of things about hate sex, and tomorrow, I expect you to know a thing or too, as well...and I want all the details."

We pile into the kitchen, and as I feed the townsfolk, I try to keep one eye on Colin, to make sure he's okay. A strange uneasy feeling moves through me as he makes his way across the room to chat with Caleb. I sure hope he's not checking to see if he's of drinking age. Constable Davis already did that at one of our parties, and I was a little mortified.

I check the cooler, and step into the pantry off the kitchen where I keep a small chest freezer. Cool air rushes over me as

I grab one of the ice trays. Before I can turn back, warm breath trickles down my neck and pushes back the burst of cold.

"Hate sex, huh?"

I suck in air, as every nerve in my body tingles in awareness. I take a fast moment to pull myself together. Earlier, when Emily blatantly stared at him, she made it clear he was the topic of our conversation. He's a smart man who can easily put two and two together. "We were discussing a book for book club."

I turn and he has a smirk on his face. Yeah, like I said, I'm an open book, an easy read but when it comes to this guy, I should be careful. I like him, and the last thing I want to do is fall for him. Everyone leaves Annapolis, and he's not even hiding the fact that he can't wait to get back home.

"The name?"

Crap, is he asking the name of the guy I want to have hate sex with?

"Ah, what?"

"The name of this book."

"Oh, ah...shoot, I can't remember it right now. I'll let you know when I think of it, though. Do you need another drink, a sandwich perhaps?"

"Violet..."

"What, did you think we were talking about you?" I say breezily, teasingly. "You know I already told you I liked you, as a friend, of course."

His eyes darken, and so help me God, Emily is right. I should be helping myself out. A brief affair with the hot Brit before he tears down our park and heads for home sounds like the most ridiculous idea ever, and one I should explore more. If he's here to take everything from me, why shouldn't I take something back in return? I just can't let him take my heart when he walks out of this place.

"Here, let me help you." He takes the tray of ice from my hand and pops an ice cube out. "You're doing too much. You're all flushed." He runs the ice over my forehead and along my hair line and I gulp. It might be an innocent gesture, but it sends my mind careening down a path I know better than going. Me in bed, Colin rubbing that ice all over my body, cooling all my warm parts as his mouth follows, to heat me back up again.

A sound I have no control over crawls out of my throat, and his hands stills. "Are you okay?"

"Ah, yeah…" Nope, not okay at all. Might not ever be okay again for as long as I live and then even when I die, and I am not exaggerating.

The noise level in the kitchen rises. "I guess I know why they call it a kitchen party."

He presses the ice to my bottom lip. "No matter how big or small a house is…" *Way to sound breathless, Violet, like the man is giving you more pleasure with a melting ice cube than any other man has given you with his entire body.* But it's true, so damn true. "Everyone eventually finds their way to the kitchen."

"We should get back out there then."

"Yes, you're supposed to be making friends and charming these people." I lick my wet bottom lip as the last of the ice melts.

"Yeah, I know." His head dips and I'm sure he's going to kiss me. Heat arcs between us, and I part my lips in invitation.

"Where is my lovely daughter?" My mother's voice bursts in my ears and the door to the pantry flings open. "Oh my." Her hand goes to her chest as Colin and I quickly break apart.

"Hi Mom." I snatch the tray. "Just getting more ice for the cooler."

"It is rather warm in here. Everything is melting fast."

Way to be subtle, Mother.

I head out of the small room and Mom backs up to give me room. She blocks Colin. "You must be Colin Parker."

He holds his hand out to shake hers and I don't miss the way Mom gives him a once over. Twice.

Mom nods. "Ah yes, now I understand."

Oh, God. What is she about to say?

"Understand?" Colin asks.

"Why my daughter has been so scarce." She puffs up her hair. "I haven't seen her all week."

"I haven't been scarce, I've been busy showing Colin around," I intervene as I dump the melting ice over the drinks.

"What exactly have you been showing him?" she asks with a grin.

"We found a cat," I blurt out.

"A bare pussy," my ex-best friend Emily pipes in as she stands next to my mother, and munches on a cucumber sandwich. "You know, those nice smooth hairless ones. I believe it was Colin's idea to cover all the costs, so they could keep it."

"How very kind of you," Mom says.

Emily's lips quirk. "He must like bare pussies, to go through all the trouble."

"It's a sphynx Emily," I blurt out before I can stop myself. "Stop calling it a bare pussy."

Emily snickers, and puts her arm around my mother. "Come on, Belinda. Let's go see what Chester is up to. Let's bring Lucky, see what he thinks of him."

I am so going to kill her.

I toss Colin an apologetic glance, and he just shakes his head and laughs. At least he's a good sport about all this. "Go mingle," I say.

I turn my attention to my guests, and we all chat and drink and eat. Soon enough, many begin to excuse themselves. It is almost nine and well past their bedtime. I look for Caleb. He must be wondering why I ignored him for the best part of the night, but he's nowhere to be found. What did Colin say to him?

Even though it's early, I'm tired by the time the last of the guests leave. Watching over Colin and making sure everyone played nice and had a good time was exhausting. Dishes clang in the kitchen, and I push off the door.

"Hey," I say when I see Colin loading the dishwasher. "You don't have to do that."

"You threw a party for me, it's the least I can do, don't you think? I just have one plate left. You head on up." Since I'm enjoying the view so much, I stand and watch as he rinses the plate, sets it in the dishwasher, and closes it. He turns back to me, and his gaze moves over my face as he leans against the counter.

"I didn't win over any of the town's influencers tonight, did I?"

"I don't know if I'd say that." He definitely won me over as he mingled, and deep down he's a good guy, sent here to do a dirty deed. He honestly wants these people to understand how good the school can be for the community. I need them to understand it too, or I'll be ousted as mayor, and I actually like my job. I'm good at it, and I care deeply for the community I love and call home. It was my father's wish that I follow in his footsteps as well, and I don't want to let him down.

"Good to know I'm not totally hated."

Girl, do not think about hate sex.

"Colin."

"Yeah."

"Do you want to get Lucky?"

13

COLIN

I stare at the gorgeous woman leaning against the wall, a come-hither look on her face, as she asks me if I want to get lucky. One of two things must be happening here. Either I'm in bed dreaming, or I'm hearing things.

"Colin, lucky..." she says again.

Fuck yeah.

I drop everything I'm doing. "You don't have to ask me twice."

There's a playful gleam in her blue eyes as she cocks her head and says, "I'm pretty sure I just did."

I walk across the room, each step determined, and put my arm around her waist. "You won't have to ask a third time." Her eyes go wide as I pull her to me, press my growing dick against her soft body and dip my head until my lips are just a breath from hers. My heart pounds a little faster in my chest, and I'm seconds from kissing her when I note the shock in her eyes. I inch back. What the fuck? Okay, maybe I really was hearing things.

"Violet?"

"The cat...Lucky. I meant do you want to get Lucky. You know our cat Lucky, and bring him upstairs for bed." I try to settle my rattled brain as she rambles on, and the second understanding hits, I unravel my arm from around her back and step back until I hit the kitchen table.

"Jesus, sorry. I thought you...must be the allergy medication. Messing with my brain." I adjust my cock in my boxers, and her gaze drops.

"And your...pants."

"I think it's from the dry weather here."

A laugh bubbles out of her throat. "Yes, it's usually wet where you come from, isn't it?"

"Wet...yeah."

Warmth crawls into her throat. Even though I read her all wrong, once I had her in my arms, I was pretty sure she wanted to snog. She might be saying one thing, but her body, the way it molded against mine, warm and pliable and so damn needy, tells an entirely different story.

Should I drag her to me again, finish what we started? Will she kick me in my bits, or let me take my fill of her. I guess we'll soon find out. I take a step toward her and Lucky weaves himself between my legs, and I nearly trip.

I grab onto the kitchen chair before I face plant. "See, he's trying to kill me."

She drops and scoops up Lucky, who snuggles into her and tosses me a *fuck you, wanker* look. "I think it's his way of showing affection."

"Like this?" I say and hold my wrist out to show her the scratch he gave me last night, for no good reason. "I woke up to find him standing over me, and when I jumped up, he scratched me. He's trying to kill me and make it look like suicide."

She laughs but it's deep, throaty and needy. "He's a sweet cat. You probably just startled him when you jumped up."

"Why was he standing over me?"

She holds Lucky and looks him in the eye. "Lucky, why were you standing over Colin?" The cat purrs and rubs his cheek against hers. "Aww, you are so sweet. Let's go get you tucked in."

"Not with me."

"I really don't know how he got into your room. Did you leave your door open last night?" She turns and heads toward the stairs. When she reaches the top, she flicks the hall light on, and I adjust my dick again before I dart up.

"My door was shut."

"Maybe you got up in the middle of the night and forgot." She carries Lucky into the spare room and sets him on the bed we purchased for him. He scratches at it, and snuggles in, looking all innocent, but I know better.

"Yeah, the mother ship was probably here to collect its spawn and I was probably hypnotized, and opened my door as I was drawn into the white light. They probably did all kinds of probing things to me before depositing me back in my bed."

"Maybe they dislodged the stick with their probing."

"What?"

"Nothing." She flicks the bedroom light off, and halfway closes the door, so Lucky can come and go as he pleases. She turns to me, our bodies close, and heat arcs between us. "There are no aliens coming for Lucky," she murmurs quietly, softly. "Get some sleep." She turns the hall light off, and we both stand there for an extra second, the mood shifting in the dark, sexual tension taking up space between us.

My eyes adjust and I see the outline of her face as she stares at me. "Night."

"Night," she says and backs away. I stand in the hall until her door closes, and I'm pretty sure I'm going to have to beat the bishop if I want to get any sleep. I turn and go to my room, securely shutting the door behind me. Nothing or no one is getting in, unless it's Violet. She's welcome. Not that I expect her to ask me if I want to get lucky a third time. Sure, I'd like it, and probably, stupidly, take her up on it, but I'm pretty certain that's not going to happen.

I make a quick trip to the bathroom to get ready for bed, and crack my window to let the cool night air in before I strip off, neatly lay my clothes over my chair, and climb into bed. The sheets are soft against my body, and I can't help but think what else would be soft next to me. Bollocks. *Go to sleep, mate.* I spend a long time tossing and turning and finally fall into a fitful sleep. As the breeze blows in, bringing the fresh scent of hay with it, it wakes me up and I start a sneezing fit again. Bloody hell.

I push to my feet, and in the dark room search for my medication, when I remember I left it downstairs in my brief-case. I tug on my boxer shorts, and quietly open my door. A quick scan lets me know the alien cat is nowhere to be found, but he's a stealthy bastard that moves like a ninja, so I best be careful.

Miraculously, I make it downstairs without being attacked, and pop a few pills. I swallow them down and quietly tip toe back up. I'm on my last step when the hall light flicks on and blinds me. "What the..." I trip up the last step and fall against a very soft body.

"Are you okay?" Violet asks, as I pin her to the wall.

"I'm not sure who's going to take me out first, you or the cat." I push off her and right myself, even though I would have loved to linger against her a little longer.

She arches a brow, a challenge in her eyes. "See, you do get up in the middle of the night."

"I needed allergy medication. I left it downstairs in my brief-case," I say and that's when I become fully aware of her barely there pajama tank top, and loose fitting pajama shorts. "What are you doing up?"

"I heard a noise. I wanted to check to make sure Lucky wasn't trying to smother you in your sleep."

I glance to my left, and out my bedroom window. "No sign of the mother ship yet."

"I wonder if you'll remember getting up come morning."

Getting up...yeah, seeing her all sexy and sleepy and half dressed...I'm getting up.

"I'm never going to forget this, Violet."

I step into her, unable to help myself, and she backs up, until she's pressed against the wall again. Her breathing changes, becomes faster, heavier, and as my eyes adjust, I glance down, and take pleasure in her deep breaths.

"Why...why not?" she asks.

"Because I ran into you." My body still burns everywhere it touched hers. "Literally."

She frowns and nods her head. "Yes, I suppose a good shock is memorable."

"That's not it." My voice is thick with need, even to my own ears.

She blinks up at me. "No? What is it then?"

I touch the thin spaghetti strap on her tank top, and slowly drag my finger along the underside. Her muscles tighten, little goosebumps forming. My gaze goes to hers. "This."

"You're going to remember my tank top?"

"I'm going to remember how it clings to your body, and the way your nipples are poking against the material." I take a small step closer, until we're almost touching. I swear we're generating enough electricity between us that we could light my entire castle for a month straight.

"Oh..." She moves her hips forward and a little welp catches in her throat. "I'm sure I won't forget it either."

"Because of the shock?" I ask.

"No, because of this." She moves her body again, until her stomach presses against my throbbing cock. I clench down and work to keep myself together as she massages my dick. I put my arms on either side of her head, and pin her to the wall. Heat flashes in her eyes, and I lower my head.

"Maybe we should really give ourselves something to remember."

She wets her lips. "What are you suggesting?"

"A right and proper shagging."

Her chuckle is full of need as it wraps around me and strokes my growing dick.

"We probably should try to remember everything about tonight. That way, tomorrow we'll know if Lucky really is an alien and the mother ship is trying to find him." I move my hands to her ribcage and brush my thumbs over her nipples. "Oh, I see you have no trouble finding things."

"Want me to show you what else I can find?"

"I think I do."

I put my knee between hers to force her legs open. Eyes locked on hers, wanting to see all her reactions, I slide one hand down her body and dip into her sexy shorts. I run my finger over her lips, and nearly sob when I find her completely shaved. I widen her wet lips—Jesus, she's so fucking wet for me—and lightly brush my finger over her clit. She gasps, and her hands go around my neck to hold on.

"You're very good at finding things."

"I think I might have been an explorer in another lifetime," I tease, as I lightly stroke her clit, and groan with pleasure as it swells beneath my fingertip. I lower my head and press my lips to hers as I touch her deep between her legs, and she pushes her pelvis against me, clearly wanting more. You don't have to ask me twice. Well, sometimes you do.

I pull my hand from her shorts and she whimpers. "My place or yours," I ask.

"Yours."

Okay, she's going to allow me into her body and not her space. Keep a level of personal separation. I can understand that.

I step behind her, put my hands on her hips, and guide her into my room. A cool breeze rushes in and I shut the door behind us. The light from the hall seeps in through the door-frame, and the moon outside slants off the walls giving me enough light to see the beautiful woman standing next to my bed.

"Your room is freezing."

I take one step toward her. "I know, but I can think of plenty of ways to warm up."

"Me too." She darts to the left, and for a second I think she's leaving, but then she goes to the closet, pulls out a big plastic tub and opens it. She tosses me a pair of wool socks. "These should fit you." I stare at the socks as she sits on the edge of my bed, sexy and enticing as she pulls a pair on herself.

"I'm used to undressing for sex, not dressing for it."

"That's because you never had sex in Canada before."

I'm doing a lot of things in Canada I've never done before. I shake my head, and wonder what I'm getting myself into as I tug on the socks. Oh, wow, they're nice and warm. Shagging with socks. It's a first, but I think I'm going to like it.

"If it was later in the year, we'd both be wearing toques."

"Toques?"

"Wool knit hats."

Chuckling, I walk to my window and close it. Sitting on the ledge, I take my time admiring Violet and pray this isn't a dream. Should I pinch myself? Nah, if it's a dream I don't want to wake up.

I wave a finger up and down her body. Up until this moment, I never thought anyone could make wool socks sexy. "Other than the socks, you're totally overdressed."

"I thought you liked my tank top."

"I do, but I'll like you better out of it." She pushes to her feet, and there's mischief in her eyes as she stands there. "Christ, don't tell me you shag with your clothes on, because dammit, woman, I need to see you naked."

14

VIOLET

"We're Canadian, not contortionists, Colin." I step closer, and his muscles bunch. Dear God, he is one hell of a fine specimen. They don't make them like this in Annapolis, and maybe not even in Canada. If they do, they've eluded me.

Dying to touch him, I put my hand on his chest and don't bother to hide my little whimper of pleasure as I span my fingers and touch all his delicious hardness. I examine his valleys and hills, and a rush of joy goes through me when he quakes from my slow but needy exploration.

His big warm hands slide under my tank top and he runs them up my sides. This time he brushes my nipples without the cotton barrier and I moan and lean into him. God, I want this and right now, I don't even care about the consequences of our actions. That's a thought for tomorrow when I'm not a quivering mess of need.

"So good," I whimper, my lids fluttering shut.

"I want this off." My eyes open wide at the need and demand in his tone. Emily is right. Colin is a man, not some fumbling college boy. "Now."

I lift my hands over my head, and in a quick movement he peels it off, leaving me standing there in nothing but my shorts. My pulse jumps at the way he admires my naked breasts, like he's about to worship them.

Worship away, my prince.

His head dips and he bends to take one hard bud into his mouth. He licks and sucks so thoroughly the sensations go straight to my bare pussy.

Bare pussy.

Get out of my head, Emily.

I slide my hands around his head, run my fingers through his thick dark hair, and hold him to me as my entire body quivers with a need it hasn't felt in...ever. His hands go around my back and he slides them down to grab my ass. He kneads my flesh and his mouth finds mine again.

"I want to see your beaver."

Ohmigod!

Despite the heat in my body a laugh bubbles up in my throat. He inches back, confusion dancing in his eyes, and I work to pull myself together.

"What? What's so funny?"

My lips twist and I try to fight back a giggle. "We don't really call it that."

"But you said you did," he counters, his voice serious. "You specifically said, a beaver is something you call a woman's naughty bits."

We're really going to have to work on his interpretation of our slang and I can't forget how he takes things literally. "Yeah, no."

"What is it, yes or no?"

"We call it that jokingly, not...you know, when we're intimate."

"I was trying to use your language." He looks away, sheepishly. "I just thought..."

I cup his face, the vulnerability about him at this very second doing the craziest things to my heart. "I know, and I love that."

"I should call it a pussy then. A bare pussy."

Okay, that shouldn't turn me on quite as much as it does, but when it's said in his sexy accent, what's a girl going to do but go with it.

"Yes, that's exactly what you should call it."

The heat and hunger are back in his eyes, and he cups my sex in his palm. "I want to see your bare pussy. I want my mouth on it, and my cock inside it."

I back away from him, and he angles his head, not at all sure what I'm about to do. I slide my fingers into my shorts and wiggle as I pull them down. His growl curls around me and gives me all the encouragement I need. Once I'm naked, I kick my shorts toward him and he catches them. He bunches them in his hands, and I back up until my legs hit his bed.

Shimmying backward, I climb on, and lay myself out like I'm a buffet for his pleasure.

"Fuck, you are gorgeous," he murmurs and carefully drapes my shorts over his chair, like they're a prized possession.

He stalks toward me, in his boxers and wool socks and I love everything about this. I hold out a finger, and rake it up and down his body. "I believe you're the one overdressed now."

"I believe you're right." He makes fast work of his boxers, and I go up on my elbows as his gorgeous cock springs free.

"Now that's a right and proper cock," I say and it brings a smile to his face.

"You like right and proper cocks, Violet?"

I examine his girth as he takes his cock into his hand and strokes. My heart speeds up, eager to touch him, take him into my mouth. "Can't say." His head angles, the question he doesn't need to ask lingering in his eyes. "Never even seen one before now." He chuckles. "I'm probably going to have to play with it a bit, to see if I like it. What's the return policy?"

He shakes his head as he climbs onto the bed, grips my legs and pushes them wide open. "I'm afraid there's no return. You'd better decide right here and now if you want to take it out and play with it."

"Is it mint in box?"

He laughs out loud. "Hell no. I take it out and play with it all the time. Now I'm going to play with you, see if my little Canadian girl tastes like maple."

My chuckle dies a slow and painful death when he lowers his head and swipes his tongue over my throbbing clit. "Oh, yes, please play with me."

I grip the bedsheets and lift my hips, banging my sex against his face, and he grunts as he swirls his tongue all over me. As I grow wetter, he dips inside and moans with pleasure as he tastes me.

He sucks my clit into his mouth, and as stars dance before my eyes, I fight the urge to start belting out the British national anthem. God save the King. Yeah, because there's no saving me. I'm in elbows deep with the man who's here to tear down the town's beloved park. The good folks of Annapolis would no doubt run a traitor like me out of town. He slides a thick finger into me.

"Oh yes, just like that."

I lift my head to see him, and he's so lost in pleasuring me, he's completely oblivious to anything else. Most of the guys I've been with are more concerned with their own climax. Honestly, Colin is a guy who's rigid and reserved, but he's brought none of that to the bedroom and now I want to sing Oh, Canada.

His head lifts, and I take in the moisture—my moisture—on his face as our eyes connect. The second they do, my stupid heart starts pounding, like it might want to get involved in this hook-up, but I swallow down everything it's trying to push up.

I reach down, put my hand on Colin's head and guide his mouth back to my bare beaver. His chuckle reverberates through me, and I lay back down, and close my eyes as another finger joins the first.

"Colin, my God..."

My body burns from the inside out, as he finger-fucks me and swirls his tongue over my clit. My brain shuts down, nothing existing but the pleasure building and centering between my legs. I'm so close to release but I fight it. I don't want this to end...ever. But I have no choice in the matter, because he's controlling my body like I'm a puppet on a string.

He runs the rough pad of his finger over the bundle of nerves inside me, and eats at my clit like a man starved. The combination takes me to the top of the mountain, and I stand there for a brief second as all the pleasures morph into a powerful climax. I let go, freefall over the cliff, and soar in the clouds with each hard pulse. He stays between my legs as I ride out my release. I slowly sail back to the Earth and I open my eyes to find dark, intense eyes looking up at me.

I take a few deep breaths, my legs like jelly as he inches back and lightly rubs my sex, petting me softly. "Wow," I say for lack of anything else, and his lips quirk. "I need to take that out and play with it more often."

His laugh curls around me as he climbs up my body and presses me into the mattress. "I can give you a hand with that. You know, while I'm here."

Oh, he's suggesting we do more of this?

"Fancy me, do you?"

"Yeah, I fancy you," he says, but there's no teasing in his voice, as his gaze moves over my face. He shifts his body, his cock between my legs, pressed up against my sex. Yeah, I want more of this, too.

"Wait, don't you have a fiancée back home?"

"No, pet. I never would have put my mouth on you if I had. I'm not that guy."

My stupid heart wobbles. Colin is one of the good guys, and there is zero chance in hell that we could be more than shagging partners. I'm not from his world, and he's not from mine, and clearly, from the picture his mother sent him, I'm not the kind of girl a guy like him could even contemplate bringing home. Imagine me showing up in my overalls. Now that would cause an international incident.

"Something on your mind?"

His words pull me back. "As a matter of fact, there is." I put my hand on his chest and shove him. He falls to his side, worried eyes on me. What, does he think I'm the kind of girl who takes and doesn't give in return?

"I believe you said something about me taking it out and playing with it."

"Aw, fuck," he curses as I take his big cock into my hand. I squeeze my fingers around it, and size him up. He tucks one arm under his head, and I nearly orgasm again just from the sexy and masculine way he's lying there, his jaw clenched, like he's not quite prepared for me to take him into my mouth. I like that he's a little off balance. I'd hate to think I'm the only one who's a mess here.

I move my hand up and down his long length, and play with him. He groans when I dip into the pre-cum and swirl it around his crown.

"Having fun, Violet?"

"Gobs of fun. Wait, aren't you? I mean, if you're not, I can stop."

His eyes darken as he reaches down and puts his hands over mine, holding it to his cock. "I think the better question is, do you enjoy torturing me?"

I move my hand up and down and his follows. His groan fills the quiet in the room as I bend forward and take him in my mouth. He curses, using British slang I've never heard before and if I could smile I would. It's a bit difficult to do with a mouthful of cock. I rock into him, take him to the back of my throat and he grabs a fistful of my hair and moves it to the side to watch.

I work him in my mouth and my hand follows the motion. He easily slides in and out as I wet him and enjoy the tang of his arousal. His veins swell beneath my exploring tongue, and his hips piston forward. I whimper, and take him deeper down my throat, deep enough that I gag. He tries to tug me off but I'm not ready to stop. In fact, I want to taste his cum. But since he's bigger and stronger and has other ideas, he grips my shoulders and moves me, sliding my body under his like I'm a rag doll.

"I wasn't done," I complain.

"I almost was, and that's the problem."

"I'm not seeing a problem." He puts a hand between my legs, and presses a finger into me.

"Oh yes. I like that."

"I need my cock in here."

I spread for him without hesitation, and in a move filled with tenderness, he brushes my hair back and asks, "Do you have any condoms?"

"Condoms, right?" With my brain on hiatus, I hadn't even considered protection. What is this man doing to me? At least he's got a few working brain cells thinking for the two of us.

"My bedroom. Nightstand." I go to push him, but he pins me down. "Ooh."

He angles his head, aware how much I liked that. "You wait here. I'll be back in a jiffy." He slides off my body and I immediately miss his weight and warmth. Wait, is there anything in my nightstand that I don't want him to see? He's back in a flash, giving me no time to dwell on it, and he's ripping into the condom as he climbs back between my legs.

"Do condoms expire?" I ask as he starts to slide it on his big, beautiful cock.

"Yes."

"You didn't happen to check the date, did you?"

"You mean you haven't...you and Caleb?"

I shake my head and my hair knots on the pillow. "No. It's been a while." He slides the condom on. "Why are you smiling?"

"No reason."

"You don't like Caleb, do you?"

"I don't know him."

I make a move to go up on my elbows but he puts his hand on my chest and pins me beneath him. Dammit I like this take-charge Colin.

"You were talking to him tonight. Then he disappeared. What did you say to him?"

"I told him to bugger off."

My pulse jumps. "Why would you do that?"

"I didn't like the way he was looking at you."

Was Colin jealous of Caleb?

"What business was that of yours?"

He falls over me, his lips lightly brushing mine and it's all I can do to keep my thoughts focused. "None at all."

"Colin, you had no right." He puts a finger back inside me, and rubs his palm against my clit.

"Yeah, I know. So, are we going to talk about Caleb or can we get onto a right and proper shagging?"

"We'll talk more..." He pulls his finger out, and pushes his crown in. Um, what was I just saying? What are we going to talk about later?

Pleasure zaps every brain cell and my arms circle Colin's back, my nails dragging skin as I run my hands all over him. His body is solid, rock hard as he powers forward, filling me in a way I've never been filled before. Moisture breaks out on my skin, and I moan as my body opens for him.

"You are so tight," he murmurs into my throat, as I move my upper body and rub my hard nipples over his chest, no doubt scoring his skin.

My sex muscles take the shape of his cock as he gives me every last inch and once he's seated high, he lifts his head and his eyes find mine. He stares at me, no words said as he begins to move his body, rocking into me. His pace is slow at first, as he learns my body, and when my breathing changes, grows a little more labored, he angles his body and drives a little deeper.

"Oh, God," I cry out as each thrust hits my cervix and brings a new kind of pleasure to my body. I lift my hips to meet each thrust, and he buries his face in my neck and presses hot, open-mouthed kisses to my skin.

"You taste so good." He kisses me some more, his hot breath seeping under my skin and burning through my veins, and while I've never come twice in one night before—sometimes I question if I'd even come once—my body begins to vibrate, pleasure mushrooming inside me.

"Colin..." I cup his face, and his forehead presses against mine as he pulls almost all the way out and drives back into me, hitting my cervix and bringing on an entirely different kind of climax. What is going on with my body? "Oh my God." My muscles clench around his cock, hugging him tight and he throws his head back and clenches down on his jaw like he's in total agony—like he wants to hang on but can't.

I pulse around his pistoning cock, soaking the condom and my thighs, and he dives for my mouth, kissing me with a passion and hunger I've only ever read about. I kiss him back, and our tongues tangle, and as my body begins to relax, he changes the way he thrusts.

"Yes, fuck me, Colin."

He rams into me, hard blunt strokes as he chases his orgasm and I study his face, loving the deep need and concentration. I lift my hips and run my hands down his back until I'm cupping his tight ass. I hold him, and he grunts, driving into me hard and deep and staying high inside.

His eyes open, meet mine, and nothing but pleasure exists on his face as he spills himself inside me.

"Yes," I murmur, as he balances on his hands, his ass tight beneath mine as he comes and pulses so hard inside me, it brings on a full-body quake.

"Fuck yeah." He drains himself and collapses on top of me, and his strong heart pounds with mine as his lips linger over mine, our breaths mingling. We hold onto one another, the moon no longer slanting on the walls as it rises in the night sky.

I run my socked feet over the back of his legs, and he quakes on top of me. "That tickles," he murmurs, and moves his body, so my legs are spread. He stays inside me, and I like that. The guys I've been with pull out and bail once they're done. But Colin here, he's no college boy working at the park for the summer, and while it's not hate sex like Emily suggested, it's still the best sex I've had in my entire life. Not that I've had a lot of experience, but I'm pretty sure anything after Colin's Olympic performance—the man has stamina—no other guy will make the cut. Basically, he's screwing me two ways here, and only one brings pleasure.

His body becomes heavier as he relaxes and he turns his head to the side. The next thing I know, he's screaming like a girl, and practically clinging to the ceiling.

"Meow."

"I told you he was trying to kill me." As I go back on my heels, a rather hasty exit from the warmth and comfort of Violet's lush body, Lucky licks one paw as he gives me the death glare. Yeah, no one can tell me he doesn't have murder on his mind. The little bastard wants Violet all to himself. Yeah, well so do I, mate, so you'd better watch yourself.

I want Violet all to myself?

Blimey, I'm guessing I do. Why else would I have told that little shit Caleb to bugger off. How dare he stand in Violet's house, like he had claim to her. Not while I'm around, you wanker. Although I won't be around for much longer, and it's a little curious how that idea doesn't sit so well with me.

I glare back at Lucky, but it doesn't intimidate him, not quite the same way it intimidated Caleb. Lucky lets out a slow meow, and focuses in on my rock-hard cock, still sheathed in the condom.

"Uh, Colin."

"I'm aware." I put my hand over myself before he decides it's a scratching pole. Violet sits up, and when a sound rises in her throat I spare her a fast glance. It's best not to take my eyes off Lucky.

"This isn't funny, Violet."

"I know," she practically shrieks, doing her best to keep herself from laughing and failing miserably.

"How did he even get in here?" My gaze jerks to the window, in search of the mother ship. "I told you he was an alien."

She lifts her chin, and gestures to something over my shoulder. "You left the door open when you went to my room to get the condom."

I glance down, take in the mussed sheets as I consider that likely scenario. "Yeah, that's possible." I'd been in too much of a hurry to get back to Violet's warmth. God, I love the way she touched me, the way her tight body opened and welcomed me in. A guy could get used to that kind of greeting. The bed creaks as I shift to the side, needing to get this condom off and into my boxers before we have an incident. "I'll be right back."

The second I stand, Lucky jumps from the nightstand and weaves around my feet. I don't want to step on him, or hurt the little bugger, despite his murderous intentions, so I move slowly, and gently push him out of my way as I try to make it to the loo. He tries to get in with me, and I use my foot to keep him out as I shut the door on Lucky, and Violet's chuckle. Once I'm alone, yet I still expect Lucky to suddenly appear on the edge of the sink at any moment, I discard the condom and grab a cloth to wash up. I grab one for Violet too, and when I open the door and find Lucky gone, I hurry my steps to get back to Violet.

"Where did he go?"

She shrugs. "Maybe to get a drink."

"More likely he's waiting at the top of the stairs for me."

I climb back into bed, and lay beside her. She pushes herself down until she's next to me, and I place the warm cloth between her legs to clean her.

Her moan of pleasure, the same sound I coaxed from her when I put my cock in her, tugs at my dick, and it swells. "Is that supposed to be turning me on again?" she murmurs.

"Depends. Is it?" Her stomach growls, and I finish washing her up and toss the cloth onto the pile of our clothes. "Are you hungry?"

She gives me a sheepish look, and my gaze roams her face, loving the flush on her cheeks and knowing I was the guy to put it there. "I was so busy entertaining tonight—"

"And watching over me."

"And watching over you," she adds. "Although you got to Caleb before I could stop you. I still can't believe you scared him away. Why again did you do that?"

Instead of answering, I ask. "You guys were a thing once?"

"Oh so we answer a question with a question now, do we?"

"I don't know, do we?"

She laughs and whacks my stomach. I take her hand, bring it to my mouth and kiss her fingertips.

She quakes, and her stomach grumbles again as she says, "A long time ago. Last year. We're just friends."

"He wants more?"

She shrugs. "Maybe, but he's leaving soon. The park closes right after the first weekend in September."

Jealousy grips my gut, and it's true, I had no right to scare him off earlier. I've never felt possessive of any woman before. There's something about Violet. She's all strength and confidence, but beneath it all, she's soft and warm...sensitive. She spends her days doing for others, and damned if it doesn't make me want to spend my nights doing for her.

"It will bother you when he leaves?" I ask, working hard to keep my tone even. I don't want her to think I'm jealous, and there is a ridiculous part of me that wants to ask if it will bother her when I leave.

"We're friends. It's always hard when someone leaves, and now with the park being sold, he has no reason to come back, right?"

Bollocks. She's enough for anyone to come back, but she obviously doesn't see that, and of course there's a history that proves her correct. Her grumbling stomach once again demands to be noticed.

"Hang on." I stand and tug on my boxers.

"Where are you going?"

I walk to the door and tentatively glance out. "To get you something to eat."

"You don't have to do that."

"If you hear a loud bang and curses, call an ambulance, because that'll be me plunging to my death on the stairs."

"You want me to go?"

"No." I step into the hall, and since the ninja cat is nowhere to be found, I head downstairs. The house is silent, much like my castle at night, but it lacks the wide-open emptiness. There's a real warmth about her place, that pushes back the cold that always resides inside me.

In the kitchen, I root around in the fridge and find some leftovers from the night. The cucumber sandwiches I'd wrapped and put away earlier look soggy. None of the food looks appealing, so instead I pour her a bowl of cereal, add milk and grab two bottles of water. I carefully make my way back to her, and she's sitting up in bed, the blankets pulled to her chin. Her smile wraps around my wobbly heart. My God, she's so incredibly sweet.

"What did you bring me?"

"Sugar."

She eyes me suspiciously, playfully. "Is that so I'll have enough energy to do this again?"

"You want to do it again, Violet?" I want her to say yes so badly, it's insane.

Her smile falls and she fidgets with the blankets. "I mean, if you do."

"Did I fail to make that clear?"

"Right, no."

I shake my head. "Right, no. Which is it?"

I hand her the bowl and her eyes light up when she sees the sugary cereal. She takes a bite and moans around the mouthful. "It's right, you made it clear, and I'm onboard. You know, while you're here."

I set the water on the nightstand. "That's settled then." She takes another bite, and her moan of pleasure strokes my dick. "Is it really that good?"

"Almost as good as sex." She taps the spoon on her bowl. "No, that's not true."

"It's better than sex?"

"Not sex with you," she says quickly. "But yeah…" My chest puffs a little, and she holds a spoonful out to me. "You have to try."

"I don't have to do anything." Except for following in family tradition and marrying.

She blinks at me, her long lashes falling slowly over begging eyes. "For me, please?"

What is it about this woman that makes me forget all common sense, or how to say no? I don't know, but I do know I want to do for her.

"Fine." I open my mouth and she squeals in delight as she shoves a big spoonful in. I chew, as the chocolaty sugar explodes in my mouth.

"Good, right?" Her eyes are wide and hopeful.

I finish chewing and swallow. "I would probably use the word tolerable."

She laughs. "Of course, you would." She eats some more, and I tug the blankets up, leaving my boxers and socks on.

"You spent your whole life in Annapolis?"

"Yes, and it was only a few years ago I moved into this house." She takes a breath and I follow her gaze around the room. "It was built by my great grandfather and left to me."

"It's very special to you."

"Very. Everywhere I look I see Grandma or Grandpa, and the room I'm staying in was Dad's room growing up."

Warmth invades my soul. I love the comfort she finds in this place. My castle is just a castle, a cold damp place where I lay my head at night. "That's nice, Violet. It's nice to have a part of them with you at all times."

She holds another spoonful out to me, and I let her feed me. Strange, I was just inside her but sitting here tucked under the covers next to her, sharing a bowl of tolerable cereal, feels...I don't know. Maybe the word I'm looking for is intimate. It's not something I've ever done before. Sex was sex, and I never much hung around afterward. I suppose that will all change when I have a wife.

"You've never wanted to leave here?"

She goes quiet, contemplative as she chews. "I've been to other places. I'm not a country bumpkin who's never been anywhere."

"I wasn't suggesting that." She feeds me again, and I adjust my pillow as I chew. "It's an aging population, here."

"Maybe that's what I like about it though, you know. I mean, I would love more people my age, and I play bingo on Sundays because what else am I supposed to do? But I love the old-fashioned values. Everyone watches out for everyone. Everyone helps their neighbor. I like the slow pace."

I nod and consider the fast pace where I live. The cutthroat world. This is the first time in...ever, that I've slowed down. I don't hate it.

She drops the spoon into the bowl and I take it from her and set it on the nightstand. "Besides, I'm hoping Emily and Trevor will start working on the new generation of kids."

"I like him."

"Trevor is a nice guy. Farm boy at heart. Most of the other people my age bolted after high school. Emily and Trevor invite me to do things with them all the time. Sometimes I do, sometimes I don't. Hell, they went to Vegas for their honeymoon and invited me." I lean into her as she laughs, enjoying this new closeness between us. The last time I felt this close to a woman was...never.

"Did you go?"

"No, I didn't want to be a third wheel."

"Maybe if you found a guy, and got married, you could all do couples things."

"Yeah, I hear Chester is looking to settle down again."

I chuckle, but it dies quickly as my brain pictures her with another guy. I really shouldn't hate the image so much. We're just shagging to pass the time. Right? "I'm not sure your're his type. I think he likes silver hair."

"I could dye it."

I laugh. "You were never serious? There's no special guy who stole your heart?"

"It was a long time ago." She goes quiet, and I sense she doesn't want to talk about it. I adjust her covers and she says, "I thought he was the one and that we'd get married after high school. Turns out we wanted different things."

"I'm sorry."

"Don't be. It's better that we found that out before we both ended up married and miserable. Everyone eventually leaves. I get that now." I hate the sadness, the quiet resignation in her voice as I sink down, and pull her to me. I hate that everyone leaves her, especially when it comes as a surprise—or at least, judging by what I'm hearing, used to come as a surprise. She now expects it. At least we both know up front that this is just a hook-up, and I *will* be leaving. I have no choice in the matter. My life, home, and future wife are all waiting for me. I have duties and expectations that I can't just shirk.

She lays her head on my shoulder, and circles my nipple with her finger. I flinch as she tickles me. "What about you?" she asks, her voice quiet. "Have you ever been serious?"

"Not really. I've been too busy for that." It's not a lie, while I might have nearly been engaged, I was never serious with Charlotte.

"Running the foundation takes all your time?"

"And then some." A moment of silence and I add, "I was almost engaged once, though."

Her brow furrows and her eyes go wide as she lifts her head and glances up at me. "Colin," she practically shrieks.

"What?"

"How can you say you were never serious when you were practically engaged, and what do you mean by practically."

"It's just....marriage is what I'm supposed to do, right? The rules I'm supposed to follow. The expectations..."

"Right, I remember you saying that."

"I was doing the right thing, and all was going okay until I overheard a phone conversation." Once again, I check my heart, search for a crack from her betrayal, but no, nothing. "She was talking about the riches and lifestyle she was hoping to marry into. In the end, I couldn't bring myself to go through with marriage. I broke things off with her." I go quiet, and Violet touches my face. "What?"

"That must have hurt."

Balls. Do I tell her? I guess we've both been honest up until now and she might as well know what kind of guy I really am and that we can have no future, not that she's asking for one. We both know what this is and what it isn't. "I wasn't sad, and that kind of concerns me."

"Did you love her?"

"No."

"Then maybe that's why you weren't sad. I'd say you probably felt relief. That gave you the out you were looking for."

"Maybe," I say, hoping she's going to let it go, but this is Violet we're talking about. She's not about to let anything go.

"And..."

I scrub my chin and consider the best way to tell her. *Blurt it out, Colin.* "I think I'm a psychopath." She stares at me long and hard, and blinks once, twice, and then bursts out laughing. "That's funny to you."

"Why do you say that?"

"They say psychopaths can't love, right?"

"Colin..." She pauses, climbs a little higher on my body and gives me a kiss. "You are not a psychopath."

"How do you know? All signs point to it. I'm dissociated from love. I can't seem to form a strong emotional bond with—"

"I hear the way you talk about your brother, and I know you love your parents. You might not like some of their expectations, but you love them, right?"

"Yes."

"Colin, you saved Lucky. If you were disassociated from your feelings, you never would have saved him."

"That's different, though."

"No, it's not. You did it for him, and you did it for me." She splays her fingers on my chest, her skin warming mine as she smiles at me, so much gratitude in her eyes, my heart pounds and possessiveness grips me.

I shake my head. "Maybe I'm just incapable of loving a woman, or being loved in return. Charlotte didn't love me. She was using me. I really don't like being used."

She kisses me again, and it's soft and sweet and for the first time in my life, there's a strange kind of pounding in my heart. "You have nothing to worry about, Colin. The right woman just hasn't come along for you."

As I gaze at her flushed face, and revel in the warmth in her eyes, new sensations overcome me. I can't explain them; all I know is maybe I do have something to worry about. She takes a huge breath and my body relaxes entirely—have I ever been this unwound—as she lets it out.

"Are you enjoying the break, here in Annapolis? I know you wanted in and out, and that didn't work out, and this town is probably far too sleepy for you, but maybe it's nice to slow down for a bit."

"The place is growing on me," I say.

She lifts her head and glances up at me. Her eyes are full of light and laughter when she says, "Like a wart, or a bad toe fungus?"

"Yeah, like a wart or bad toe fungus. I was sent here as punishment, you know."

"What?"

I chuckle. "When we were kids, Mum used to say if we misbehaved, she'd send us to Nova Scotia to live."

"That's terrible."

"That's what we thought."

She whacks me. "That's not what I mean."

"I know and it's not so terrible. But they've not been pleased with me since Charlotte, and any lawyer from the foundation could have come to oversee this deal. This is all about what happens if I don't toe the line, so to speak."

"Are you sad it was you?"

"Not anymore."

Unable to help myself I cup her face and press my lips to hers for a deep, slow, intimate kiss. Our lips linger, and she breathes out a happy sigh, her eyes closed as she places her cheek back on my chest. Will she notice that my heart started beating a little faster?

"Do you think Cameron will have the paperwork ready for the next meeting?"

"I hope so, but you need to prepare for a mob," she answers and chuckles against my chest. The vibration strokes my cock. "I'll check in with him tomorrow, to make sure he has everything in order."

Why does the idea of him having the paperwork ready bring a knot to my stomach? "If he doesn't—"

"You'll have me fire him?"

"Yeah, that's right," I fib. What I was really going to say is, that it wouldn't be so horrible. But that's ludicrous and she seems anxious to get it done and over with. Honestly, I'm here to get a job done, not fall in love with the sleeping town, the crazy townsfolk, or their most adorable mayor.

As they say in North America—FML.

16

VIOLET

My body is sore in the most delicious ways as I open my eyes and turn my head to find the other side of the bed empty. My chest tightens, and I can barely get in air as I sit up straight and glance around Colin's room, but he's nowhere to be found. The bathroom door is open, and it too is empty. Maybe he's gone for his early morning run, so neither of us had to do the awkward morning after sex.

Would it be though? Would it be weird and awkward because he's a guest and the lawyer overseeing the land deal? Sure, he said he wanted to do this again, and I agreed. Last night something happened between us, some intimate shift in our relationship that brought us closer together, made me feel safe and cherished.

This morning, with the sun rising in the sky and giving a different perspective, maybe he's had a change of heart, realized sleeping with me was a huge mistake, and ran first chance he could. He thinks he can't love, but maybe he just hasn't met the right girl. Maybe he felt something more last night... Maybe he didn't. It's not like I want more from him—not because he's not loveable, I'm sure he is. Anyway, none of these thoughts are helpful, and it's a path I shouldn't be exploring.

Get it together, Violet.

I go still and listen for sounds. Cripes, I hope Lucky didn't trip him on the stairs, and I'm going to find him battered and broken on the living room floor because he cracked his noggin on my low stair header. I do not want to get sued by the man I just slept with.

A noise from outside reaches my ears, and that's when I realize it's Colin, and he seems like he's deep into negotiations with someone. Oh, God, I was hoping after last night the townsfolk were going to warm up to him. I push to my feet and pray they're not out there with their pitchforks as I step up to the window. A laugh bubbles in my throat when I spot Colin, both hands on his hips, standing in my vegetation carrying on a conversation with my two goats. His clothes are dirty, and I can only guess Waffles knocked him to the ground again.

He reaches into a basket and produces a bell pepper. "I'll give you this if you let me pass."

Waffles, the alpha, lowers its head and butts at him. "Oh God," I say and rap on the window. Colin glances up at me, relief on his face. I open the window. "I'll be right down."

"Hurry," he yells back.

Since I have no idea where my clothes are from last night, and I see a pair of Colin's sweats in the closet, I tug them on, and yank on his discarded dress shirt. I button it up as I dash downstairs, slide into a pair of flip flops, and hurry into the yard.

"What are you two up to?" I say to my goats, and they sidle up to me. I bend and pet them. "Are you giving Colin a hard time?"

As I think about a hard time, my body quakes in memory of last night. Colin definitely gave me a hard time in the most glorious ways.

"You guys leave Colin alone. I know, I know, he's shutting down the park, and that's why you both live here now instead of the petting zoo, but there's nothing we can do about it, and there's no need for us to be mean."

"They used to live in the petting zoo at the park?"

"Yeah...they're still getting used to this place."

His head lifts, his eyes meet mine. "What happened with all the animals?"

There's a look of horror on his face, like we might have eaten them. I shake my head and internally laugh at that. How could he even entertain the idea that he was a psychopath? "We relocated them to other zoos. The female goats are now at a farm that makes soap. These guys, though..." I frown. "No one wanted them, and I didn't want to see them turned into dog food...or human food. So here they are, living their best life in my garden."

"I'm sorry, guys," he says so quietly, his voice so full of pain and vulnerability, I can't stop my heart from getting involved.

"I think they're happy here."

"Why wouldn't they be? They get to torture the guests."

"You're the only one they've tortured so far, Colin."

"I guess they know I'm the reason they're here, missing their friends."

Popcorn bites at my shirt, and I stand to stop him. "Next time, you come out here, you should put on the overalls in the shed. Save your clothes." I brush my hands together. "Okay, now you two, go play and stay out of trouble." I turn to Colin as they scamper off. "That's how you negotiate with goats, Colin."

I expect him to laugh, but no, he's not laughing. Nope not laughing at all. But you know what he is doing? He's examining me from head to toe as I stand there in his clothes.

"Oh, I'm sorry," I say quickly. "I didn't want to take the time to run to my room to get clothes. I just—"

Before I can finish the sentence, he slides an arm around my back and pulls me to him. As my softness meshes with his hardness, his head dips, and he claims my lips with a kiss so hard and hungry, one would think we didn't spend last night having sex. Or maybe the kiss is because we did spend last night having sex. Nevertheless, all I know is my body is reacting, and my arms are sliding around his back, ready to hang on for the ride.

He breaks the kiss. "Don't ever apologize for wearing my clothes."

"When it pulls that kind of reaction from you, I won't."

He grins. "Oh, you liked that, did you?"

"Maybe I did."

"Maybe there's more from where that came from."

"I hope so," I say, and remember I have an early shift at the restaurant. "Can I take a rain check?" I gesture toward the house. "I need to go." His arm goes slack around my back, and he backs up an inch, like I wounded him. I tug on his hand. "Work. Restaurant. Frank's surgery."

"Thank God."

I plant one hand on my hip. "What's that supposed to mean?"

"I was worried you were going to try to make crumpets again."

"Were they that bad?"

"Yes."

"Colin," I say and whack him. "I was interrupted while making them. It's not my fault they were so chewy."

"It was entirely your fault."

I shake my head and look at the basket at his feet. "What are you doing out here, anyway?"

His forehead bunches, and he has that look on his face again, the one that suggests I might not be all there. "Gardening."

"I know you're gardening. Duh. I mean why are you gardening?"

"That's not what you asked."

"I know, I know. My fault. Why are you gathering vegetables?"

His face lights up. "When in Rome."

"Look at you, accepting our way of life so quickly."

There's a new kind of excitement about him when he pulls the gorgeous bell peppers from the basket. "When I was a boy," he begins and I grin, imagining Colin as a young lad, a curiosity about the world he always took so seriously. "One of the cooks used to make an English breakfast using peppers."

"You were going to make breakfast?"

"Yes, I didn't want to wake you. You were sleeping so soundly."

A tightness forms in my chest as I remember waking up to an empty bed. "That was...considerate."

He angles his head and eyes me. "Bloody hell."

"What?"

"You woke up, and I was gone. I should have left a note, or texted your phone. I'm not used—"

"I'm not used to it either, Colin, and it's okay. I shouldn't have thought...I'm sorry."

"You have nothing to be sorry for." He kisses the top of my head. "I can be a bit daft at times, which I'm sure you already know." We exchange a smile. "Won't happen again."

We head inside. "Do you want to come to the restaurant and have breakfast?"

"Sounds good." He holds the basket of peppers up. "I can save these for tomorrow."

"I can't wait to try your English breakfast. I bet it's delicious." He drops the basket off in the kitchen.

"I'd better shower." He nods and I dart upstairs and into the bathroom. I shut the door behind me, but don't lock it, as I normally would when I have a bed and breakfast guest. Oh, and why aren't you doing that, Violet? Oh, I don't know, maybe there is a part of me that hopes he'll follow me up and hop in the shower with me. I snort. Yeah, no. That wouldn't be a great idea. I need to get to the restaurant and that would only make me late.

"Hey." As I undress, I turn to find Colin stepping into the bathroom with me.

Then again, being on time is overrated.

"What do you think you're doing?" I ask, unable to hide the pleasure in my voice.

"Heard about the water shortage, so I thought..."

I'm about to correct him, and consider I might be the one with the brain tumor. "Yes, we need to save the water for the farms. Good thinking."

Completely naked and aware of his hungry eyes roaming over my body, I turn on the spray, adjust it to hot, and as it heats up I step in. The cool water falls over me, but it does nothing to push back the heat as Colin quickly undresses and follows me in. He's so big, his presence so overwhelming, a shiver wracks my body.

"You're cold." He adjusts the temperature, and the hot water starts flowing. I moan with pleasure as it falls over me, and he slides his hand around my neck, and kisses me fiercely. As he sucks the breath from my lungs, I put my hand around his back, and step closer, until his cock is pressed against my stomach. He breaks the kiss. "Everyone is slow moving here, but I can be quick, unless..."

I laugh at that. "I don't mind quick."

His growl of need teases the want inside me, and he grips my wet hair, and tugs until my mouth is open to his again. "I need to go get a condom but I don't want to move."

I bite my lip. I don't know him, not really, and I shouldn't say what I'm about to say, but here goes nothing. "I'm on the pill."

He goes perfectly still. Shit, too soon? "I...uh..."

"So last night, you let me go get a condom, running the risk of letting Lucky sneak into the room. You're both in cahoots, aren't you?"

I chuckle. "I need to be at work in twenty minutes. Do we want to have this conversation, Colin, or do you want to shag?"

"Shag, definitely shag," he says as he catches me by surprise and spins me, placing both of my hands on the tile wall. "But don't think you're getting off that easy."

"I thought you said you were going to be fast," I tease.

"That's not what I'm talking about."

"So you're going to get me off fast then."

His mouth goes to my ear as he slides a thick finger inside me and my legs go weak. "Fast and easy are two different things, darling." He fucks me with his finger, and while I want to come back with some smart-ass response, I suddenly have no idea what we were talking about. He pushes his finger into me, and presses his palm to my clit and I nearly come right then and there.

"Colin..." I murmur.

His other hand cups my breast and he massages and toys with my nipples. I move my hips, wanting more...wanting everything. I moan with want and frustration as my body burns all over.

"Need something?" he asks, his hot breath falling over my neck.

"Yes," I cry out and he doesn't tease me or keep me waiting. Instead, he pulls his finger out, positions his cock and slides into me with one hard push. "Ohmigod..."

His big hands close over mine on the wall, and our fingers thread as he moves his hips, pumping in and out of me, with zero finesse and one hundred percent determination to take me where I need to go in seconds flat. I do love a man with single-minded determination.

Love?

Like, yeah, like is what I mean.

"You feel so good," he murmurs, his thrusts hard, blunt, meant for my pleasure. His hand travels downward to play with my clit, and in no time at all, every ounce of pleasure in my body centers between my legs and I come all over his cock.

"Jesus," he curses as I clench around him, and the next thing I know he's moving at a faster speed, chasing his own release. I hang on to the wall, and gulp as he pistons in and out of me. His growl fills my ears, shutting out the sound of water running as he puts both arms around my body, and hugs me tight as he pushes deep and lets go high inside my body.

I gulp air, but can no longer breathe. Not from the amazing sex, but from the tight hold he has on my body, like he might die if he lets go. The warm water falling over us turns cooler, and he slides out of me. Big hands spin me, and he snakes one around my neck and holds me as he kisses me, his mouth firm, demanding, hungry for something I'm not even sure either of us are aware of. Why do I love that move so much?

"That was—"

"Amazing," he says.

"I was going to say fast," I tease, "But yeah, pretty damn amazing."

"Fast and thorough, I aim to please."

He pulls me into the cool water and I shriek. "I need to get a bigger hot water tank."

"This is what happens when you dally instead of washing."

"I'd take a cold shower any day if it meant I got to dally with you."

His chest puffs up a little as he squirts a generous amount of my grapefruit soap onto his palm and lathers me up.

"Great," I say.

His hand stills. "What?"

"You're turning me on all over again."

He laughs and continues to wash me, and once I'm all soaped he puts me under the cool spray and rinses me. "How about tonight? I'll make up for going fast."

"Slow and easy?"

"Didn't I say you weren't going to get off easy."

I laugh, so light and easy, loving this new warmth, easiness and comradery between us. I finish rinsing and move so he can step under the spray. Even though I need to get my ass in gear, I stand there, enjoying the view, and once we're done, we both step out and towel dry.

"Emily asked me about a foursome," I say and as soon as the words slip from my mouth, I realize what I've said.

His brow raises. "Didn't know you were into that kind of thing."

"You know that's not what I meant." He follows me to my bedroom, and stands there, leaning against the doorjamb as I drop my towel and start to dress.

"Great, now *you're* turning me on all over again."

I grin at him over my shoulder as I dress. "I know we're not a couple or anything, and we don't want that." He holds his hand up to stop me from speaking. "I just mean, it might be nice to go do something fun, where I'm not feeling like the third wheel."

"I think we could do that."

I finish dressing and he walks to his room as I comb out my hair. Now it's my turn to lean against the doorjamb and take pleasure in watching him dress. He really is a beautiful male specimen.

"You don't have to."

"No, I want to. I want to see what kinds of things you do for fun. It's not like I have anything else to do. I might as well immerse myself into country life until the next town hall."

I smile, liking that...maybe a bit too much.

"Come on," he says. "We need to get you to work. I'll drive for practice, then I'll come back here, change Lucky's litter box and take him for a walk."

"You're seriously going to walk him?"

"A good way to get in with the influencers. As long as he doesn't eat my face when I try to put the leash on him."

"Okay, but try to stay out of trouble."

We head to my car, and it's weird, I kind of like him taking care of me this way. I realize it's a simple gesture, and I'm capable of driving myself, but still, there's something very comforting in letting him do it for me.

He parks and we walk inside, the morning crowd filling the place up. "You've got a busy day ahead of you."

I go to the break room, grab my apron and come back to find Colin at the counter, reading over the paper menu.

"You can take my car, do whatever you want. I'm off around three. Try not to get lost. I don't have a navigation system."

"The town has one road. I hardly think I'll get lost."

Emily plops herself down beside Colin, her gaze bobbing back and forth between the two of us. I pour both her and Colin a cup of coffee and grab my notepad, ready to go take some orders. I'm about to go, but Emily reaches across the counter and captures my hand.

She has a shit-eating grin all over her face when she says, "One question."

"What?" I ask, and wish I hadn't as I glance nervously at Colin as he takes a big drink of his coffee.

"Tell me everything you've learned about hate sex," she says, loud enough for everyone to hear, even Colin...which is, of course, why he's spewing coffee all over my clean apron.

17

COLIN

Emily's words ring loud and clear in my brain as I drive the short distance back to Violet's house, on the wrong side of the road, I'll have you. But I think I've mastered it. I haven't killed anyone or hit a tree, so I call that a win. I wave to Clara as she steps from her house. Her actions are like clockwork.

Seriously, I can't believe Emily announced that we had hate sex to a restaurant packed with people. She's got it all wrong, though. There was no hate involved. At least not on my part. There could have been on Violet's end. I'm sure she hates what I'm doing to her beloved park and town. I park and hurry inside, in search of Lucky. I find him grooming himself on my pillow. That's bloody disgusting.

"Hey," I say to stop him, and he gags, like he's about to bring up a huge hairball on my side of the bed. "Want to go for a walk?"

Wow, if looks could kill.

Okay, Colin. Come on. You've got this. You're bigger, and higher on the evolutionary food chain, surely to God you can wrangle one hairless cat.

Puffing up my chest to show dominance, which pretty much brings a smirk to Lucky's face, I step up to him with the leash behind my back, and scoop him up. He hisses at me, and I hook the collar to his neck as he scratches at my arm.

"Ha," I say. "Who's smarter now?"

Yeah, I know, you are.

I set him down and practically drag him outdoors. He stretches and glances around, raising his face to the sun. "Yeah, it's nice out here in the real world, isn't it?"

He inches back, and that's when it hits me. Shite. Maybe he's afraid. After getting dropped off in the middle of nowhere, he probably thinks I'm going to do the same to him. I sink down on the stoop, and sit there for a long moment, giving him time to adjust and maybe trust me a little. He clearly has men issues and I'd like to get my hands on the guy who did this to him.

"Hey, mate," I say quietly and shift to face him. "I'm not going to leave you anywhere. I promise." He sits against the rail his back braced like he's in fight or flight mode, and I get it, he strikes out at me because he's afraid. "Do you have any idea how lucky you are?" I shake my head and smile. "You're the smartest cat I know, to find your way to Violet. She's going to be a wicked cat mum, even to a cat with no hair, and you're going to have a brilliant life here with her. Just don't touch any of her mice. They're off limits. Though, I must say you don't strike me as the mouse hunting kind of cat. That's a bit beneath you."

I grin as I think of Violet's protective nature. Honestly, I've never met another woman like her. She's definitely not the kind of woman who'd go after a man for his wealth and stature, or want to live in a gilded cage and throw fancy parties. No, she throws fun kitchen parties, where the atmosphere is relaxed and no one puts on airs. Well, it would have been more relaxed had I not been there. But that was the whole reason for the party, and really, I don't want these good people blaming Violet. She's doing her job and cares deeply about this community. I don't want this to be any harder on her than it already is.

Lucky extends his paw toward me, and I hold my breath because this time his claws aren't extended.

"There we go, mate. You believe me now, do you, that Violet will take good care of you and you'll have a brilliant life." As soon as the words leave my mouth, my gut clenches. I'll be leaving here soon enough, and oddly enough that thought doesn't sit well with me.

Someone on the sidewalk clears their throat and I spin to find Clara standing there, Molly in her hands. "I...didn't mean to interrupt," she says, and I cringe. How much did she hear?

"Sorry, I was just chatting with Lucky."

"How are you today, Lucky?" A smile reserved for everyone but me crosses her face. "Are you taking him for a walk?"

"I was planning on it."

She pinches her lips and lines form around her mouth. "I suppose you could join us. It might be best for Lucky."

What, does she think I'm going to set him free? I stand, and give the leash a little nudge. "Such a shame he was dropped off."

"Best thing that ever happened to him."

Aghast, Clara's hand goes to her chest. "Excuse me?"

"I'm just saying. Why would we want him with an owner who didn't want or respect him, merely because he has a small murmur. He's much better with Violet...and me." I don't know why I added that at the end. He's only mine for the next week or so.

Her lips pinch into a white line. "Yes, I suppose when you put it that way."

"Do you think he's going to be okay with Molly?"

She sets her little white dog on the ground, and Molly looks him over as Lucky, naturally, ignores her. "He's obviously been around dogs before." She gives a very efficient clap of her hands, and it totally reminds me of Mum. "Very well then, let's go join up with the others."

We head down the walkway and spot the others coming up the road. As we walk toward them, Clara turns to me. "What is this I hear about you and Violet having hate sex."

And just like that, I no longer have a tongue, you know, having swallowed it and all. "I...uh, Emily was just playing around. You know what she's like." Is that global warming increasing the temperature in Annapolis or is it the scowl on Clara's face?

"Yes, I do know what she's like. But she has a good heart."

"She does, I'm sure."

"Violet has a good heart too." She waves a very gnarled finger at me. "I don't want to see you hurting her."

"Not my intentions. Ever."

A good heart is a big thing around here. I'll have to remember that. Also, I'd never purposely hurt Violet.

Her face relaxes slightly and it's good to know Violet has so many people who are protective of her. I just pray they don't turn on her once this deal goes through.

"She'll do the right thing, you know. She'll stop you from tearing down her park."

I want to tell her it's too late, and that they should all stop holding out hope. The deal is as good as done. Maybe I should hold a town meeting myself, show them the plan and what it can do to bring jobs and income into this town. They don't like change. Change can be scary. What if I eased their worries? That might make it easier on Violet.

Eugenie, Audrey, Irene and Chester all give me a once over, when we reach them. Their attention is quickly turned to Lucky and he lifts his tail as they fuss over him, much like they did last night.

I fall silent as we walk, and conversation turns to the weather. Obviously, I'm not in their circle of trust so they're not about to discuss important issues in front of me. We walk by Lisa Landry's house. Apparently, she's a recent widow in her sixties, and the rest of the walk is filled with conversations on how she's blowing through her husband's money by running to the bars in the city. It's an outrage really, someone her *age* thinking and acting like she's in her twenties. After I hear every salacious detail, true or not, about Lisa Landry's 'affairs' in the city—two towns over, which really isn't the city at all— and the kind of men she's luring with her money, our walk is over. I quickly, happily bid them a farewell, and take Lucky home.

I stare at the wall for a good ten minutes, trying to figure out what the hell just happened, and why I'd so easily got caught up in the drama of Lisa's life. I think I might have PTSD. But seriously, did she really bring a young bartender to a nearby hotel and have her way with him? According to the front desk clerk, she did, but how good of a source was she, really?

Bollocks.

What the hell am I doing? I feed Lucky and fill his water bowl, and decide to take a drive through town to waste time and explore until Violet finishes her shift and we can do something fun. I grin, unable to help myself. Last night was fun. This morning was fun. Does she have more of that in mind? I sure as hell hope so.

Back in the car, I leisurely head through the one street town. I wave to people walking by and they're about to wave back until they realize it's me behind the wheel. I go through construction, and love how there are no other vehicles on the road, but they stop me for a good five minutes, simply because they can and Canadians are wankers.

Once I'm back in motion, I decide to explore a few towns close by and check out the real estate market. Not for me, but maybe the families of the students might want to buy vacation homes so they can be closer to their children.

I drive along the shore and note all the working fishing boats and traps along a long dock. There's a gorgeous stretch of beach not too far from the working waterfront. Going further inland, I head up the south mountain which really is just a big hill, and look for For Sale signs as I explore the orchards, and even stop at a few of the u-picks and markets. I grab some jellies and spreads for my mother, and handknitted scarves for my brother and father. I think many of the families would find this a quaint place to visit.

It's getting later in the afternoon by the time I decide to turn myself around and head back. I drive for a few miles, and check the signs. I think I'm close, but since I'm not one hundred percent sure, I decide to stop to ask a man about to jump on his tractor, if I'm on the right road.

I park, and climb out into the warm sunshine. "Excuse me," I say and the man turns to me. "I was wondering if you might be able to help me."

"I'll do what I can."

"I'm looking to make my way back to Annapolis. Do I take a left at the four-way stop up ahead?"

He eyes me, and for a brief second I think I see a spark of recognition. Word travels fast around these parts, and I do have a British accent, so yeah, he probably knows exactly who I am.

"Yup, yup, just about any road will get you there. Some just take longer than others. If I were headed to Annapolis, though, I wouldn't start here."

I narrow my eyes and try to wrap my brain around that, as the man puts a piece of hay between his teeth and looks off. Is he all there? Should he be behind the wheel of a heavy tractor?

"The name's Mack."

"I'm Colin," I say and leave off the last name or the organization I'm representing, because maybe there's a slight chance he doesn't know who I am. Yeah, sure just like there's a slight chance that Mum isn't back home making my wedding arrangements.

"Just about to cut me a corn maze." He chuckles. "Been doing it for the last fifty years. Kids around these parts love it."

I'll have to take his word on it, since I haven't seen too many kids. Just at the park, and they were visitors from elsewhere, I'm sure.

"That sounds like fun."

He eyes me, and I straighten up. Maybe he's sharper than he's letting on. "You think so?"

"Sure, sounds like great fun. Is cutting a maze hard to do?" I glance behind him, to the massive corn field in the distance.

"Not too bad when you have all the right equipment. This old zero turn tractor gets the job done lickedy split."

"I'm guessing it does."

He spits the hay from his mouth and wipes his hands on his plaid jacket. "Care to join me? Go for a ride, see what it's all about." I reach for my phone to check the time, but it's in the car. "Too much of a candy ass?"

Candy ass?

What the hell?

"Yeah, I get it. A city boy like you, who doesn't know his ass from a hole in the ground, wouldn't be caught dead on a tractor." He waves his hand. "Go on. Go back to where you came from."

Doesn't know his ass from a hole in the ground?

What the hell did I ever do to deserve these kinds of insults. "That's not true. I was—"

"Get in then. Come along, I'll even let you ride it."

"I..." Bollocks, he's not really giving me a choice here, and I guess if I'm trying to get on the good side of the townsfolk, I better go.

"Let me grab my phone."

"No time for candy-ass phones on a tractor, boy. Hop in before I leave without you."

I debate on quickly grabbing my phone and locking my car and decide against it. No one is going to steal anything and if I make any sudden moves, I'm afraid he'll back his tractor up on over me. As much as I'd like to shoot Violet a text, I leave my phone, walk to the other side of the tractor, and climb in. I don't suppose we'll be all that long.

Mack jumps in beside me, and puts his hand on this stick, and I grab on to the seat and hold on as the bumpy tractor takes us up into the huge corn field.

"Been doing it so long, I have the whole route planned out. All right son, you ready for a lesson?" He fixes his hat and fixes me a glance.

"Sure."

For the next two minutes, he gives me a fast rundown on how the tractor works. Yes, two minutes. That's all a candy-ass city boy like me gets, apparently. "You ready?"

"Ready," I say. I'm a fast learner sure, but come on. This is out of my wheelhouse. I study him carefully as he cuts through the stalks, and I make note of the way he drives, hoping I'm one tenth the driver he is when he finally forces me to take the wheel, which I'm sure he's going to do. He sings along to some imaginary song in his head as he cuts a path in and out, and backs up to leave numerous dead ends so the kids can get lost. He chuckles to himself at times, and as the time ticks by I wonder if he even remembers I'm beside him.

"It must take hours to get through this maze."

He casts me a glance. "Only if you're a dumb ass."

Why do I get the feeling I'm the one he's calling a dumb ass? "All right, son. Your time to drive."

I want to protest, tell him I'm enjoying the passenger side, but he's climbing out and coming around my way.

"Scooch on over, now."

I throw a leg over the gear shift and take a seat. Not too bad, pretty comfortable. Since it's still running, I work the gears and clutch, and turn when he tells me to turn, back up when he tells me to back up, and if I didn't know better, I think I might have impressed the man.

We ride for what seems like hours, and my arse is growing a bit numb, and my stomach is growling. "How are we doing?" I ask, so turned around and lost that without Mack guiding me, I'd be properly lost.

"Looks like we're done. You did a fine job, boy."

I beam, truly proud of myself. At least one person in this town doesn't hate me. "You want to ride it out of here?"

"Sure, I've gotten the hang of it. Just tell me how to get back."

He frowns, and glances in the side mirror. "Dagnammit, I think there's a corn stalk stuck in the wheel. Give 'er a look, will ya?"

"Yeah, sure."

I climb from the tractor, and circle the back of it, to check the wheel. "I don't see much from back here."

The tractor starts moving, the loud hum of the engine filling my ears, as Mack turns it around for me. How nice of him to set me back on the right track. He moves ahead a bit, and I start walking toward him, ready to jump back in but he picks up speed.

"Hey, wait for me."

I run after it, but he's already too far ahead, and cutting the corner until he's out of my sight. I run faster, and faster, until I'm out of breath and completely turned around. I go still and listen, trying to follow the roar of the engine. Just when I think I know where he's going, I turn and come to a dead end.

Bollocks.

You have got to be fucking kidding me? Why the hell did I get out of the tractor, and how did I not see this coming?

Because Mack was right, and I really am a dumb ass.

18

VIOLET

I finish my shift, having stayed much later than planned, since Angie was home with her sick son and I couldn't find anyone to replace her. I stand at the counter, and pull my phone from my apron as the door opens and in walks a few locals. Dammit, I was hoping to get out of here before the dinner rush. I check my phone, but there are no texts or messages from Colin. I messaged him earlier to let him know I'd be staying late, and that he might have to do dinner on his own. I thought I would have heard back from him by now. Worry trickles through me and I pray the townsfolk don't have him strung up somewhere.

A couple of guys step up to the counter and flip over their mugs. As I pour their coffee, they laugh and joke with each other, and I breathe a sigh of relief when Tamara comes in to replace me. She's been working here for at least thirty years and I'm not sure she's missed a shift yet. I fondly remember her serving me milkshakes when I was young.

I note her heavy blue eye shadow as she comes closer. Most can't pull it off, but with her long silver hair, it totally works on her. "Hey Violet, what are you still doing here?" she asks as she grabs her apron off the hook and ties it around her waist.

"Angie's son wasn't well, so I stayed on."

"You do too much around this town." She waves a finger at me. "You're going to end up sick if you don't start resting and taking care of yourself."

"I'm fine," I say, and stifle a yawn, because that would just fuel her fire. "The park is shutting for the season." Actually, forever. "So that's one less job I have to worry about."

Her eyes narrow, and she steps a bit closer, like the conversation is for my ears only. "This bloke, as they say in Britain, have you gotten rid of him yet?"

"No, Tamara...it's not that easy." God, these people are going to run me out of town if I let this sale go through, but I'm not really *letting* it, now am I? I can't stop it, but they won't see it that way at all. My stomach clenches. What the hell am I going to do? One thing I can't do is let the townsfolk know that there's a part of me that needs this to happen. I do the books for the foundation. I know we're failing miserably, and short of selling the house left to me by my grandparents, there's nothing I can do. The influx of short-term money won't help in the long term, anyway. Selling it is the only feasible solution.

"Hey, did you hear what Mack did to your bloke?" Todd pipes in from the counter.

I stop breathing. I could correct him and say he's not *my* bloke but while he is here, he sort of is under my protection... and in my bed.

"What are you talking about, Todd?" He takes a sip of his coffee as I untie my apron and try not to panic. No one would really hurt Colin, right? "What happened?" I ask again.

He starts laughing so hard he can barely speak. I glare at him and he pulls himself together. "He's lost in the damn corn maze." He checks his watch. "Apparently, he was helping Mack, and he drove him to the back and left him there. It'll be dark soon enough. Don't expect him back any time soon."

"Probably won't find his way out until morning, and maybe not even then," Russel adds as he adjusts his ball cap and swivels on the stool beside Todd.

I slam my apron onto the counter. "This really isn't funny."

"Depends on who you're asking," Wild Willy says as he saunters up to the counter and plunks himself down beside Russel. The man got his name from all the wild stunts he pulled as a kid around these parts, so of course he'd find it funny and while my father got along with everyone, there was always tension between Dad and Willy and I never knew why. "I guess if I needed him to solve a problem for me, I'd be mad if Mack was trying to run him out of town too."

Needed him to solve a problem for me?

I have no idea what he's talking about and I'm not about to stick around and find out. Not when Colin is lost in a damn corn maze. That thing is hard to find your way out of on the best of days and the brightest of mornings.

I grab my purse, clock out of my shift, and head outside. Great, Colin has my car. How the hell am I going to get to the corn maze? Emily. I start walking, and pick up my pace when I reach her farm. I'm practically running, which is great for my step counter, but not my lungs, when I see her house.

I'm out of breath by the time I get there, and she opens her big farmhouse door, tons of tractors dotting the horizon in the distance, and glances at me.

"Are you okay?"

"No," I wheeze. "Colin is lost in the corn maze up at Mack's place."

"What the hell?" She turns to her driveway. "Did you walk here?"

"Ran might be more accurate. Colin," I say and gasp for air. "He was helping Mack cut the maze and Mack left him at the far end."

"Wow, I didn't know Mack had it in him."

"He shouldn't have had it in him and he's going to hear from me. But Colin has my car and I have no way to get there. I need to borrow yours."

"Hey Violet," Trevor calls out from the other room as Emily disappears for a moment.

"Trevor," I say managing to sound somewhat normal again.

Emily comes back and hands over her mess of keys attached to far too many key chains. She angles her head. "Do you want me to drive? You don't look so good."

"I ran here. I'm fine," I assure her.

"You're kind of pale."

"I know, I need to exercise more."

"I don't think it's that. Maybe you're pregnant."

"My God, Emily." Through clenched teeth, I grumble. "We only slept together last night." I leave out the shower sex, without the condom, as I turn and head down her driveway toward her car. "I am not pregnant."

She hollers something back, but I'm already in her car with the door closed. I back out of the driveway and head up the mountain toward Mack's place. Why on earth would he be so cruel to Colin? I thought the townsfolk were better than that.

Twenty minutes later I spot my car at the end of Mack's driveway, and I pull in beside it and kill the ignition. The sun is low on the horizon as I march up to Mack's door and pound on it. I listen and when I hear nothing, I pound again.

"Hold your horses, I'm coming, I'm coming."

Mack's voice comes through the door, along with the sound of feet shuffling on a wooden floor. The door finally opens and when he sees me standing there, a scowl on my face, he backs away, his look sheepish...guilty as hell. "What brings you by, Violet?"

I put my hands on my hips. "You know very well why I'm here." He takes his hat off, and scratches his head like he's searching the recesses of his brain. "Mack," I warn. "Why would you do that to Colin?"

He gives up the charade and says, "He's got no business being here."

"Yes, he does. His business is to buy the park and he has every right to do it, and you know it."

"You can put a stop to it."

"I don't control the Hanson Society, Mack. This deal was between them, the government and the Waltonstound foundation."

"You could if you wanted to."

"No, I can't." He opens his mouth, but I hold my hand off. "You don't have to like him, or like why he's here, but of all people, I expected you to at least treat him decently." Mack's been a pillar of our community forever, and would do anything for anyone at the drop of a hat. "I never expected this from you."

He glances down like a reprimanded child. "I'm sorry. I'll go get him."

"No, I'll go get him." I walk away and he apologizes again. I head to the back field. I've been running through his corn fields since I was a child and I know the pattern so well I can do it with my eyes closed. As I approach, a loud sneeze, coming from the maze, startles the crickets silent, and I call out, "Colin, are you there?" High on the mountain, my voice carries in the quiet night.

"Violet?" Another sneeze. This maze can't be good for his allergies. A flash of anger grips me.

"It's me," I say and start into the maze. "Keep talking to me and I'll come find you."

"Oh shite."

I quicken my steps as I follow his voice. "What?"

"I just got a corn in the face."

"Stop moving. I'll come to you." I run my hand along the cornstalks as I walk, and the sky grows darker and darker. "What were you doing out here anyway?"

"Oh, you know, just looking for the tallest peak on the tallest mountain so I can hurtle myself off, to save the townsfolk the trouble."

My heart pinches. He doesn't deserve any of this. "Didn't I tell you to stay out of trouble?"

He makes an oomph sound, like he's totally given up and sitting this one out. "Funny how trouble seems to find me everywhere I go in these parts."

"I'm sorry for what Mack did. We had a talk."

"Got into a right and proper kerfuffle, did you?"

"Let's just say I don't think he'll try this again."

"That sort of makes it sound like you think I'd fall for this again. I'm not that daft."

I chuckle. "Of course, you're not, I just meant...tell me why you were up here. The truth this time."

"Do you think I can eat one of these corns?"

"They're not ready yet. Mack cuts the path before they're ready for eating." I walk along and nearly trip on a few loose corn husks rolling around on the ground. I slow my pace so I don't faceplant. "It's easier that way. Are you hungry?"

"Starving."

"I'll make you something when we get home."

Home.

Wow, that sounded weird and oddly wonderful, inside my brain. "I'm really sorry everyone is giving you a hard time."

"I was just out for a drive. Thought I'd explore the community, see what kind of fun things the students could do once the school was built."

I switch direction, his voice a bit hard to detect in the vastness of the mountain. "Maybe you can keep some of the things in the park, like the paddle boats, and even the treehouse."

"No, don't want the kids shagging in it."

I chuckle at that, but I'm a little sad to think a part of my youth is going to be destroyed. I love that treehouse.

"Thought I'd check out the real estate market."

"Oh, the park isn't enough for your foundation. You need to buy up a few farms too," I tease, but he goes silent, the only sound around us is the stalks crunching beneath my shoes. "Colin, I'm kidding," I say but I'm pretty sure I hit a sore spot. Truthfully, teasing or not I shouldn't have said that.

"How did you figure out I was here?" he finally asks, breaking his silence.

"Couple of the locals came into the restaurant and told me about the bloke left in the corn maze and there's only one bloke I know, so I put it together quickly. I'm not daft," I say, hoping to pull a chuckle from him, but it doesn't work.

"At least I'm giving them a good laugh." A long moment of silence and then, "Maybe I should just leave."

My heart lurches, and my instant reaction is to scream *no*. But Colin leaving is what everyone wants, right?

Is it what you want, Violet?

Well, crap.

"Maybe I can talk Grandfather into giving up this idea. I'm sure there is land elsewhere in the province, and we wouldn't have to tear down the park, and everyone can stop hating me, and stop blaming you and things can remain status quo."

Nope, not a psychopath, although I already knew that. But seriously, he wouldn't care what others thought of him, or me, if he was, and it warms me that he doesn't want to upset the townsfolk.

"I'm sure your grandfather did his research and picked the park for a reason. It has some great old buildings on it, very castle-like, and a lake, and the orchard. If I had a kid, I'd want them going to a school like that."

He grunts. "Sounds like you want this deal to go ahead."

I swallow, and come up behind him. "Boo," I say, and he jumps to his feet and turns. As the moon fills the sky, it silhouettes his handsome face.

"Scared me." His hand slides around my waist, and he pulls me to him. My entire body quivers as it meshes with his and his big hands push back the cold as he runs them down my back to rest on the curve of my ass.

"Um, is that a corn on the cob in your pants, or are you just happy to see me."

His warm chuckle curls around me and makes my heart happy. "Have you ever shagged in a corn maze, Violet?" he asks.

"No, but I think that's about to change."

I roll over in bed, not at all angry that Mack left me in the corn maze. Hell, I wouldn't have had such an amazing night with Violet, getting her naked under the stars. That's one for the books, that's for sure. I take pleasure in the sight of her as she sleeps, and unable to help it, a big smile crosses my face. I lightly touch her hair, and with a chill in the air, I cover up her naked body as I recall all the ways I touched her last night.

"Creeper much?"

My gaze flies to hers. "Creeper?"

"Watching me when I sleep like some weird stalker."

"Call me any name you want, as long as I get to stare at you naked."

I fall over her, and kiss her deeply. As I do, my heart pounds a little faster, and a ringing sound circles my brain.

"Are you going to get that?"

"Get what?"

"Your phone, it's ringing."

"Bollocks, I thought that was in my head." She grins. "See what kissing you does to me?"

She laughs, obviously pleased by that and I roll toward the nightstand and see that it's Mum calling. I groan, and flop back onto my back, my phone in my hand. I'm not surprised she's calling. I've been ignoring her messages since I arrived in Nova Scotia.

"She's going to think we kidnapped you or something."

I drop my phone. "I can't deal with this. It's too early."

She pushes her blankets off. "You're right. It's a lot for..." she glances at the clock. "Eight in the morning."

"It's noon there."

"Oh right." Her gorgeous breasts draw my attention and I ache to take her nipple into my mouth.

"See something you like?"

"Yeah, I do."

She laughs. "Rain check?"

"Don't tell me you have to work at the restaurant again."

"Nope, need to take care of the goats, and to be honest I have a bit of a headache. Maybe I'm developing allergies from all that walking in the corn maze yesterday."

"You look a bit pale."

"I'm fine," she says and pushes to her feet. She pulls a bottle of medicine from the nightstand and takes two pills, washing it down with the water she set there last night. "This will work quickly."

"I'll take care of the goats while you rest and get rid of that headache, then I'm making you breakfast."

She flops back down, which surprises me. "If you insist. Oh, and I have today off, so after breakfast, we're going to have some fun and break some rules."

"Violet, the rulebreaker. Can't wait."

I tuck her in, pull on some clothes and snatch up my phone before I leave the bedroom. Lucky is right there, waiting for me at the top of the stairs. "Hey mate," I say, and he weaves in and out of my legs, but this time he's purring. I think we've come to a truce but it's a bit too early to tell. It's best I stay cautious. There's still a chance he's luring me in with kindness, and once he gains my trust he's going to attack.

I head downstairs and Lucky follows along. I feed him, and refill his water, and he follows me outside. I take a basket with me and pluck a few ripe vegetables. I then head to fill the water bowls for the goats, put some carrots and seeds in their food bowls, and by the time I actually find them, they're sitting there facing Lucky.

"Am I interrupting a meeting here?" I ask, and Lucky starts licking his paw. I prepare for a goat attack, and when one doesn't come, I grin. Okay, I guess we're all friends now. I turn and Lucky is tight on my heels as we go back inside, and he dashes upstairs, like he's checking on his mum.

Speaking of mum.

I pull my phone from my pocket and find oh, approximately three thousand messages, all about finding me the perfect wife. In the last message, she threatens to fly here herself and find out what I'm up to and what's taking so long. The women she's approved aren't going to wait forever. She's right. They're going to wait even longer than that if I have any say.

A growl rumbles in my throat. Who am I kidding? Tradition and responsibility be damned, but the truth is, one of them isn't going to wait at all. Why can't I be more like my reckless brother?

You're being reckless now, aren't you, Colin?

In a way, I am. Running around town, doing what I want and shagging the prettiest girl in the entire province, quite possibly the entire universe. What she sees in me I'll never know. I'm about to set my phone down, when another text comes in, another warning that Mum is going to pay Annapolis a visit to see what I've gone and gotten myself into. I know she won't. She spent a lifetime threatening to send us here if we were bad. She's not just going to show up. Right?

Bollocks.

The truth is she has distant relatives here. Cousins who are affiliated with the governing premier of the province. I'd better call her back later. Right now, I need to make a right and proper English breakfast for the woman who does so much for others, and so little for herself. For as long as I'm here, I plan to do for her, and no I'm not going to examine that ache in my gut as I think about flying back across the pond.

I go straight to work on cooking breakfast, and serving it up. Hurrying my steps, I go upstairs and find Violet and Lucky snuggled in bed. My heart misses a beat as I watch them, hating to wake her. I start to back out of the room, going quietly. Her breakfast can be reheated. It won't be quite as good, but that doesn't mean I can't make it for her again.

"Still at it, I see."

I stop going backward and start toward her. "Still at it?"

"Creeping me."

I sit down beside her on the bed. She rolls my way as the mattress compresses beneath my weight. "Did you want to sleep longer?"

She inhales. "When the house smells this good, no."

I chuckle, as she shrugs out from the blankets, her face still a bit pale. "Are you sure you're feeling okay?"

"I think I'm just tired. It will do me good to have some fun today." She glances out the window. "It's gorgeous out, perfect for what I have in mind."

"Does what you have in mind involve getting out of our clothes?"

"Actually yes, but not like that."

"Care to elaborate?"

"Not really." Lucky moves to my pillow, where he begins to groom himself, but since we've come to a truce, I let it go. Violet tugs on the T-shirt she was wearing last night, and glances at her jeans on the floor.

"Here," I say and hand her my sweats. Once she's dressed and looking completely adorable, we head downstairs, and I pour her a much-needed cup of coffee. She glances at my phone as she takes a seat at the table.

"Did you call your mother back?"

"No, but I will. Later."

I put her food in front of her, and her eyes go wide as she drools over the big red pepper filled with mushrooms, eggs, and bacon and tomatoes. "Colin, this is amazing."

A measure of pride wells up inside me. I like cooking for her. Back home, I rarely—okay, never—get a chance to play around in the kitchen now that I'm grown.

"I hope you like it."

"What's not to like?" She slides her fork into the pepper, takes a bite and moans around it. My dick thickens. "It's not Tim Horton's cereal, but—"

Before she can finish, I lean into her, and kiss her, some weird desperation to be close, to be physically connected, overcoming me.

"Wow, what was that for?" she asks when I break the kiss and drop down into my seat.

"You don't like being kissed at the table?" I ask, unsure how to answer the question. What am I supposed to say, the universe made me do it?

"No..." She takes another bite and eyes me. "I like it. In fact, I kiss all my boyfriends at the table."

She's being cheeky, but that doesn't stop the jealousy from surging. "Oh, you and Caleb kiss at this table, do you?"

She tilts her head and bats her eye lashes, playfully. "Maybe."

"Sorry, but I don't think that will be happening again anytime soon."

"Yeah, because you scared him off."

"I didn't say much. I think he left because his nappy was full."

"Nappy?" She takes a sip of coffee.

"His diaper," I explain and then next thing I know, she's spewing coffee all over me. I deserved that, after doing the same thing to her yesterday.

"Colin, I can't believe you said that. He's not that much younger than me. Just because you're ancient...and...and..." She stands, tears a piece of paper towel from the roll, and moves to my side of the table to clean the coffee from my face. "...and...you could have waited until I swallowed."

"That's what she said."

Her hand goes still and her eyes lock on mine. She stares for a long second, like she's processing my words.

"Did you—"

"Yeah." Another moment passes then she bursts out laughing.

"Where did you ever hear that? That is definitely not something I ever expected to hear you say."

"You can thank Nate. You should check out his social media sometime. He's quite funny. We're obviously very different."

"I think you can be funny."

"Yeah, it's pretty funny getting lost in a corn maze, eh?" I say and she laughs some more. I love the sound, love the way it wraps around my heart and tugs tight. As her body jiggles from laughter, my thick dick jumps up to take notice. I capture her hips and position her body over mine. Her laughter dies down, and when it stops completely and she realizes she's straddling my lap, my hard dick to be precise, she swallows. Hard.

"Oh."

"For the record, I'm happy to see you." I push my plate away, and reposition her until her back is on the table and her legs around my waist. I decide a right and proper *Canadian* breakfast is what I have a craving for. "Headache?"

"Gone," she says quickly, heat flooding her gorgeous blue eyes as her chest rises and falls with her fast breaths. I run my thumb over her bottom lip, and push it inside her mouth. She sucks and I nearly shoot off in my pants.

"Fuck, Violet…" I growl.

Her look is sexy, needy when she says, "Yes please."

I run my damp thumb along her neck, leaving a streak of wetness on her delicate flesh. Moving downward, through her cleavage, I reach the string on her sweatpants—well, actually they're my pants—and untie them. She moans and moves her hips, urging me on.

Just then Lucky jumps onto the kitchen counter to watch the action. Damn voyeuristic cat. "Lucky," I murmur as my dick aches to get inside her again.

Her lids fall shut as I tug on the elastic. "Yeah, lucky," she says, her lust-imbued brain not registering what I'm saying.

I glance at the damn cat. I can't shag while he's watching on. "Come on, Lucky. Scram." He smirks at me. "Goddamn cat."

"What?" I turn back to Violet as she shifts on the table, lifting her hips so I can remove the pants.

"Lucky is watching."

Her head turns, and she laughs. "Hey, Lucky, go on upstairs. I'll snuggle you later."

Lucky purrs, jumps from the counter, and darts into the other room. "I didn't know I was about to shag a cat whisperer." She reaches out and puts her hands on my chest. "Here I thought Lucky and I had come to a truce."

She tugs on my shirt, bringing my mouth to hers, and all thoughts of Lucky disappear from my brain. Okay, not all thoughts. I'm still thinking about getting lucky. I kiss her deeply, lose myself in her sweetness as she tugs on my shirt, and that's when I understand she wants me to take it off. I stand, tug it off, and toss it to the floor, which is a little unlike me. I'm normally much tidier, and I really have no idea why I'm thinking about that right now. Maybe it's because life is a little more relaxed here, and there's all these strange new, and exciting, things stirring inside me.

"That's better," she says once I'm half naked.

"Not quite," I say and take her pants to her ankles to expose her bare pussy. She didn't bother putting underwear on, and I'm ever so grateful for that. "Now it's better."

I work the pants over her ankles, and she spreads her legs wide for me. I growl at the way she opens for me, wants me. With my mouth watering, I press it to her hot pussy and lick from bottom to top, savoring the sweet taste of her. She lifts her hips for me, grinding herself against me, letting me know exactly how she likes it. I take my fill of her heat, and slide one finger into her.

Her cry of pleasure curls around me, and my cock jumps, but I'm not ready to fuck her just yet. I want her juices on my tongue first. She cups her breasts as I slide one hand under her buttocks as I bury my face in deeper and continue to finger fuck her. Her breathing becomes ragged, and the second I suck her clit into my mouth, she explodes all over my face, and I fucking love it. I eat at her slowly, lick softly as she rides out the waves.

Her hands curl in my hair, and I lift my head to see her eyes, which are barely focused. "Inside me, now," she says her voice a low soft whisper of need.

I tear open my pants, grip my dick and stroke it as I position my crown at her warm and welcoming pussy, and in one quick thrust I'm inside her. She grasps at the table, her fingers clawing and I take her legs and wrap them around me. She hugs me to her body, and I inch out slow, only to dive back in again.

"Just like that, Colin."

"Yeah," I murmur and continue the motion, going slowly at first, building our climaxes together. I glance at the beautiful woman on the table, and there's a new kind of tightness in my chest. What the hell is going on with me? I don't know, and I don't have time to explore it because her eyes are glazing over and my body is demanding release. I grip her hips for leverage, and as I pound into her, I slide my thumb over her clit, and apply pressure.

Her eyes fly open. "Oh, God, Colin…"

She clenches so hard around me, it brings on my own orgasm, and I curl my body into her as I fill her with my seed. I fall over her and her hands go around my back. Damn I love the way she touches and holds me. It does the weirdest things to my heart.

If I didn't know better, I'd say this is what falling in love felt like. Hey, does that mean I'm capable of falling for a woman? Does that mean I'm falling for Violet, a woman I can never have a future with?

20

VIOLET

I smile at Colin, my heart swelling a little as he drives us through town. I have to admit, while I'm used to doing everything myself, it is kind of nice to hand the wheel over to him. It's nice to sit back and relax, knowing he's competent and capable and I can put my trust in him.

Unable to help myself, I reach across the seat and give his big, warm hand a squeeze. As his warmth goes through me, heating my already warm, somewhat feverish body, he glances at me and I smile back. Honestly, I'd be a fool to think I wasn't feeling more for this man. It's crazy. It's insane. It shouldn't have happened. But it did, and I don't know what to do about that. Not that there's anything that I can do to change it.

But he's leaving soon, headed back across the pond to marry some girl of his mother's choosing. Cripes, I wouldn't fit into his world anyway, even if I wanted to. I wear overalls, rescue goats and naked cats, grow my own vegetables, and barely have two dimes to rub together. I can't even imagine living in a castle. I wouldn't know what to do with myself if I had servants. I get that most girls dream of it, or at least I think after watching Cinderella, they might give it a thought or two, but I'm not that girl, and I'm okay with that. His mother certainly wouldn't be, though.

Yeah, we're two different people from two different worlds and he already told me he didn't think he was capable of falling in love with a woman. So there's that to remember. My stupid stomach takes that moment to churn, what little I ate for breakfast, before Colin took me hard on the kitchen table, sloshing around in my stomach and threatening to rise for a second viewing.

"You okay?"

His voice pulls me back. "Yeah, fine," I answer and put on a happy face. Today is about fun, and stomach be damned, that's exactly what we're going to do. "Take a left up here."

"Where are we going?"

"I told you, you'll see when we get there."

"You're not driving me out to the middle of nowhere to leave me for dead, are you?"

I chuckle, and turn the radio up a notch when a song I like comes on. "If I was going to do that I would have done it already, don't you think? Or I would have left you in the corn maze."

I start to sing along, and I appreciate Colin not cringing. He takes the turns carefully, and I look out the side window as big trees, with their long extending branches reach across the road like they're trying to join hands and form a canopy over the pavement. I look out the front window, a little queasy from the fast movement. I focus on the road ahead and try to get my stomach under control. I can't be getting sick. I never get sick. Which means this nausea is because I'm getting too close to a man I should be keeping my distance from, physically and emotionally.

"Right here," I shout as we reach the bridge, coming upon the landmark faster than I realized because I wasn't paying attention. Colin has the ability to throw me off my game without even trying.

He eyes me, his brow furrowed. "We're in the middle of nowhere, how can we possibly be breaking rules, Violet?" He leans forward and glances around. "And we're also surrounded by trees, so why would you tell me to bring my trunks? Do Canadians jump from tree to tree in their bathing costumes or something? Is it some weird custom I know nothing about?"

"You know if I ever come to Britain, I'm going to really make fun of your culture."

"So it's true then, we do jump from tree to tree. My guess is right."

"Of course not." I shake my head at him. "Just pull over, I'll show you." Not that he brought a bathing suit. We couldn't find one this late in the season, but that's okay. His boxer shorts will do just fine. He eases off the road, and since it's a narrow road, half my car is still in the lane. I'm not worried. People from around these parts know this area well.

I jump from the passenger side and wish I hadn't. My head spins a little at the fast movement. I grip the side of the car until it passes and when I blink my eyes open, Colin is standing in front of me, worry all over his face.

"I don't think you're okay. Did you eat enough this morning?"

"I just got up too fast. Low blood pressure."

There's uncertainty in his eyes as his gaze moves over my face, a careful assessment. I pull off my T-shirt and shimmy out of my shorts. He makes a noise like he might have swallowed his tongue and I grin. The man just saw me naked, made love to me on my kitchen table. Correction, shagged me on my kitchen table and now he's standing here drooling over my bikini. I kind of like it.

I snatch up his hand and drag him to the rail on the bridge, the river running fast below it. "You might want to strip off."

He blinks once, then twice, as he reads the sign, 'No Jumping Allowed'. "You can't be serious."

"Sure, it's fun. I've been doing this since I was two apples high."

"It says no jumping."

"Pfft, that's just a suggestion."

He steps up to the sign and points at the small print. "Right here, it says town ordinance. It's a local law, Violet."

I wave a dismissive hand. "Oh, you can just ignore that."

"Aren't you the mayor?"

I climb onto the metal rail, and sit on it, my feet dangling some ten feet from the water.

"Get down from there before you kill yourself."

"Okay, *Dad.*"

"Violet."

"Do it with me."

"I am not—"

"Fine, I'll do it alone." When I catch the mortification crossing his face, I laugh. "It's safe."

"I'm not doing that."

"You're afraid of heights, are you?"

"No," he says, a little uneasy. "It's against the law."

"Right and you don't break the rules. I remember. I'm not asking you to go skinny dipping. I know how you feel about that, but when in Rome…"

I stand and balance on the rail and he curses under his breath. "Wait," he says, and starts tearing off his clothes. I watch, pleased with the view, and a moment later he's glancing up and down the road, like he's worried we're about to get arrested, but he has nothing to worry about. Constable Ben Davis has made this jump at least a thousand times.

I know he'll love it if he tries, but if he's truly afraid, I'd rather him stay on the pavement. "You don't have to if you really don't want to."

"Of course, I have to. This has peer pressure written all over it."

I blink at him innocently. "I would never subject you to peer pressure. I can't anyway, you're not my peer, you're far too old for that."

"I'm your peer, it's Caleb who isn't."

"You really don't like that guy, do you?"

"No," he says without any further explanation, and hauls himself up beside me. I reach for his hand.

"Let's do it together."

"My mother once asked me, if my friend jumped off a bridge would I do it too?" He looks so handsome as he glances at me, a small smile on his face. "Until I met you, the answer was no."

"I'm a bad influence, huh?"

"The worst."

"Excellent. Okay, on the count of three, we go." He nods, and I hold his hand tighter. "One, two, three." We both fling ourselves off the rail and jump into the river. Our grip breaks as we hit the water, and I go down and down and down. I eventually kick my legs, propelling myself upward, until I reach the surface, but Colin is nowhere to be found. Crap. Did he drown?

I look down for him and a second later, he's right in front of me. "Violet," he screams so loud, I fear he might have punctured my ear drum. I seriously can't hear well at the moment.

"What?" I yell back, and that's when the water drains from my ear. Ah, that's better. I take in his childlike wonderment.

He grips my shoulders. "That was so much fun!"

I laugh and hug him. "I told you. You need to trust me. I won't lead you astray."

"Can we do it again?"

"Of course, we can."

He kisses me quickly and takes off for the shore, and for a moment sadness invades my soul and my throat squeezes tight. I hate that his upbringing was so strict, that doing the right thing, always, has been so ingrained into him that he's terrified of misstepping. As long as he's here, I'm going to ensure he has fun, with no photographic evidence to prove it.

He should be able to enjoy himself without the fear of his actions being splashed all over social media.

He reaches the embankment and holds his hand out to me. "Coming?" I swim to shore and he hauls me from the water. "I had no idea breaking the rules could be so much fun."

"Maybe that's why your brother does it all the time."

"Maybe," he says but there's skepticism in his eyes, which makes me wonder more about this reckless brother of his.

We head up the embankment, and climb back onto the rail. I wobble a bit, once again dizzy, but I have to say, the cool water felt good against my hot skin. Colin's big hand captures mine and a smile lights up his face, and he does the count-down. We jump in, and over the next hour or so, it's rinse and repeat. Colin can't seem to get enough of the jumping, and well, I can't seem to get enough of him.

After our millionth jump, I climb from the water, exhausted. "I think that's enough for me. I'm totally waterlogged."

"Okay," he agrees. "Can we come back again, before I fly back home?"

"Sure, if the weather stays nice." We head to my car, and I grab us towels from the back. Mr. Barker drives by and honks his horn at us.

"I still need to get a whittling lesson from him. Maybe I could bring a beaver back home with me."

He's grinning as he says it, and I get the gist. "It would have to be a small beaver if you're taking it on the plane."

"Well, yeah. No one wants a gigantic beaver, Violet."

"Ohmigod," I say and whack him with my towel.

He yelps. "Hey what was that for?"

"You want another?"

Laughing, he darts to the driver's side and I grin as I watch him. I love this playful, funny side of Colin. Heck, when I first met him, I had no idea he had it in him, or that he'd be in me. Life is crazy sometimes, and comes with its own agenda, apparently.

I dry off and pull my clothes on over my still damp bathing suit, and hop into the car. Colin's stomach grumbles. "I don't think you had enough to eat this morning."

He wags his eyebrows at me. "You're right. I might need another bite."

I laugh at his playful antics and note that I'm not at all hungry, which is odd. I can always eat, especially after exercise. He starts my car and pulls onto the empty road. His hand finds mine and he squeezes. "That was so much fun, thanks for taking me."

"My pleasure."

"You're hot."

"Why thank you," I respond.

Confusion moves over his face, and I stare at him until the lightbulb goes off. "Oh, I get it. While yes, you are hot, or as we say in Britain, fit, you're also hot hot. Your skin is on fire, even after all the cold dips."

"I don't think I'm feeling all that well," I finally admit, and his face goes serious.

"Bollocks. Why didn't you tell me? We didn't have to jump off the bridge." He shakes his head and grips the steering wheel.

"This is my fault. I knew you looked pale."

"Maybe it's just something I ate."

"You barely ate a thing this morning. Let's get you home. Do you have a thermometer?" I blink as he dives deep into protective mode.

"I don't know. Probably. Somewhere."

"Then I'll stop at the drugstore and get one." He reaches across the seat and puts his hand on my forehead. "Do you think you're going to hurl?"

"Hurl?" I laugh and put my hand over my stomach. "No, I don't think so." The trees go by in a blur as he picks up speed. "I don't have time to be sick, Colin. I have shifts at the park, and at the café, and the town hall meeting is coming up soon."

"I can take your shifts, and forget the town hall meeting. We can put it off a little while longer if you're ill."

"Colin, you can't—"

"Nonsense." His phone pings and he ignores it, but I recognize the sound well enough to know it's his mum calling again. He casts me a fast glance before turning his attention back to the road to take a sharp turn. "I'm not just going to leave you when you're sick. What kind of guy would that make me?"

My heart does a big tumble in my chest. Does he want to stay longer to be with me or is that wishful thinking? Either way, he's incredibly sweet, offering to take my shifts, which of course is ludicrous. What does he know about server work, or running equipment at the park? Nothing. But if he stays longer, I could run the risk of really losing my heart, and while he might want to stay because we're having a ton of fun, we have no end game here, and his pinging phone is a sober reminder of that.

21

COLIN

After stopping to get a thermometer and buying nearly every type of fever reduction pill on the shelf, I pull into Violet's driveway, and hurry around the other side of her car to help her out. She's still warm and working to stifle a yawn, but all the jumping from the bridge wore her out whether she wants to admit it or not. She's stubborn, I'll give her that.

"Why did you buy so much?" she says as she looks at the bag in my hand. "If I take all of them, I'll be a rattle in the wind."

"I didn't know what you liked to take for fever, so I got one of everything. I didn't want to risk getting the wrong kind, and having to leave you and go back to the store."

"I'm a big girl, Colin. I'm quite capable of taking care of myself when I'm healthy and when I'm sick."

"I know that."

"Then why is your arm around me, practically carrying me to the door when I can walk."

That's just it, she can do all these things on her own, has been doing them all on her own, and I want to be the guy to help her when she's down. "Humor me, okay?"

"Okay," she says the fight draining out of her—another sign that she's plenty sick—as I open the door and usher her in. Lucky comes running down the stairs and meows loudly when he sees Violet.

"Hey Lucky, we need to take care of Violet. She's not feeling so well."

I scoop her up, and she gives a little yelp as I carry her upstairs. Lucky jumps onto my side of the bed. Yes, I put her in my room as she reserves this one with the big bathroom for guests. Her room isn't quite as equipped, forcing her to use the loo in the hall and I don't want her to have to walk that far.

She moans as I set her down. "My bathing suit is still wet. I'm going to make a mess of your bed." Her movements are clumsy as she tries to get out of her damp clothes.

I touch her forehead again. "Let me help you, and then I'll give you something for fever."

She stops struggling, and sits up as I take off her T-shirt, and reach around her back to unhook her bikini top. I toss it away for now, and get to work on removing her shorts and her bikini bottoms. Once she's naked, I make a quick trip to her room, root through her dresser drawer and find a T-shirt and pajama shorts. I hurry back, help her into them, and she blows a strand of hair from her moist forehead as I tuck her in. My heart clenches as I gaze at her. I'm not happy that she's sick, but I do like taking care of her. I dump the medicine on the bed.

"Which one?"

"It really doesn't matter. Whatever is going to take the fever down." She moans and rolls to her side.

"Should you see a doctor?"

"It's the flu, Colin. Not Ebola."

"You do too much around here." She carries far more stress than she lets on. "You've worn yourself out." I grab a bottle of ibuprofen, pour two in my hand and press them in her palm. "Hang on." I grab the glass on the nightstand and dart to the bathroom where I rinse it, and fill it up again. "Can you sit up?"

She moans as I help her up and she swallows the pills. She flops back down again, her eyes glazed as they search mine out. "Colin, can you call the café, and let them know I don't think I'll be able to make my shift Wednesday. You'll also have to call the park. I'm supposed to work the paddle boats on Thursday. Give them the heads up I might not be able to make it in, but I'm hoping to be better by then. The contact numbers are in my phone, and my phone is in my bag, which is still in the car."

I tuck the covers around her. "What's your passcode?"

"I don't have one."

"Violet, you can't go around without a passcode on your phone. What if it fell into the wrong hands? Anyone could go through your stuff."

"This is Annapolis, and I have nothing to hide. If you want to go through my phone, go through my phone. I'm boring with a capital B."

"I never said I wanted to and you're the least boring person I know." Although, it might be interesting to look at her pictures and see what else she does for fun. "Any other calls?"

"I don't know. I can't think right now."

"Don't worry about a thing. I'll take care of it all. You just rest and get better."

She rolls over and I stand over her for a moment, until her breathing levels out. "What do you say, Lucky? Let's get out of here and let her get some sleep."

I head toward the door and Lucky follows along. I don't shut it tight behind me—I want to hear her if she calls out—and I quietly go downstairs and head outside to get her phone. I grab it and I'm about to go back in the house when I spot a bunch of people hurrying toward me, each person has something in their hands.

Have they brought out the pitchforks and torches? I stand tall, and fold my arms across my chest as they approach, but as they come closer, I noticed they're all carrying casserole dishes. What the hell is going on?

"Clara," I say as she approaches, her face pinched tight with worry. "What's going on?"

"Where is she?"

"Who?"

"Violet, who do you think?"

Okay, she doesn't have to be so mean.

Irene comes up the driveway, a casserole dish in her hands. "How high is her fever?"

I stare at them for a second until Eugenie, Audrey, and Chester join the fray. "You're talking about Violet?" Chester shakes his head, looking at me like I'm daft. "What?"

"Of course, we're talking about Violet. We heard she was sick. We brought our flu shakedown remedy."

Clara points at the individual dishes in everyone's hands, and says, "Chicken soup, chicken casserole, turkey soup, turkey casserole, and of course chicken cacciatore, because it's Violet's favorite and Audrey makes the best chicken cacciatore in town." Audrey beams at Clara.

"But...but..."

"Out with it," Chester says.

"How did you know? We just got in the door."

"Ronald, at the pharmacy, he called to let me know," Clara explains, like I should already know that.

Word really does travel fast here.

"How did you make these dishes so fast?"

"We keep them in the freezer, at the ready," Chester says. "Now are you going to let us in, or keep us standing out here until dark."

Chester can be quite the arse at times.

"Come in. She's sleeping, so we need to be quiet. I haven't taken her temperature yet; she just wants to sleep but I did give her something for the fever."

Inside they take all their food to the kitchen, and everything about this warms my heart. Violet doesn't ask for anything, but she has a town full of people who care about her, and that's comforting to know.

I hold her phone in my hand. "She asked me to cancel her shift at the café."

Eugenie frowns. "Oh, dear that's not good."

"Why not?"

"Frank is home, and he'll insist on coming in. He's not up to it just yet. He needs to be off his feet for at least another month, but he won't want to leave them short."

"If I didn't have these bunions," Clara says.

Chester grabs his lower back. "And my sciatica is acting up again."

As they go around the room, comparing ailments, I pipe in. "I...well...maybe I could do it for her." I scrub my face. "But I don't want to leave her alone either, you know."

Five sets of eyes stare at me, like I might have just suggested we all go skydiving without a parachute.

"I don't—" Chester begins but Irene cuts him off.

Her milky blue eyes narrow in on me. "Have you ever worked at a café before?"

"No, but—"

"It's not as easy as it looks," she says, her back clearly up.

"I never thought it looked easy. I'm a quick learner, and I'd like to help out if I can."

Chester nods as he thinks about it. "I don't think Brian would turn down the help."

"Brian?"

"The owner," he clarifies.

"It's settled then," Clara says. "You take her shift, and when you're gone, we'll sit with Violet. Now let's get these things in the freezer, and I'll leave instructions on how to heat them up." I'm not as daft as they think I am, but I allow her to go over the instructions.

Once I finally get them out of the house, I call the café and talk to Brian. He seems okay with the plan, and it's kind of shocking how easy going he is, the way he takes things in stride. But I don't mind helping out. I'm stuck here, so I might as well put myself to good use. Although I'm not quite sure I'd use the word stuck anymore.

I'm about to tiptoe upstairs to check on Violet when my phone rings. Seeing that it's Mum and knowing I can't ignore her much longer, I slide my finger across the screen and answer.

"Hello Mum," I answer in a quiet voice.

"I thought you'd fallen off the end of the earth."

"I'm in Nova Scotia, you know that."

"Same thing as the end of the earth as far as I'm concerned."

I open my mouth, about to defend the place, but decide against it. It's funny really because until I arrived in Annapolis and started exploring the small town, I thought Nova Scotia was the armpit of the western world. Why wouldn't I? That's all I've ever heard, but since I've been here, I'm starting to form my own opinions.

"I messaged Grandfather and told him there would be a delay in getting home."

"The sooner the better, I say."

"It might actually be a bit later than I thought." I lower my voice even more and walk into the kitchen.

I hear a spoon clanging in her teacup when she says, "Do tell me, what dreadful thing is going on now."

"Violet is sick," I say without thinking.

"Violet?" she asks and I can just imagine she sat up a bit straighter in her favorite Queen Anne's chair.

Bollocks.

"She's the owner of the bed and breakfast, where I'm staying. She's come down ill, and she's also the mayor so the meeting might be postponed." Mum goes too quiet, and I pace around the kitchen. "Are you still there?"

"I thought you were staying with a man named Bryant."

I chuckle, but it's uneasy sounding, even to myself and my Mum is quite astute when it comes to matters of the heart. *Matters of the heart?* Am I saying that's what's going on between Violet and me?

"She has no one to take care of her, so I'll be staying on until she's better." A little white lie, for sure. She has lots of neighbors who want to help, she just won't ask. With me, she doesn't have to ask and I'm taking care of her whether she likes it or not.

"You're expected home, Colin." Her voice is stern, her tone no nonsense. "We have many important matters to discuss about your future."

"I know." What was that Violet said about moving to Canada? "How is Nate?"

She gives an exasperated sigh as I redirect the conversation, feeling a tad guilty at pulling my brother into this to save my own hide. "That boy needs to settle himself down."

"I'll message him," I promise. "Give him a talking to."

"Have you seen my cousin Beatrice?"

"Nova Scotia is a big place, Mum."

"Hmm, you know, maybe I should pay her a visit myself, see what's really going on with the paperwork."

"You don't have to come here. I have everything under control," I assure her as I pinch the bridge of my nose.

"Do you now, Colin? Do you have everything under control?"

Nope. Not even a little bit. Or as Violet would say, yeah, no.

22

VIOLET

I wake up soaked, my hair stuck to my face. With great effort, I peel my tongue from the roof of my mouth and pull the wet curls from my feverish flesh. I glance around and try to orient myself but my head spins with the fast movement. I can't believe I've been sick for days, barely able to keep anything down.

"Whoa," I say and put my hand on my forehead. My stomach takes that moment to churn.

"Hey."

The soft voice comes from the doorway, and I wince as light filters in through the crack in the curtain and stings my pupils.

"What time is it?" I ask.

"Eight o'clock."

"But it's still light out."

"That's because it's eight in the morning."

I go to shake my head, shocked, but remember that will just make me dizzy. "I don't remember ever being in bed this long."

He crosses the room, sits on the end of the bed, and puts his hand on my forehead. "You're still warm. I shouldn't go."

Go? He's leaving?

I take in his freshly shaved face, his combed hair, and his clothes. He's dressed in khaki pants and a polo shirt, like he's going to a meeting or something. But it's only Wednesday, which means our meeting isn't for two days, unless he managed to get it moved up and is planning on heading to the airport afterward. But wait, no, he travelled here in a very expensive suit, and he'd likely travel back home in it, right? I try to sit up and shake the fog from my brain.

"Go where?" I ask and try to sound casual and airy, not at all freaked out that I don't want him to go.

God, I don't want him to go.

"You need to get more medicine in you." He reaches for the acetaminophen bottle and shakes out two. "I freshened your water a half hour ago. I can do it again—"

"No, that's fine." He hands the pills to me and my throat is swollen and scratchy, making it painful to swallow them down. I set the glass on my nightstand and try to fix my hair, but the effort proves futile and only exhausts me.

"Do you think you can eat something?" He peels a strand of hair from my cheek and tucks it behind my ear. "Maybe toast, or some eggs."

"Ugh, no." My stomach rebels at the thought and I slowly lay back down. I sink into the pillow, the bedding damp from my sweat. "Where did you say you were going?"

"To Annapolis café."

"Yes, of course, you need breakfast. I should make you breakfast. That's what you're paying me for." I try to sit up again, and he puts his hand on my shoulder and pushes me back down. I like it. A lot. I might be sick, but I'm still a woman and his touch does crazy things to me.

"You're not going anywhere, and I'm not looking for breakfast. I'm taking your shift at the café."

Okay, clearly I'm hallucinating from this fever. "For a second there, I thought you said you were taking my shift."

"I am taking your shift. Clara is downstairs. She's going to stay with you until I get back."

"Colin, wait what?" I shimmy backward and try to get up, but he stops me.

"I called Brian and he was okay with it."

"You can't just take my shift."

"Seems I can." He adjusts the blankets around me. "What about soup, does that sound like something you could eat?"

"No, I just want to sleep until November, but I have too much to do."

"No, you don't. I'm going to take care of everything for you." I pinch him and he jumps. "Why did you do that?"

"I wanted to see if you were real."

He chuckles. "You're not used to anyone doing for you, are you?"

"That's okay. I don't mind." Truthfully, I like when Colin does things for me. But taking my shift? Insane, right?

"It's okay to count on someone else once in a while."

"Until they leave," I say quietly without thinking.

"What?"

"Nothing."

He takes my phone from his pocket and sets it on the nightstand. "Call me if you need anything."

"Are you going to wear my frilly apron too?" I don't know why I asked that. Maybe I'm stalling, wanting him to stay here with me a bit longer.

"Yes."

"Pics or it didn't happen."

"Are you twelve?" he asks as he shakes his head and while I might be feverish, I can't help but think how cute he looks at the moment.

"Only in my head."

"Fine, I'll send you a picture if you like."

I smile, as my heart thuds a little faster. "You're crazy."

No, I'm the crazy one. Crazy about him.

"Yes, well, I've been called worse around these parts."

"Colin...I...I just want you to know I'd wouldn't sell a pic of you to the tabloids."

His smile is soft and warm. "I know."

I nod. "Tell Clara she doesn't have to stay. I'm just going to sleep and if I need anything, I can call her or you."

"You sure?"

"Positive. I don't like an audience when I hurl," I tease.

"At least you still have your sense of humor. The fever didn't burn that out of you."

"How are the goats, and Lucky?"

"All taken care of." A sense of comfort comes over me, and my lids briefly fall shut.

"You get some sleep."

His lips land on my forehead. "Don't get too close, you don't want to catch this, whatever it is."

"I'll take my chances."

My stupid heart does a little happy dance. He stands and I open one eye to take in the view as he walks to the door. "Colin," I murmur.

He turns to me, his face full of concern. "Yeah."

"Thank you. I'll make it up to you when I'm better. We'll do something really fun. I promise."

"I'm not sure you could top the other day at the river..." A low growl catches in his throat when he adds, "Or in the shower, or the night in this bed."

His words hug my aching body like a comforting blanket, and I give him a small smile. He smiles in return and says, "I'll check back on my break, and I'll bring you back something to eat tonight. Maybe you'll feel like it then. Try to get some sleep, and I'll let Clara know she doesn't have to stay. She'll probably fight me on it."

"I'm pretty sure you can handle yourself, Colin. Except if there's a corn maze involved...or a goat."

His soft chuckle fills the air and lingers as his footsteps sound on the stairs. The next thing I know, my eyes are opening and it's midafternoon. I move my body, and my muscles ache, but I don't feel nearly as bad as I did when I woke this morning. I turn slowly and reach for my phone. The image staring at me after I run my hand across the screen brings on a big, belly laugh. He kept his word, put on my apron and sent me proof. I'm beginning to believe he's too good to be true.

The door downstairs opens and Lucky's meows filter up the stairs and reaches my ears. I want to call out, to see if it's Colin but I don't have the energy. I send him a text instead, and he instantly answers letting me know he's home and on his way up to check on me.

I toss the thermometer into my mouth just as he steps into the room. "How are you feeling?" He quickly crosses and the second the thermometer beeps he takes it and checks it. "You're doing much better." He pours two pills into my hand and refreshes my water for me. My stomach growls as I drink.

"I brought you back soup."

"Thank you." My heart wobbles. "You're home early."

Home. Why is it I like the idea of Colin and home in the same sentence?

"Things quieted down after the lunch break, so Charlie let me go. He told me I did a great job."

I grin as he beams at me. "Did he give you a sticker?"

"Sadly no, but you know what, I really enjoyed it. I got to talk with a lot of people today. I think I even brought a few over to the dark side."

"The dark side, huh?" I ask with a laugh.

"Once I explained how the school would bring in profits, and boost the economy, they started to see where I was coming from."

I put my hand on his arm. "That's great, Colin."

"I considered a town hall meeting. To really help the towns-folk understand what we're trying to do. I get they love the park. It's been a part of their life for thirty years, but things change over time, whether we want them to or not. Sometimes good things just come to an end, the natural evolution of life." His other hand closes over mine and as he gives it a squeeze, I wonder who he's trying to convince of that, me or himself. "I can't wait to tell you more about my day, but I'm not sure you're up to it. Your skin is damp."

"I need a shower."

"I don't think you're in any shape to stand in the shower."

I groan. "I'm disgusting."

"I could join you, make sure you don't fall, or you could have as sponge bath. I can help with that too."

"I want to wash my hair, so how about you join me." Isn't it crazy how getting naked with him is like second nature to me now? In the past, I'd never let anyone see me like this, especially not a boyfriend, not that Colin is my boyfriend. Still, there's a real comfort between us, an easy trust, and intimacy I've never shared with anyone before.

He stands and pulls the blankets to my feet, exposing my damp pajamas. "Just because I'm going to help you shower, does not mean I'm putting out, Violet." I laugh and it hurts my head. "Easy..." He puts his arms around me and carefully leads me to the ensuite bathroom. I used to use this room as my own until I turned the place into a bed and breakfast, and I must say, I do miss having a private bathroom.

He sets me on the counter, and backs up. "You're not going to fall if I leave you, are you?"

Oh Colin, I am so going to fall if you leave me.

I swallow down the lump in my throat and force a smile as I remind myself he is going to leave. He has to leave and we're not a couple or anything, so really, he's not leaving me, because I was never his. "I'm okay." He eyes me for a second and I glare at him. "I'm fine."

"Okay, okay." He turns the water on, and I struggle to get undressed. I tug my T-shirt up and it's so damp I can't get it over my head. Warm knuckles brush my skin.

"Let me." He easily removes it and I'm exhausted by the time I put my arms back down.

"I wish I'd gotten the license plate of the truck that ran me over. Although it feels more like it was a Zamboni."

"Zamboni?"

"Machine that cleans the ice before and after hockey games."

"Canadians and their hockey."

Offended, I say, "You don't like hockey."

"The only game worth playing is football, Violet."

I'm about to complain, but getting undressed has simply exhausted me. "That was a workout, and I'm not even getting the benefits with my Fitbit. Maybe you could wear it for me."

"No, that's cheating."

I nod. "Right, rule follower."

"I think a sponge bath would have been the better choice."

"Hair, remember?"

I expect him to say of course he remembers, I'd only mentioned it seconds ago, but he doesn't—hey, maybe he's finally starting to understand our language and has stopped taking things so literally. He helps me off the counter and removes my shorts, and a second later I'm under the spray, which is gloriously on the cooler side. Colin strips down and climbs in with me. He goes straight to work on washing me, while I struggle to keep my hands off his hard, gorgeous body. But this is so incredibly nice.

"Doing okay?" he asks when I sigh.

"Living the dream," I respond, and his chuckle vibrates through my body. He washes me all over, and gets to work on shampooing my mess of hair. "I already feel so much better."

He removes the nozzle from the hook, and I close my eyes as he rinses my hair. "Do you think you could eat?"

"Soup does sound good."

"The triple G's brought turkey and chicken. Both are in the freezer. You also have casseroles."

I sag against him, and he holds me to him as he turns the water off. "That was so nice of them."

"You live in a great place, Violet. Charlie told me tomato soup was your favorite so that's what I brought home from the café." We step from the shower and he snatches a big fluffy towel from the small closet and dries me. He wraps me in it and quickly dries himself off. Back in his bedroom, he gives me a big pair of sweats and one of his shirts to wear. After he dresses, we head downstairs and he insists I sit in front of the TV, and he'll serve me on a tray.

My heart is far too unsteady when he comes back in, walking slowly so he doesn't spill the soup on the tray. He's completely adorable as he struggles to balance everything. I put my legs on the floor so he can place the tray on my lap. "Oh, crackers too."

"Charlie said you can't have tomato soup without crackers. I didn't know that was a thing."

"It's yummy."

"Crackers go with cheese, not soup."

"Yeah, well you eat beans on toast, so I don't think you're an expert on what goes together."

He laughs and sits next to me, and while we're so very different, from different worlds, we sort of fit together nicely. He puts the spoon into the soup, and brings it to my mouth. I open my mouth and let him feed me. Honestly, I could really get used to this kind of attention and care. But since I've been in this town my whole life, and know a thing or two, like the fact that no one ever stays. I'm not stupid enough to let myself get used to it.

After watching a movie with Violet last night, her falling asleep in my lap, I brought her to bed and crawled in with her, being careful not to wake her. As I look at her now, the early morning sun shining in through the curtains, I take in her flushed cheeks. I don't know what hit her, but it hit her hard. Maybe she picked up the same bug that laid up Tucker Clements. I'm just glad I was here to help take care of her. Sure, she had her neighbors, and her mother isn't far, and while I love the sense of community all caring for one another, I was able to stay through the night and get her water and medicine when she needed it, and I know she wouldn't have asked anyone for anything. It's in her nature to give, not take.

Honestly, it's hard to believe how much I want to do for her. It was less than two weeks ago, I couldn't wait to get out of this place, and now, I don't know. I'm not really in a hurry to leave, and it has nothing to do with my Mum trying to marry me off, and everything to do with the sweet woman opening her glassy eyes beside me.

"Good morning," I say quietly.

The smile that tugs at her lips squeezes my heart. "Have you been awake long?"

"No, just woke up. How are you feeling?"

She stretches out her limbs. "So much better. My head isn't pounding anymore." I let loose a loud sneeze and she grimaces. "Okay, it is now."

"I'm so sorry," I say quickly. "I forgot my allergy meds last night." I push her hair from her face and lay my palm on her forehead. "You still feel warm."

"If I have to spend one more day in this bed, I might jump out the window."

"Is it that bad?"

She rolls toward me. "Yes, I mean no. It's been nice to just sleep off the flu, and not having to worry about my obligations. Although you're my obligation, and I've not been keeping up my end of the bed and breakfast."

I scrub my chin. "You're right. You haven't been. I might have to put that in my review." She whacks my stomach and I exaggerate an oomph. I snatch her hand, bring it to my mouth and kiss each finger individually. "I really am glad you're feeling better."

"I should be able to make the town hall meeting tomorrow." She sits up a tiny bit, and smiles, but it doesn't reach her still feverish eyes. "Then you can get on your way."

"I don't want you pushing it. There's no need for you to go to the meeting if you're not well. I'm sure we can reschedule."

"I don't know—"

"Who knows if Cameron even has the paperwork, anyway."

"I've messaged him a few times, left a few warnings. He's not responding, so that doesn't bode well for you, Colin."

"You know this sale has to happen, right?"

"I do. It doesn't mean I have to like it, but the park isn't thriving. You know, the park was actually built for me."

My head rears back at that revelation and the entire universe closes in on me, sucking the air from my lungs. I'm not just buying her park, I'm buying something that was built for her. I had no idea. "Are you serious?"

She chuckles. "Yeah, we didn't have much for kids to do in the area, and when Mom and Dad got married and were trying for kids, it's when my grandfather came up with the idea for the park."

I push to my feet and pace to the window. "Jesus, Violet. How can I possibly tear it down after hearing that?" I turn to face her, and sit on the window ledge. "How do you not hate me?"

"Because...I just don't. I know all good things come to an end."

Just like we're going to come to an end...

I walk back toward her and sit on her side of the bed. She shifts to face me, and I hate everything about this situation. If I don't get the land secured, it'll be a huge blow to the foundation, and hell, I wouldn't put it past Grandfather to fire me. I don't want to lose my job or fail the foundation, but Violet loves the park. It has special meaning to her, and I know it will gut her once it's gone.

"I have your shift at the park today," I tell her.

"Colin, you don't have to do that. You've done enough for me as it is. Don't you have your own work to take care of?"

"No, I want to take it. I'm looking forward to it, actually."

"It will be a long and boring day. No one goes to the park on Thursday, and we're gearing down to close it next week anyway. Just don't bother."

"Would you have gone in?"

"Yes."

"Then I'm going in. Right after I take care of the goats, and get you something to eat."

"What am I going to do with you?"

"When you're better, I'll give you a detailed list."

She chuckles as I climb from the bed and tug on a pair of sweats. It's funny, my sweats were only ever used for running, but here I find myself in them more and more. Back home, my picture would be blasted all over social media if I wasn't in my usual suit. I kind of like the laid-back easiness of it here, though. I don't have to watch my every move. Maybe that's not true, there are still plenty of townsfolk out to get me despite Violet's efforts.

She groans as she climbs from the bed, and I hold her a robe to pull on over her pajamas. She snuggles into it. "I need coffee."

I open the bedroom door, and Lucky is sitting there waiting for us. He purrs and slides in and out of Violet's legs, and she picks him up to assure him she's feeling much better. We head downstairs and she gets comfy on the sofa with Lucky, and picks up her phone as I make her some toast and coffee.

I carry it to her on a tray and set it on her lap. She smiles up at me, and my world tilts on its axis.

"Emily is coming over. She wants to plan the annual lobster boil for Saturday night."

"Do you think you'll be up for it by then?"

"I feel so much better, Colin. Thanks to you taking such good care of me."

My chest swells. I like being the guy she can count on. "What exactly is a lobster boil?"

"Oh, it's so much fun," she begins, a new energy and animation about her as she starts waving her hands around, and it's clear to me that she's feeling better, and can probably make tomorrow's meeting. There shouldn't be a knot in my stomach because of that, but there is, and I can't do anything about it.

"It sounds like a lot of fun."

"We do one every year on the beach, as the end of park season approaches. It usually starts out with just a few of us, but by the end of the night, half the town can be found laughing around the bonfire. You're going to love it." She claps her hands together. "Your very first lobster boil. I can't wait for you to taste how good the lobsters are when cooked in the sea water over an open fire."

My heart dips into my stomach. "I probably won't be here, Violet. If you're up for the meeting tomorrow...and we get the papers signed, I'll be headed back."

She goes completely still for approximately two seconds, then she shakes her head and waves me off. "Of course, I don't know what I was thinking." She goes into complete professional mode. "You'll need a ride?"

"Yes, but if you're going to the lobster boil, I can find alternate arrangements."

"No, it's fine." She frowns, and her brow furrows. I know her well enough to understand she's working through something. "If I can't get you to the airport and back in time, I'll make arrangements with the cab company in Bridgetown." She turns her attention to breakfast and takes a big sip of coffee and I hate the way my stomach is churning, and it's not because I'm catching her flu. Bollocks. We're having a little fun while I'm here. Nothing serious is going on and by the sounds of things, she's not one bit bothered that I'll be out of here shortly.

"Do you need me to bring you anything back after work? I can stop at the café and get soup."

"No, I'm good, thanks though." I turn to head upstairs to shower for work, and her soft voice stops me. I spin back around, and she has a completely different look on her face, a soft vulnerability about her as my eyes meet hers and for a second, I think she's feeling whatever this thing blossoming between us every bit as much as I do.

"Thank you."

I nod. "You're welcome."

"I..." She frowns and glances at her toast. A second later, her head lifts and she says, "I'll have supper ready for you when you get home." I stare at her. Is that what she really wanted to say to me? Why do I get the sense that it wasn't?

"No, I want you to rest—" She opens her mouth and I shake my head. "Promise me. Hey," I add. "You don't want a relapse and not be able to make the meeting, right?"

"You're right," she says quickly and my throat closes over, as a rush of emotions I wish I didn't feel career through me. I'd be lying to myself if I said that wasn't the answer I wanted to hear.

"I'd better go get ready." I dash upstairs, shower, shave and pull on a comfortable pair of khaki trousers and a polo. Back downstairs, Violet is flicking through the stations and I'm happy to see that she's eaten most of her toast. "Say hello to Emily for me."

"You really don't have to go, Colin."

"If a kid shows up and wants on the paddle boats, they're getting on the paddle boats." She chuckles softly. "Besides, I do want to go and have another look around the park. This gives me the opportunity to size things up."

"Okay," she says quietly, and I stand there for a brief second, the sudden need to explain everything to her again tugging at me, but she already agreed that the place needed to be sold. Before I get in her car, I make sure the goats are fed and have water. Twenty minutes later, I pull into the very empty parking lot of Annapolis Park.

I head into the open-air building, and spot Caleb behind the counter. He lowers his head when he sees me. I get it, we're not friends and I sort of told him to take a hike at the party. I head his way despite all that.

"Hey," I say.

"Hey," he responds and looks over my shoulders. "Where's your girlfriend?"

"She's ill. I'll be taking her shift at the park today," I say, not bothering to correct him. Violet and I do not have a label and if we did, it wouldn't be boyfriend/girlfriend. His brow raises and he looks like he's about to make a rude comment, until I glare at him. "Can you please point me in the direction of the park manager."

"Yeah, just a second." He pulls his phone out and shoots off a text. I glance around the place as he waits for a response. "Donna will be here in a few minutes."

"Can you let her know that I'll be at the old stone house on the hill."

"Whatever."

As he rudely dismisses me, I walk outside, and look over the big map of the park. I run my finger along the perimeter, and note that just across the street there used to be another park, but it has a closed sign over it. I guess I thought the zoo was inside the park. I didn't realize it was on a completely different parcel of land.

I head back inside, and Caleb lifts his head from his phone. "Lost?" he asks.

"What's the zoo being used for?"

"Nothing. The animals were relocated months ago."

My mind races. Does Grandfather know the sale of Annapolis includes the empty zoo? Does he have plans for the land?

"Thanks." I head back outdoors, and walk through the park—Violet's gift. My stomach knots as I think about the changes we're going to make to the place. I walk the windy path, and the fresh scent of flowers fill the air. I sneeze. In the distance,

I see Mr. Barker whittling in front of his shop, and I walk toward him.

"What are you working on today?" I ask, making polite talk.

"Working on a couple of whistles." He has a whole box of them beside him. I guess business is slow these days and the whittling keeps him busy. "Did Violet ever show you her beaver?"

I grow hot under the collar. "Uh, yeah, it was spectacular."

He eyes me for a second, and I bet back in the day he was a guy no one messed with. "She's a good girl, that Violet."

"Yes, I know."

"She'd give you the shirt off her back if you were cold."

I nod. "She's very kind and generous."

"Unless she's cold too. Then you're shit out of luck." He bursts out laughing and I chuckle along with him.

"I think she'd give the shirt whether she's cold or not."

"Probably right." He turns back to his whistle. "Don't hurt her, Parker."

Hurt her? How could I not hurt her? I'm taking her park out from underneath her. It might be failing to make a profit, but it's still her park, something she treasures deeply.

"I won't," I say around the lump in my throat.

"Good, then you'll find a way to do the right thing."

I nod, and realize he's telling me the right thing to do is not turn the park into a school, but what he fails to understand is that it's out of my hands. There is nothing I can do to stop it.

With that thought sitting heavy, I say, "I'll be on my way then."

He gives me a nod and I continue up the hill until I come to the old stone building. I try the door, but it's locked tight. What's the purpose of the building if it's not being utilized?

I glance over my shoulder, like a schoolboy about to get caught doing something he's not supposed to, and I try one of the windows. It's pretty much sealed shut. I walk around the building, run my fingers over the aged stone.

"It's quite a lovely building, isn't it?"

I turn to find a middle-aged woman standing there, her arms folded as she watches me.

"It is. Can I have a look inside?"

She shrugs. "Not much to see, really." With a handful of keys all dangling from a large ring, she steps up to the building and puts the key in the lock. The old door creaks open, and disturbs a layer of dust. "It's just a bunch of old equipment, and papers and pictures."

I sneeze into my elbow as I glance over the pictures. "Do you know who these people are?" I take in the man standing next to an ox as it drags some heavy looking piece of farming equipment through the soil. "This land must have been an old farmer's field at one time."

"It's been in the Bryant family for as long as I can remember." She sighs heavily, no doubt hating me as much as everyone else.

I walk around the stone house, and examine the farm equipment from the dawn of time. I have no idea what half of it is.

Let's be honest, I don't have a clue what the other half is either.

"Are you okay?" Donna asks.

"Yes, perfectly fine," I respond.

"Good, let's get this locked back up and get you to the paddle boats." I step from the building, my mind racing with a million questions—like how this building was overlooked, and if it could mean what I think it might mean...

24

VIOLET

"You're in a strange mood," I say to Colin as I find a parking spot across the street from the town hall, the meeting about to start shortly. He's been grinning like the village idiot since he got back from the park last night. I guess he's happy his time here is coming to an end. Why else would he be so damn happy?

"Just working on some things," he says, completely distracted.

Yeah, like getting the paperwork filed and flying back home. I get it.

I put the car into park and shake my head. "Great."

He finally lifts his head from his phone. "What?" He glances across the street, as a dozen or so townsfolk walk back and forth in front of town hall steps, holding signs that say, 'Save Our Park'.

"I'm sorry," I say and reach for my door. "Let me go talk to them."

"No." He captures my arm. "You shouldn't even be here, Violet. You're still pale. I told you we could postpone."

I so want to believe he wants to wait, because he likes being here with me, but again, what can come of it. His life is overseas, as is his future fiancée. He doesn't belong here and I simply don't fit into his world.

"I don't want to put this off any longer."

"You keep reminding me of that," he responds, his voice a little deeper, a hint of something I can't seem to identify lingering in the depths. "I'll handle the crowd. I don't want anyone coming at you. None of this is your fault."

Before I can stop him, he jumps from the car, and dives head first into the mob. Technically, they're not a mob. Just a bunch of elderly people having their say. I keep my eye on him as he talks to everyone, and tries to explain what a new school will do for the community. I'm about to go to his rescue when my phone pings, and I get a message from Cameron that he's come down with the flu and can't make the meeting.

I don't know whether to believe him or not—I did just get over the flu myself—and I don't know whether to laugh or cry. Without Cameron, the meeting can't go on, and that means Colin will be stuck here until we can reschedule for next week, and if Cameron gets better before that, I can't imagine anyone will agree to an earlier meeting. They want to make things as hard as they can for him. But the truth of the matter is, if Colin stays longer, I'm going to get in deeper and that's not going to bode well for my heart.

I take a big fueling breath and get out of the car. I spot Wild Willy, leaning against one of the pillars on the steps, his white hair an untamed mess as he grins at me, looking like trouble with a capital T. As I approach, he pushes off the wall and heads toward Colin. Colin turns toward Willy, and I really don't want Willy causing a scene, so I call out, "Meeting is canceled."

Willy stops in his tracks, his eyes going back to me, and I'm caught off guard by the mean gleam I see there. What is he up to and what was that he said about me being mad at Mack for trying to run Colin out of town? I'll have to think about it later, because right now, my announcement changes the mood of the protestors, and cheers ring out around me. A few people pat me on the back, like I had something to do with the canceled meeting.

Colin turns to face me, and frowns when his eyes meet mine. "I'm sorry," I say as I walk toward him. "For the crowd...for Cameron stalling. He said he has the flu, but I don't know. I'm afraid you won't be headed home today."

He nods, and the muscles along his jaw clench as he goes quiet, thoughtful. What the hell is going through his brain? His head lifts. "Do you mind if I borrow your car for a bit this afternoon?"

His question totally takes me by surprise. "I...sure...why?"

"I'd like to go to the city."

"If you need a drive—"

"No," he says so quickly it's like a slap to the face. Okay, clearly he needs a reprieve from the town and after being accosted here, can I really blame him? We all need a bit of quiet time right, and maybe he's worn out from taking my shifts and taking care of me. I hand the keys over.

"Do you want me to drive you home first?" he asks.

"No, it's okay. I could use some fresh air." He touches my face, runs his thumb along my cheek. My entire body reacts, and I lean into him, despite the people watching us. Cripes, if they knew I was sleeping with the enemy, they'd really run me out of town.

As if reading my mind, he says, "I really want to kiss you right now, but everyone is watching. They already hate me, and I don't want them hating you too."

I nod and step back, still a bit weak. Worried eyes move over my face. "Are you okay?"

"Yes. Will you be back for supper?"

"Don't worry about supper." His gaze drops to my mouth and he wets his tongue like he's dying for a taste. I turn and catch the way Willy is watching us, far too carefully. "If I'm not back in time to cook, I'll pick something up in the city for us. You need to go home and get some rest."

I inch back. "Okay, text me if you get lost and need directions."

I move to the sidewalk as he walks to my car and stuffs himself in. "That's right, go back to where you came from," Mr. Shelby calls out and I just shake my head. My phone rings. I slide my finger across it, my mood lightening, happy to talk to my mother. She stopped by to check on me yesterday when Colin was working, and obviously, she's gotten the wrong—or rather the right—idea about us. I never could keep anything from her.

"Hey Mom."

"Are you feeling better?"

"So much better." I move along the sidewalk and can still feel Willy's eyes burning into my back.

"Sorry about the ruckus at town hall."

I shake my head. "Aren't you at work?"

"Yes, Mrs. Fraser came through the drive through and told me all about it."

"Of course, she did."

"That's why I'm calling. To make sure you're okay. I know what the land means to you, pumpkin. I know this is heartbreaking."

"Cameron didn't show. Apparently, he caught the flu bug that I caught, so Colin has to stay for a little longer."

"Does he now?"

I can hear the pleasure in her voice. "Mom, don't start...we're just friends." Yesterday she put it in my head that maybe we could be more, but she just doesn't understand all the reasons we can't be together. I mean, his mother is picking him out a bride, and he's a rule follower so he's going to go along with it.

He wasn't a rule follower when he jumped into the river, Violet.

But he has a life in Britain, and I have one here.

Logistics, Violet. Logistics.

But he's here to take my beloved park away.

But it's not his fault.

As I argue with myself, Mom's chuckle pulls me back. "Friends who shag, you mean."

I nearly choke on my own saliva. "Mom!" I yell. "I am not having this conversation with you," I tell her, but I do like how open and honest we can be with one another. Dad died just a couple of years ago, in a terrible car accident on an icy road. Mom and I were always close, and relied on each other heavily after that. We're more like sisters than mother and daughter. Nevertheless, even if she guessed that I was having sex with Colin, that it was written all over my face when she stopped by yesterday, I still don't want to discuss it.

"Hey, Mom," I say, switching topics. "What's up with Wild Willy?"

She exhales. "What's he done now?"

"Nothing he's just...I don't know, creepy. What happened between him and Dad?" Mom goes quiet, and since Mom never goes quiet, the hairs on the back of my neck rise. "Mom?"

"Oh, Pumpkin, it was a long time ago. But I dated Willy for a hot minute, before your father. He's always had a grudge."

"You dated Wild Willy?" I ask, incredulously.

"I was young and foolish," she says with a musical laugh.

Just like I'm being young and foolish with Colin.

"I guess the apple doesn't fall far from the tree." A car horn blares through the phone.

"Hold your horses," Mom yells. "I'm talking to my daughter."

"You'd better go. I just got home and have something to do."

"Okay, talk to you soon," she says and begins to berate the customer as she hangs up. I laugh. How she can get away with that and not get fired is beyond me. Then again, she doesn't have to work, she wants to work to fill her time and keep up on the gossip.

I head inside and pull on my overalls. Over the last few days, I've neglected my garden, and it's a tangled mess of weeds. I head out and get straight to weeding, but I'm antsy, my mind on Colin and why he needed to go to the city, alone. After working in the garden for the better part of the day, I head inside, wash my hands and check the fridge to see what I can toss together for the lobster boil tomorrow. Will Colin want to go, or has he had enough of this town—enough of me? My throat squeezes tight at the thought, and I mentally scold myself for getting involved with him in the first place.

My stomach grumbles and that's when I realize it's nearing supper. I shoot a text off to Colin, to let him know I'm feeling well enough to cook. Yes, he told me not to worry about it, but he's been so kind, taking care of me, that I want to do something nice for him. I wait for an answer and when none comes, I dash upstairs to wash the day off me before I begin to cook and prepare food for tomorrow's lobster boil at the beach.

The warm water feels glorious against my skin and I soap up, and rinse off. I'm about to shut the shower off when movement behind the glass door catches my attention. A little yelp crawls out of my throat, but then I realize it's Colin and the noise turns to a moan as I wipe the glass and admire his body as he strips. I could definitely get used to this view.

The door slides open, and his grin sends heat straight to the needy spot between my legs. "We need to stop meeting like this," I tease.

"Actually, I was thinking we needed to meet like this more often." He looks over my naked body. "Am I too late?"

"Never," I say and crook my finger to invite him in. As his big body takes up space beside me, I squirt body wash into my hand and start soaping him up. He moans and tilts his head back as I take my time, my hand going to the swelling member between his legs.

"Violet..." he murmurs. As I take in his handsome face, I want to ask him where he went, what he did, but he's not volunteering, so it feels a bit intrusive, and I'm already in deep enough as it is. Honestly, he doesn't owe me an explanation. We're not a couple. We're just having sex, and earlier this morning, he was gearing up to leave the province.

"Are you upset that you didn't get the papers signed?" I ask as I stroke the long length of him, and enjoy the way he's thickening in my palm.

"What's a few more days?" he murmurs. "And hey, about that foursome..."

"What?" Good Lord, where was he today and what was he up to?

He laughs, and his cock jumps. "You know, Emily had mentioned a foursome."

"Right, right." I go back to stroking him, and he puts his hand on my shoulder, and runs his fingers down my arms. Goose bumps break out on my flesh despite the steamy shower.

He cocks his head and I'm certain he couldn't look any more adorable if he tried. "What did you think I meant?"

"That," I say quickly. "I thought you meant that."

His lips quirk like he doesn't believe me. "This way I get to go to the lobster boil you love so much."

"You want to go?"

"When in Rome," he says, and my heart beats faster, both happy and sad that he's staying and wants to go to the lobster boil. I love spending time with him, I'm just terrified he'll be packing my heart in his designer suitcase when he leaves. But right now, I can't think about it. I don't want to think about it. I'm going to put it out of my mind, and enjoy these last few days while I can.

"When in the shower..." I say with a chuckle full of want and need as I tease his cock.

"You're thinking a twosome, huh?"

I chuckle and his eyes go serious as his gaze moves over my face. He places his palm on my cheek and his thumb lightly brushes my bottom lip. "Are you feeling better?"

"I am. I think all the fresh air today just tired me out."

"Then let me take care of you."

"You have been taking care of me."

"Not like this," he murmurs, his mouth capturing mine for a slow simmering kiss that nearly takes my legs out from underneath me.

"Ah, you want to shag in the shower."

He turns the water off. "No, I don't want a quickie in the shower. I want to take care of you tonight, slowly, thoroughly...all night long."

"I can get behind that."

He grins, slides his hands around my body and captures my ass. He gives it a firm squeeze. "I can get behind this behind." The next thing I know my legs are around his waist and he's carrying me to his room.

25

COLIN

I set Violet on the bed, kicking the door shut behind us so Lucky can't scare me to death in the middle of the night. Completely naked, I stand back to look at the warm, welcoming smile spreading across Violet's flushed face as she goes up on her elbows, her gaze moving over my trembling body and throbbing cock.

My heart thumps hard, and I shake my head, unable to believe I get to sleep with this incredible woman again. I'm not sure what I did in this lifetime or a past one to get so lucky. I chuckle quietly as her blue eyes glisten with want and beckon me closer. To think I thought she was a man when I first arrived in Nova Scotia, or that this province was the armpit of the western world. Honestly, I never expected for any of it to grow on me at all, let alone so quickly.

It's true, I haven't been here long, but there's been an undeniable shift inside me as Violet and the town have shown me a completely different way of life, shown me what home and hearth really means, even though it was the last thing I expected when Grandfather sent me here to secure the land

—as punishment for not getting married when it was expected of me.

I still plan to get his deal done, and while Violet showed me that it can be fun to break the rules, I'm not breaking anything when it comes to the boarding school. Bending the rules, yes, but not breaking them. At least, I'm hoping to bend them. I need a few more days before I can report back to my grandfather, but in the end, I'm hoping everyone gets what they want—Violet included.

Right now, however, I'm going to give her body what it's begging me for. I move to the bed as an early evening breeze rolls in through the open window and washes over my damp, naked skin as I slide onto the bed, and fall over her. For the first time in my life, I feel like I'm where I'm supposed to be. Her arms go around my back and her light caress warms me from the inside out. There's no denying that I want to be touched by her every day and touch her in return.

I find her lips with mine and kiss her deeply. Our tongues tangle and play and while my cock is anxious to be inside her, I want to draw out this moment, savor it for the next few minutes before I bury myself in her and lose myself just a little bit more. Her legs wrap around my waist and tug me tight against her and my cock presses against her warm, wet opening.

"I need my mouth on you first," I murmur, and slide down to her breasts, take her nipples into my mouth one after the other. I suck, and lick and spend a long time teasing her buds. She writhes beneath me, and her hips lift, letting me know exactly what she wants. I want it too. I press wet, open-mouthed kisses to her damp skin as I kiss a path downward. I reach my destination and bury my face between her legs and eat at her like a man starved. She is an addiction that I don't want to quit. Can't. Which means we need to have a right and proper chat—right after I bring her pleasure. I just pray she feels the same way about me as I do about her.

I circle her clit with my tongue, the way she likes it, and she lifts her hips, bucks against my face. "That...is so...good, Colin." Her words come out rough and broken, as she gasps for her next breath, lost in what I'm doing to her. "Colin..." she moans again. "More."

My chest puffs with pride. I love that I can do this to her, love hearing my name on her tongue. Giving her what she wants, I ease a finger into her tight opening and small quivers begin in her core.

"That's it," I say, encouraging her to take everything she wants from me. She rides my finger and my face and I glance up to see her take her perfect breasts into her palms.

She is so close. I move my finger inside her and rub her tight bundle of nerves until she's chanting my name and gripping the bedding. Applying a tiny bit more pressure to her clit with my tongue is all she needs to push her over. She cries out as she tumbles into orgasm, her hands going to my head, to hold my mouth to her sweet spot.

I lap at her, drink in her sweetness, and my heart is somewhere in the vicinity of my throat as I slowly bring her back from ecstasy. I am so into this woman. So goddamn crazy about her, and her fun-loving nature, there's no way I can return home like the obedient son I once was and follow in footsteps that don't belong to me.

I'm not that guy anymore. I'm not the guy who thought he couldn't love a woman. Everything about Violet changed me and set me on a new trajectory. I don't know what the future brings, I'm only sure it has to involve the woman who had a good laugh over me buying a beaver. After Charlotte, I didn't think I could trust again, didn't think a woman could want me for me, instead of what I could do for them. Violet isn't even asking me to save her park. Which makes me want to save it all the more.

"Colin, I want you inside me."

I crawl up her body. In one long thrust I push into her, and I swallow her moan as I kiss her with all the hunger inside me. Tight muscles squeeze around my cock and as much as I want to draw out this sweet lovemaking until morning, I'm already fucked. But that doesn't mean I can't take her a few more times through the night. I don't want to wear her out, not when she's recuperating after being knocked on her arse, knackered from the flu, but I somehow can't get enough of her. I want her in ways I've never wanted another woman.

Her moans soothe my soul and bust open my heart just a little more. I push into her, each stroke bringing a deep pleasure to every inch of my aching body. Her hands cup my face, her half-lidded eyes drawing me in deeper to a place I never thought existed as we come together as one. My heart crashes harder. I've had sex plenty of times, but the intimacy in what we're sharing here was never a part of it. This is what love feels like. I'm sure of it.

Her muscles squeeze my cock as she climaxes, her hot juices soaking me and pushing me over the precipice. "Violet," I say and bury my face in her neck, never in my life so content with anything as I freefall into the abyss.

"So good," she says quietly, her voice low and sleepy, but contented just the same. After I fill her with my seed, I'm about to inch out quickly. Dammit, maybe I should have waited another day before I ravaged her. Her arms lock around my back and she holds me to her, and I settle myself down. She wanted this every bit as much as I did. I move my weight to the side so I don't crush her as our breathing regulates.

With our legs in a tangled mess, I note her feet are a bit cold —bollocks, I should have grabbed our shagging socks. I chuckle. I never thought I'd get dressed to have sex, but when in Canada... She lets loose a contented sigh and I lift my head as her lids drift shut. I smooth her hair out, and let her fall asleep. Inching out of her, I make a quick trip to the bathroom and nearly jump out of my skin when I turn the light on and find Lucky on the sink, a shit-eating grin on his face.

"You're a pervert," I say to him quietly, and he licks his paw, like he's very well aware of his voyeuristic tendencies and quite proud of them. I wash myself up and grab a cloth to clean Violet. She moans in her sleep and I wash her quickly, and crawl in beside her. Lucky jumps onto the foot of the bed as I pull Violet to me and tuck her in tight to keep her warm. Crickets chirp in the garden outside, the sound lulling me to sleep as she settles against my shoulder. I let my lids drift shut, hoping to wake in an hour or so, so I can take her again. The next thing I know, there's a heavy weight on my chest, waking me up.

My lids fly open, and I gasp as I struggle to breathe. Am I having a heart attack? I rub the sleep from my eyes and find Lucky sitting on my chest, his face inches from mine.

"Meow."

"Shite," I say and quickly turn to check on Violet, hoping I haven't woken her.

"Meow."

"What do you want?" I whisper. He continues to meow, and I turn to the clock to see that we both slept in. "I guess you're hungry?" More meowing as he stretches, and for a second I think he's going to swat at me. "Fine, I'll feed you if you get off me."

Lucky jumps to the floor, and I ease from the bed. He eyes my dick and I cover it. "Piss off, mate." I quickly tug on a pair of sweatpants and a T-shirt and head downstairs to feed the supreme ruler of the house. He circles my legs as I fill his dishes, and once I'm done, I stretch out my knackered body and check my messages, hoping to hear more on the amendment to the land use bylaws for the park.

Unfortunately, it's Saturday and now I'll have to wait until Monday when the office is open again. I scan my other messages and open one from my grandfather asking what's taking me so long. I quickly message him back and let him know there have been more delays. Even if Cameron had showed up yesterday with the paperwork, I wouldn't have signed it. Even if I had, it might not be legally binding. That's what I'm waiting to find out.

I open the fridge and consider breakfast. We didn't even eat supper last night. I guess that's why my stomach is grumbling so hard, but I'd skip supper every night if it meant climbing between the sheets with Violet. Bollocks, she's going to be ravenous when she wakes and that means I need to make a big omelet with fresh vegetables from the garden. I step outside into the mid-morning sunshine, and Lucky follows me. I notice the shed door is open. Violet must have been in there yesterday and forgotten to close it. I step inside the dark space, hoping nothing jumps out at me, and notice a few pairs of blue overalls hanging on the hook. These are the overalls she must have been talking about.

I take a pair down, and size it up. They're big enough to fit me, so I climb into them. If Waffles decides to attack me again at least I'll be able to keep my clothes clean. Though he should be used to seeing me around by now. But Canadians have a mind of their own, so I have to stay on my toes. I head back to the garden and my pantlegs make a chaffing sound as I walk. Back home I wouldn't be caught in overalls, and that brings on a chuckle. If the paparazzi could see me now...

"What do you think, Lucky? Does this look work for me?"

He meows, and I bend to pat him as he rubs up against me. He hisses the second my hand lands on his head. "Hey," I say, I thought we were friends now. He hisses again and I realize it's not me his distress is directed at.

"What in the name of God is that thing?"

My head lifts, and air leaves my lungs in a whoosh when I find my mother standing there, a suitcase at her feet, as she glares at Lucky, like he's, well....some sort of alien.

"Mum," I say, and blink my eyes, sure I'm still asleep, and having a nightmare. No way is my mother standing here, looking completely flawless—despite the long flight—in Violet's back yard. Or maybe Lucky sat on my face and suffocated me and I'm actually dead. That might be better than my Mum showing up when I was getting ready to tell Violet how I feel about her. "What are you doing here?"

Her disapproving glance moves over the overalls I'm wearing. "I could ask the same about you."

"I'm...the paperwork is taking time," I explain, as Lucky settles at my feet, like he senses the tension and is siding with me. Thanks, mate.

"That's not what I mean." She holds a finger out and waves it up and down. "What is this?"

"Oh," I say, and laugh, but it sounds strained. Probably because I know why she's here and it's to get me back home, on the path to marriage and grandchildren—for her. "I was getting fresh vegetables from the garden, and Violet has these two goats… Shite!"

At the mention of the goats, they come out of nowhere, and Waffles hits mom from behind and sends her flying forward. She lands with a hard thud, and I drop my basket and run to her, praying nothing is broken.

"Mum, are you okay?"

Shite. Shite. Shite.

She grumbles something under her breath, deep brown eyes narrowing in on mine as she lifts her head, dirt on her cheek. "Do I look okay?"

I put my arms under her and help her to her feet. Flustered, she begins to wipe the dry dirt from her coat. I'm not sure whether to tell her she has a spot on her face or not.

"We can get that laundered."

"I'll take care of it when we return home. I doubt it could be laundered properly here."

I didn't miss the way she said *we*. But I'm not even all that sure I want to go home, at least not to some random girl who wants my hand in marriage because I can offer her the world.

"I'm so sorry. Popcorn doesn't like adults, and Waffles likes to protect him. I landed in the mud when I first got here. At least the ground is dry today…" As I mutter on, Mum shakes her head and pats her coiffed hair. "Canadian goats," I explain. "They're mad."

"I think you've gone mad," Mum says. "It's a good thing I came when I did."

"I'm fine, I'm just collecting some vegetables for breakfast."

"Are you not a guest in this bed and breakfast?" I nod and she continues with, "Then why are you preparing your own meals."

"I just...I don't know. Violet hasn't been feeling well, so I've been helping out." Her eyes narrow in on me, and I brace myself for a lecture.

"This Violet you've mentioned a time or two. Who exactly is she?"

26

VIOLET

I wrap my arms around myself as I step up to the window and listen to the exchange between Colin and a woman who could only be his mum, based on her accent and her very expensive wardrobe. From the look on her face, she's not too happy, and of all the people for Waffles to attack and knock over, did it have to be a stoic British woman dressed in a coat that must cost more than my house? I curse under my breath, because yeah, we're off to a lovely start here, and I'm sure, without having even met me yet, I've made a huge impression on her—too bad it wasn't a good one.

My stomach clenches, worry invading my body. Why again is it I want to impress his mum? I'm not sure. All I know is I don't wear fancy gowns and jewelry, which means I'm not the kind of girl she'd want with her son. Heck, I could probably ride a tricycle through town while spinning a fiery baton and singing their national anthem and she'd be less than impressed. As they turn to come toward the house, I push from the window and dash into my own bedroom, which hasn't been occupied in a few days.

I dress quickly, tugging on jeans and a T-shirt, the fastest things I can find, and check my face in the mirror. *Calm down, girl.* I take a deep breath, hold it until the count of three, and let it out slowly. Why am I so nervous? It's not like I need Colin's mother to like me or that I care what she thinks of me, right? But one look at Colin and then one look at me, it's easy to tell we've been having incredible sex. Something tells me she's too astute for that to go over her head—and she's not going to like it.

Bollocks.

Great, now I sound like Colin. But seriously, Colin is a grown-ass man and can sleep with any woman he wants. He's not married yet—heck, he's not even engaged. A wave of protectiveness comes over me. I get that he was raised differently than me, but he should be allowed to make his own decisions in life. I don't care about their stupid customs and duty.

He does, though...

Heck, not only that, he doesn't think he has the ability to love a woman. Not only does that mean he could never love me—but it also means he'll be stuck in a loveless marriage, and I hate that for him. I did tell him though, that when he found the right woman, he'd know what love was. Dammed if I didn't want to be the right woman. He's been doing nice things for me, but it doesn't mean he's falling for me, the way I'm falling for him.

My heart sinks a little at that last thought, and I step from my bedroom, plaster on my best smile, and walk to the top of the stairs. I grip the rail tightly, and give myself a second. Lucky runs up to meet me and hides behind my legs. Great, Lucky isn't afraid of anything or anyone yet he's hiding from Colin's mum.

"Go get under my covers," I tell him. "I'll probably be joining you later."

Lucky darts off and I hurry downstairs to find Colin and his mum in the kitchen. Colin is rooting through the cupboards, searching for God knows what, and his mother is seated at the table. Her stern eyes pin me in place as I skid to a halt.

"Good morning," I say in a chirpy voice that makes me want to strangle myself. "You must be Colin's mum."

She cocks her head, and I can almost hear her brain spinning as she forms an impression of me. A beat passes before she says, "You must be Violet."

Chuckling nervously—what is wrong with me—I smooth my hand over my mess of hair, and nearly jump ten feet in the air when Colin slams one of the cupboards shut and turns to me. I cast him a quick glance, almost afraid to take my eyes off his mother, and I know him well enough now to read the worry in his eyes. What, is he afraid I'm going to tell her we've been shagging?

"That's right. I'm Violet," I say and extend my hand for a firm shake. What I get in return are limp noodle fingers in my palm.

"Violet runs this place and is also the mayor," Colin says, and something about the way he added mayor, like being a mere bed and breakfast owner isn't impressive enough, sends a cold chill through me. Clearly looking down her nose at me—his mum, gives me the once over, taking in my jeans and T-shirt. Alrighty then.

"What brings you to Annapolis, Mrs. Parker?" I ask.

"I'm here to see family. My cousin Beatrice lives in the city, and I've been promising her I'd visit. It's been far too long."

Why do I get the sense she's not being entirely honest and that this trip has everything to do with Colin?

She turns to her eldest son, the rule follower, the man who stands by duty. "Did you find that tea?" He opens another cupboard.

"I'm sorry, I don't have tea." I walk to the sink to fill up the carafe. "I can make you a coffee."

She crinkles her nose in distaste. "Who doesn't have tea?"

"Canadians," Colin teases as he leans against the stove, but the humor is lost on his mother. I snatch my purse off the counter.

"I can run out and get a box, or we could head to the cafe for breakfast and tea."

She waves a dismissive hand. "No need to trouble yourself. I'll just have water, it's been a long flight and I'm rather parched."

"No trouble at all."

Please...I want to go...to get away from your sneer.

"Why exactly are you here, Mum?"

She taps the seat next to her. "I told you, to visit my cousin, and since you're here, I thought we could do it together. Now come sit, I want to hear all about what you've been up to. It must be horrendous being stuck here in the middle of...." Her words fall off and she makes a tsking sound. "I still don't understand why Father insists on building a school in this province." Her gaze goes to me, "No offence, of course."

"No, of course. I'm pretty sure that was a compliment." Colin turns from me, but not before I catch his smirk. I bite mine back. "Will you be staying long? You're more than welcome to stay here. I have a room available."

"I see." She inspects my kitchen. "I don't suppose there's a Mayfair nearby."

"No Mum, there isn't," Colin responds, his voice holding a measure of annoyance. "There is nothing wrong with Violet's place. The beds are comfortable, and it has everything you need."

"It doesn't have tea."

Colin cringes, glances at me, and I can read his apology. I grin and nod, knowing exactly what is going through his head. Yes, Colin, that is exactly what you sounded like when you first got here and I didn't serve you a proper breakfast.

"I'll be right back. You two probably have a lot to catch up on anyway. I'll make crumpets to go with your tea when I get back."

"Violet," Colin says, like he's about to stop me and I shake my head.

"I have to grab a few things for the lobster boil tonight anyway." It's a lie. The only thing I need is a moment to myself. I have no idea why this woman is rattling me so much.

Oh, maybe because you really like her son, and you want her to like you too.

Before anyone can stop me, I dash out the door and jump in my car. I adjust the seat and drive straight to the grocery store. I park, and I don't know why I was worried about her liking me. There was no way she was going to, anyway. I am everything she's not looking for in a future wife for her prince —even though he says he's no one's prince.

I hurry into the store. Shoot, I should have asked what kind of tea she'd like. I pull my phone out and do a quick Google search, on what kind of tea stuck up British women drink. I doubt our small store would have the first three on the list, so Tetley it is. I grab a bottle of salad dressing for the lobster boil, just to cover my lie. Will Colin even be coming now that his mother is in town? It's certainly not an event I could ever see her attending.

Back in the car, I take my time driving home as my mind races. Colin disappeared yesterday for hours, and now his mother is in town. Was he behind it? His way of letting me know he has duties and obligations at home, and that's where he belongs. Nah, that doesn't sound like him at all. But I have no doubt she's here to put pressure on him to come home and marry.

I park and leisurely walk to my front steps and inside, Colin and his mother are talking quietly, their words not meant for my ears. I bang the table near the front entrance to let them know I'm back and when I step into the kitchen, his mother is gathering up Polaroids. I didn't even know they made those anymore.

"I got Tetley," I say. "I hope that's okay with you, Mrs. Parker."

I meet Colin's eyes. "Her name is Isabella," he says.

"Mrs. Parker is fine," his mum says, and Colin takes a fast breath. He rolls his eyes, which are dripping with apology.

"You must be exhausted from your flight," I say. "And hungry."

"Tea is fine. Then I'll take a short nap and Colin and I will head to the city to see Beatrice. She's expecting us." She taps

Colin's leg. "She's arranged dinner tomorrow night with the premier of the province. I believe we'll be going to a place called the Shore Club."

"Oh, it's a great place," I say. "Great music, and lobster. Did you know that Prince Charles and Lady Diana dined there years ago?"

Her face lights up. "Then we must go, Colin."

He hesitates. "I…"

"Violet will come with us, of course."

My heart jumps into my throat. "No…I don't want to intrude."

"Of course, you'll come. You're the mayor of this town, are you not?"

"Yes, but—"

"Then it's settled."

She waves a dismissive hand as I walk to the counter and turn on the kettle. I face Colin to gauge his reaction. Does he or does he not want me there? Dining with the premier isn't something I always do—or ever do. I might be a small-town mayor, but I'm really just a country girl at heart and the premier is not the kind of guy who runs in my social circles. I'll be in way over my head, out of my league.

You already are, Violet.

He reads the question in my eyes. "If you have other plans…" he begins, giving me an out. Is it because he doesn't want me there?

His mother clears her throat and we both turn to her. "What could be more important than dining with the premier, Colin?"

I'm definitely not getting out of this one, and honestly, I can't tell how Colin feels about it. Does he think I won't fit in and he's trying to keep our two worlds separate?

I place the tea in front of his mother. "Do you take sugar or milk?"

"A spot of milk."

I hand her the big two-liter cardboard container and she scrunches up her nose, and stares at it like it's a cow with two heads and I just asked her to milk it.

Colin unscrews the lid and pours a dash into her tea. "I'll finish this, have a nap and then we'll be off, Colin."

"I'm afraid I won't be joining you this afternoon," Colin says and his mum arches a perfectly manicured brow. "I have plans," he adds.

"What could be more important than spending time with your mother and cousin?"

"Violet planned a lobster boil."

"You're welcome to come," I blurt out.

Mrs. Parker takes a sip of tea, and over the rim of the cup asks, "What on earth is a lobster boil?"

"Oh, it's so much fun," I begin, becoming more animated, and it brings a smile to Colin's face. "We cook lobster on the shore, and everyone usually joins in. Sometimes we go swimming, or boating. There's a bonfire..."

Her eyes hold a measure of aversion, when she says, "Yes, while that sounds lovely, dear, I have prior commitments. Colin, you'll be joining me?"

"No, I can't. I promised Violet I'd go, so I'm going. I wasn't expecting your sudden arrival. Had you informed me you were coming, I could have planned differently. I can arrange a drive for you to the city, but I won't be accompanying you. Violet and her friend go through a lot of trouble putting this on every year."

"Perhaps I'll put off visiting Beatrice."

Colin shakes his head and reaches for his phone. "No, I won't hear of that." He turns to me. "Is there a driver you can recommend?"

"Yes, over in Bridgetown, you can get a taxi or a limo."

"I'll book it." He stands and goes into the other room, leaving me alone with his mother.

She smiles at me, and opens her purse. "While you were gone, Colin and I were discussing his future back in the UK."

"Oh, that's nice."

"He's soon to be married, you know?"

"He did mention something about that." I stand and pour a cup of coffee. This is a conversation I don't want to be having, but since it's forced upon me, I'm going to need copious amounts of caffeine.

"I was quite surprised to find him dressed in those dreadful overalls and working in your garden. It's so not like him. He has servants for such things."

"I didn't ask him to do that. It's just that I haven't been well, and he's been sweet to help me around here."

"That's why your cheeks are flushed, you haven't been well?" As soon as those words leave her mouth, memories of last night bombard me, and I grow hotter, my cheeks blazing.

"Fever," I say and to justify the coloring of my face, I add, "I might still have a touch of it."

With her teacup halfway to her lips, she pauses and says, "I do hope Colin and I don't get it. It would be dreadful flying home unwell."

I swirl the coffee in my cup. "When exactly is it you plan to leave?"

"The second the papers are signed. Colin says the meetings take place every second Friday." She sets her teacup down with a bang. "As mayor, surely you can speed that up?"

"I'll see what I can do." I suppose the sooner Colin leaves the better. Then again, is it possible that I can be more deeply involved. My heart takes that moment to clench, and I feel it all the way into my throat. I swallow but it's difficult and painful. I grab my phone and shoot off a message to Cameron, asking if he's feeling better and if we can all reconvene on Monday.

Reaching into her purse, Mrs. Parker pulls out a picture of a gorgeous girl in a gown and sets it in front of me. "This is Francesca. I think she's perfect. Colin does too."

I try to keep my voice even, despite the storm waging war in my stomach. "Did he say that?"

She laughs. "In not so many words. It's going to be the wedding of the century. A gorgeous ceremony at the basilica, with many royals and celebrities in attendance."

"Is that what he wants?" I honestly don't know one way or the other. We've never discussed it, but my gut tells me that's not his style. Although, maybe back home, it is his style. When in Rome...maybe he's just been slumming it here, jumping off bridges to humor me and pass the time. Maybe I don't know him at all...

"Of course, it's exactly what he wants." Her brow raises as she looks me over, a thorough examination. Her lips are tight as she turns her attention back to the picture. "She has the perfect birthing hips, don't you think?"

Ah, was that what the in-depth inspection was all about? Is she saying I don't have great birthing hips? Wait, what the heck are perfect birthing hips anyway? Before I can answer, Colin comes back into the room and relief washes over me.

"I have a car arranged for you this afternoon."

She stands, and says, "Colin, please tell me you packed a suit for tomorrow night?"

He picks up her suitcase. "I have a suit."

"Perfect," she says with a laugh. "We can't have you showing up to dinner with the premier in those dreadful dungarees. This is not at all who you are, and we wouldn't want anyone thinking otherwise." She turns to me. "Isn't that right, Violet?"

Okay, I get it. I get what she's saying, but I'm not trying to turn Colin into something he isn't.

Right?

27

COLIN

"It's pretty full," I say to Violet as she hands over a few more drinks for the cooler.

She puts her hands on her hips, but her thoughts seem miles away when she asks, "Do you think we have enough?"

"I guess it depends on how thirsty everyone is."

She opens her freezer and pulls out a bag of ice and dumps it into the cooler. A few cubes go careening across the floor and she drops down to pick them up as Lucky darts into the other room, frightened. He's been sticking close to us since Mum arrived, and I'm still having a hard time wrapping my brain around her flying across the pond to check up on me. I'm a grown man, for Christ's sake.

She wasn't too pleased that I wasn't accompanying her to Beatrice's house, but you can't just spring that on me and I had plans with Violet. As I think about our night, about Mum showing me all the pictures of all the girls 'suitable' for me, my appetite for lobster disappears.

Violet mumbles under her breath as she walks around on her knees to gather the ice. Speaking of ice, she's been a bit standoffish since my Mum showed up, the air between us a little cooler, and I don't like it. Not one little bit.

A strange anxious ball lodges in my throat. I try to push back the unease invading my body, warning that tonight could very well be my last night with Violet. I wanted to talk to her this morning, tell her how I feel, but then Mum showed up and the time was never right. Maybe I should tell her right now, before we go to the lobster boil. A sense of urgency grips me, my heart pounding just a bit harder, reaching into my throat.

I close my eyes and take a few deep breaths before saying, "Violet."

Her head lifts, her blue eyes a bit stormy, like she's fighting her own demons, and with me here to tear down her park, I suppose she is. "Yes."

"I—"

"Let's get the party started," Emily says loudly, as she comes through the front door and straight into the kitchen. She glances at Violet on the floor, gathering up the ice. "What are you doing down there?" Emily's attention turns to me and as she snickers, I get how this looks. I'm standing still, Violet on her knees right in front of my bits. "Oh, I see you've already gotten the party started."

"Emily," Violet warns, and I reach for her hand and help her to her feet.

Emily holds her hands up, palms out. "Kidding, kidding."

The cooler closes with a thud, and Violet takes the salad she made earlier out of the fridge.

Emily turns to me. "Hey, I hear your mother is in town."

I shake my head, but I shouldn't be surprised. "Of course you did."

"Is she coming to the lobster boil?" She glances around the kitchen like she's searching for her.

I tug on the collar of my shirt, which suddenly feels a bit tighter. "No, she went to the city to visit her cousin."

Emily crinkles her nose. "Not her thing, huh?"

"Yeah, no," I say and Emily laughs.

"Look at you with the yeah, no. You're turning into one of us."

Violet's face pales a bit, a weird little noise catching in her throat. She coughs to cover it, and goes to the sink to pour herself a glass of water.

"Are you okay?" I ask after she drinks.

She wipes her mouth with the back of her hand. "Yeah, allergies."

I nod, but don't really believe her. Emily jerks her thumb over her shoulder, something I've seen Violet do numerous times. "Come on, Trev is waiting for us in the truck. He's ready to get his lobster on."

I pick up the heavy cooler and follow the girls outside. The sun is low on the horizon as I slide the cooler in the back of the truck next to another cooler and a few bags. Violet and Emily take the backs seats, and I jump into the cab next to Trevor.

"Hey bud," he says and turns the radio down. "Are you ready for your first lobster boil?"

"Sounds like a fun time." Truly it does. I've been doing a lot of firsts since I've been here, mainly, falling in love. Violet was right when she said it would take the right girl.

He puts his truck into gear as the girls chat in the backseat. Emily is excited and animated as she asks Violet what she's going to wear to the Shore Club to meet the premier. I can't tell whether Violet is excited or not, but personally I'm thrilled that she'll be accompanying us—not that she had a choice. Mother can be extremely pushy, and she very clearly wanted Violet to come, although I'm not sure why. I have no doubt she sensed something going on between us, and I would have thought she'd be trying to push us apart, not together.

"This is a nice truck," I say to Trevor, making small talk and his face lights up. His vehicle is obviously a source of pride. For the next five minutes, on the way to the beach, he talks about his truck, and I nod, listening intently as we drive by the working wharf with all the lobster boats. I grin, thinking about how much Violet loved piloting the lobster boat. She's a woman of many talents.

"What kind of vehicle do you drive?" he asks.

"Oh, it's a Bentley." Technically I don't drive it. I have someone who chauffeurs me around, but that sounds pretentious, so I keep it to myself.

He whistles, and cocks his head. "Nice," he says. "How is it on gas?"

We talk about gas prices for a bit, and my ability to drive on the right, or rather wrong, side of the road in Nova Scotia. Conversation dies as he pulls down a path that leads to the beach. There's a big table set up, and large, stainless-steel pots sitting on grates over fire pits made with rocks. A group of people are laying out food on the table, while others tend to the fire.

I step from the car and laughter reaches my ears. I have never seen such a sense of community before. Although the community did come together at the meeting, to drive me out of town. Will they welcome me here?

"Are you okay?" Violet asks.

I nod. "This is great. No one is going to toss me into the fire pit, are they?"

She laughs, and it's so warm and musical, it soothes every worry racing around inside my brain. I dip my head and press a kiss to her forehead without thinking. Her eyes go wide and she glances around. Ah, she's worried someone might see us. Right, I get it, she can't be seen kissing the enemy. The need to protect her overwhelms me and it's all I can do not to drag her into my arms. But I won't, because I'd rather the towns-folk hate and blame me, over her.

"I won't let anything happen to you." She inches back. "Can you help us get all this stuff down to the beach?"

"Sure." Trevor and I take the coolers down, and the girls carry bags with food and snacks. I get a few odd stares as I set the cooler down, but for the most part, the people here tonight are here to have a good time.

"Toss me a brew, would ya, bud?" Trevor says, and I reach into the cooler and grab him one. I kind of like being buds with Trevor. He's a nice guy, very down to earth, and of course, he's one of the few people in the town who doesn't hate me. I take a deep breath, fill my lungs with the briny air, and a sense of contentment flows through my blood as I listen to laughter mingling with the sounds of the waves lapping gently against the sandy shore. The gatherings we have at home are formal, rehearsed, suit and tie, not at all relaxed like they are here. How will I ever go back to that life?

You don't want to.

It's true, I don't. I want this, all of this. But Violet hasn't given any indication that she might want more, and Mum is here pressuring me. What if I decided to stay and my entire family turns against me, and I come to learn Violet isn't interested in more than a hook-up? A seagull squawks overhead, pulling my thoughts back to the present, and while I want a future with Violet, tonight I'm just going to enjoy our time here on the beach, and set my worries aside until tomorrow.

"Violet, Emily. Cold brew?" I ask, and they nod. I crack the cans open and hand them out. Trevor opens a few lawn chairs and sets them around one of the fire pits.

"Have a seat, bro," he calls out to me. "Watch the master cook in action." He folds his sleeves up and reaches into another cooler full of lobster. Emily brings him a pair of scissors, and she puts her arm around his waist as he cuts into the rubber bands to remove them. It's easy to see the love between the two of them and I might be a little envious at what they have. The truth is, I want what they have—with Violet. Trevor takes the blue bands off a few more lobster, tosses them into the boiling pot, checks the time and sinks into one of the chairs.

I search for Violet, and my heart misses a beat when I find her leaning against one of the picnic tables watching me, a small smile on her face. Once again, she seems like she's in a faraway place, but the coolness about her from earlier has melted. I think like the others, she just wants to let her hair down and enjoy tonight.

"Hey," I call out, and she pushes off the table and comes toward me.

I pull the lawn chair closer and she drops into it. I want to touch her, I want to kiss her—hell, I want to pull her onto my lap, the same way Trevor just pulled Emily onto his, but I don't want to bring her trouble from the townsfolk. Then again, they all count on her to 'fix' the problem of me swooping in to close their park when it's most vulnerable. Maybe they'd think she was using her charm and her body to sway me into saving it. I guess they all know her better than that though. She hasn't even asked me to save it, even though it's a big part of her history, a place that holds so many memories.

Maybe she truly wants it gone.

As that thought pops into my head, I slowly turn to her, and think back to our conversation when I was lost in the corn maze. It seemed to me she was pushing for the sale to go through. I asked, but she never answered, instead she snuck up on me and said, boo. She can't want this sale to go through though, right? I mean, it's a piece of her heritage being torn down. I want to ask her, but I don't want to talk business tonight. She's smiling and happy and I want to keep it that way.

"Having fun?" Violet asks as more people pour onto the beach and the volume goes up a notch. A few people set up tiki torches and light them, creating a fun atmosphere, and I take a sip of beer, and watch the flames lick the bottom of the stainless-steel pots.

"Isn't drinking on a public beach illegal?"

"There you go, answering a question with a question." Her warm laugh curls around my heart. I face her as she takes a sip of her beer, and I love seeing her happy, like she doesn't have a care in the world. "Yeah, it is." She tips her can and I follow the direction. "Corporal Davis is right over there. If you're a concerned citizen, you might want to take it up with him."

I laugh, and lean into her, her warm scent filling my senses. "Thank you."

"For what?" She asks, sounding a bit breathless.

My heart swells and thumps harder. "For inviting me to join you, your friends, your community. I...I've never really felt like I was a part of anything before."

My hand drops from my chair, and I run the sand through my fingers. Her hand falls and touches mine, and she lightly brushes her thumb over my wrist. "I'm glad you're here, Colin."

I let loose a slow breath, as my body beckons hers, aching to have her beneath me again. "I really like your friends."

I really like you.

"They like you too."

I want to ask her if she likes me, like I'm some kindergartener with his first crush. I nod and sit back in my chair, our fingers still touching, caressing as our arms dangle from the chairs. I smile, unable to help myself, as the heat of her fingers wrap around my heart. We sit in silence as conversations go on around us, and I love the quiet comfort between us as we each delve into our own thoughts.

Trevor taps his wife's arse, and she jumps up from his lap. "Okay y'all, it's time to show the wanker how to eat a lobster."

"I know how to eat a lobster, you twat," I say back and Trevor laughs.

"Do you now?" he reaches into the pot and pulls out a steamed lobster, dropping it onto the closest table.

A bit sheepish, I glance at Violet who is grinning at me. "I know how to eat it," I say again, determined to get the point across.

"But you don't know how to break it open, do you?" Trevor asks as he fishes another out and sets it beside the first.

"Yeah, no."

Everyone laughs, and so do I. I don't mind being the brunt of a joke when it's all in good fun like this. Trevor waves me over to the table. "Get on over here, you wanker, and I'll show you how it's done."

"Go," Violet says.

I stand and meet Trevor at one of the picnic tables. "Okay, you have to get right in there with your hands, like this." He breaks into the lobster with practiced ease, separating the claws, and tail from the body. He proceeds to show me how to crack the claws and open and clean the tail. When he's done, he nods toward one of the lobsters. "Your turn, Colin."

Since I'm an apt pupil, and can follow his instructions—hey, I mastered the tractor in no time at all—I break into my lobster, and everyone claps as I separate the parts. Violet moves in beside me, her hand on my back, her heat curling around my heart, as well as other body parts.

"Nice job," she says, her voice low and teasing. "I didn't know you were so good with your hands."

"Why don't you meet me at the other side of the beach, and I'll show you just how good I am with my hands..." I lean into her and whisper, "...and my tongue."

28

VIOLET

"Stop it," I say to Emily and whack her hand away from my hair, which is piled high on my head. The stylist thought I needed a sophisticated look when dining with the premier. But it's so not me. I don't even think you can use my name and sophisticated in the same sentence.

Emily huffs and tries to tuck the hair in again. "You have a loose curl."

"It's supposed to be loose, now stop."

She drops her arms and sits on my bed. "I don't know about that. After spending two hours getting it styled, you'd think she would have pinned it all up."

I spin, hoping to pull off casual but my stomach is so tight I have no idea how I'll be able to eat. "Does it look okay? Should I take it down? This is so not me, Emily."

"You look gorgeous, but if you want to take it down, take it down." She shrugs like it's no big deal. "No one said you had to get all fancied up."

"I look stupid. I know it."

She stands and comes up to me as I turn back to the mirror. "You're gorgeous."

"I don't know what it is about *Mrs. Parker*," I emphasize her name. "That makes me feel like my every movement, and how I look is being judged."

"Because she's a judgy bitch, that's why."

"Shh," I say and try not to chuckle. "She's in the next room."

"Maybe I should go over there and tell her to her face then."

"Stop it."

The grin falls from Emily's lips. "Come on, Violet. You have nothing to worry about. You're one of the hardest working people I know, and you care so much about this community, and everyone in it. If she can't see that, who cares?"

"I don't know why, but I care."

"Because you love her son, and you want her to like you."

My heart leaps into my throat, and I open my mouth about to correct her, when she shakes her head to stop me. "Don't deny it, not to me. I can read you like a book. Heck, everyone can. I'm sure Mrs. Parker can, and that's why she's being hard on you. She just wants what's best for her son, and she's making sure you are."

I blow out a slow breath. "You think that's what tonight is all about? Her getting to know me, to see how Colin and I are together?"

"What else could it be?"

"She's trying to marry him off to a debutante, you know." I glance down at my body, my old ratty robe dangling around my knees—the most comfortable thing I own. "I can't compete. They're totally out of my league."

"Violet, all of those women are out of your league. Do I have to remind you again how smart, kind, and caring you are?"

"It's not that. It's just they're all so, I don't know...proper? We've obviously had very different upbringings."

"Would you change yours in any way? Would you prefer fancy parties to lobster boils, and jeweled gowns over overalls?"

I give a very unlady like snort, which just drives home the fact that I'm completely different. "No, and you know what, Colin likes me for who I am—"

"Duh, obviously. I saw the way he looked at you at the lobster boil. He's totally into you, just like you're totally into him."

I grin. I am so lucky to have a friend like Emily. She might be a lot at times, but she's honest, and always has my back. She's the kind of girl who lifts other women up. I don't think too many people have friends like that. But I saw the way Colin looked at me last night too, and he fulfilled his promise in showing me how good he is with his hands and his tongue when we came back home. He followed me to my room, and made love to me for hours.

Made love?

Heck yes, we made love. Every touch, every kiss, felt more like we were making love than indulging in a brief hook-up. No one can kiss or touch the way he touched me if he wasn't feeling more, right? Afterward, he snuck back into his room, not wanting to be in my bed when his mother woke. I guess he doesn't want her to know—much like I don't want the townsfolk to know, for fear they'll disown me for sleeping with the enemy.

Am I Colin's dirty little secret?

Then again, since I'm not showing any public displays of affection, maybe he thinks he's *my* dirty little secret. Yeah, we definitely need to talk. Maybe tonight after dinner, we'll get a chance.

Emily waves her hand in front of my face. "Hey, where did you go?"

I chuckle. What was it we were talking about? Oh right, that Colin likes me for who I am.

"You know, I like me for who I am, too. I shouldn't—won't—change for anyone."

She hugs me. "That's my girl."

"But...Colin. I know we've been having fun, but what happens when he leaves..."

"What if he doesn't leave? He could live and work right here in Annapolis."

"I've thought about that. A lot. But I don't even know if we're even in a place to consider a real relationship. I haven't even known him very long." I frown, and shake my head, and a few more tendrils fall loose. "This could all very well be some made up fantasy in my brain."

"Can't be. You don't believe in fantasy or prince charming."

I'm no one's prince.

"You think?"

"What I think is you two need to talk."

"I think you're right. Colin seemed like he had something important to tell me last night when you came running into the kitchen."

"Ugh, sorry. Sometimes my timing sucks." A knock comes on my door, and I stiffen. "Girlfriend, you need to relax."

Emily jumps up and opens it, and the second I see Colin in his very expensive suit, I nearly bite off my tongue. The man cleans up nice.

"Hey," he says, his gaze going to me. A grin flirts with his lips. "Is that what you're wearing?" I pick my brush up off my dresser and toss it at him. He dodges it and laughs.

"Of course not. I'll be ready in a second."

"We'll be downstairs waiting. Mum ordered a car."

"I could have driven us."

He tugs on his tie. "It's okay."

"She doesn't like Violet's car, does she?"

Does Emily have to say everything she's thinking?

"Your car is fine. Mum would rather something bigger."

My car isn't fine. He just doesn't want to say it. But I get it, she doesn't want to show up in a small car—the bumper held on with duct tape and a prayer.

"I'll be just a second," I say, some of the wind coming out of my sails.

"Take your time."

He closes the door, and I just stand there. "Don't," Emily says. "You're perfect, and so is your car."

"Now that's a straight up lie." I walk to my closet, a burst of unease weakening my knees. "None of my dresses are good enough."

"What are you wearing?" I pull out a cute little blue dress that I actually wore to Emily's wedding a few years ago. It was only worn once, so I figured it was still in good shape. It's true, I don't dress up very often.

"I love that dress on you. Put it on."

I pull it on, and I have to suck in my stomach as Emily zips me from behind. "Great, I put on weight, and now I look like a stuffed sausage."

"It's only a tiny bit tight." She smooths her hand along my waist and hips. "It shows off all your curves."

"I don't want to look like a show girl."

She laughs. "You don't. Colin's eyes are going to bulge out of his head when he sees you in this."

"I just don't want his mother's to," I say and turn around to see the back in the mirror. Why didn't I account for a bit of weight gain, and why did I wait until the last minute to put this on. Stupid. Stupid. Stupid.

Tires sound outside and Emily goes to the window. "Ooh, fancy limo. Mrs. P likes to travel in style."

"God, don't call her that."

"Come on, get downstairs and go have a good time."

I give myself a once over again, and it's too late to turn back now. Right? As if reading my mind, Emily turns me and ushers me out the door. Maybe, if I'm lucky enough, Lucky will wind himself around my feet and send me hurtling down the stairs so I don't have to go.

"Here, kitty," I say, and Emily nudges me.

"Nice try, now go."

I walk downstairs slowly, and head to the front closet to find a pair of shoes. I slip into my black heels, and make my way to the kitchen. The second I enter, my jaw slackens. It's not because his mother has a row of pictures on the table, all the girls 'suitable' to be Colin's wife, but because she's dressed in a gorgeous, jeweled dress—I think those jewels might be diamonds—looking like she's about to step onto the red carpet at the Oscars.

Colin's head lifts as I make a throaty sound, and his gaze moves up and down the length of me. He's not smiling. In fact, he's scowling, and I hope it's because his mother was sitting there pushing a bride on him, and not because of my too tight dress.

"I'm ready," I say breezily.

Colin stands, and smooths his hand down his tie. "Perfect time. Our car just arrived."

Mrs. Parker takes her time putting the pictures back into her bag, almost making a show out of it, and in that moment, I think Emily might be wrong. If she knows what's going on between Colin and me, and if she was trying to get to know me better, to see if I'd make a good bride, why on Earth would she still be shoving debutantes down her son's throat?

With her glasses halfway down her nose, she stands, and gives me an inspection. She doesn't say anything, she just takes her glasses off and slides them into her purse.

"Shall we?"

She puts her arm through Colin's, and I back up and glance up at Emily as she sits on the top step. She gives me two thumbs up and Colin and his mum walk to the door. I follow them, and we head outside. His mum gets into the car first and Colin turns to me, his voice low, for my ears only.

"You look amazing."

"Thank you, you do too."

I slide into the car next, taking a seat opposite his mother and when Colin is about to get in, his mother pats the seat beside her.

We're all quiet as the driver heads through town and pulls onto the highway. His mother is the first to break the quiet.

"Tell me, Violet. Were you able to get the paperwork in order and move the meeting up? You can't expect us to wait until the next council meeting. That's simply absurd."

"I reached out to Cameron, but he hasn't responded yet."

"Why don't you try him again right now?" She blinks at me, skepticism all over her face, like she thinks I'm the one trying to stall the deal—steal her son.

"Okay, sure." I pull my phone from my purse, and shoot Cameron off another text. Three dots appear. "Oh, he's messaging back."

She pats Colin's knee. "Look at that, dear. We might be able to leave here tomorrow, after all."

"It hasn't been so bad."

My gaze lifts, my eyes latch on his, and he telegraphs me a secret message, one that lets me know his time here has been the opposite of bad. I keep the grin from my face, and my heart sinks into my heels as Cameron's message comes in.

I read it once, then twice.

"What does it say," Mrs. Parker asks.

I force a smile. "Looks like we can move the meeting to Monday. Cameron is feeling better and has the paperwork ready."

Mrs. Parker claps. "Excellent news. See that, son? Mother knows how to get things done."

What did she get done? Nothing. I'm the one who just texted Cameron. I supposed she pushed me to do it, but still, and you know what, I don't like her condescending attitude where Colin is concerned. I want to say something, hell I'd love to tell her what I think about her matchmaking, but now is not the time or place so I bite my tongue.

I lift my head, and find Colin staring at me, the muscles in his jaw tight as he clamps down. He's so deadly quiet I'm not sure what's going through his head. He pulls his phone from his pocket, and checks on something. He's even more solemn when he shoves it back in his pocket.

"Are you looking forward to seeing family?" Mrs. Parker asks Colin, and the two make small talk for a little while. We finally reach our destination, and honestly, I can't wait to be out of the vehicle. Maybe I'll hitchhike home.

Colin jumps from the back seat first and holds his hand out to help us both out. His mother latches onto him again and he tosses me an almost apologetic look. I glance around at all the tall gorgeous people, dressed far better than me, and I shrink back a bit, a little overwhelmed. Colin abandons his mother and comes toward me, his eyes full of concern. I shouldn't be here. I shouldn't have come. I stick out more than the pope at a grunge concert. But at least I now get why she invited me along. To make me feel out of place. To make me feel like I don't belong in hers or Colin's world.

Well done, Mrs. Parker. Well done.

29

COLIN

I toss and turn in bed, desperate to talk to Violet. She was quiet last night, and I suspect it was because she didn't know anyone. Nevertheless, when she met the premier, she was kind and gracious and even made him laugh. But of course, she did. Violet is an amazing woman and mother might have seen that herself if she gave her a chance, but no, Mum talked nonstop all the way home from the Shore Club. She spent the entire drive raving about meeting the premier, and the connections it would give her. It's no wonder Violet went straight to bed—alone—with a headache.

I roll, and check the clock when I hear footsteps in the hall. Mother's footsteps. I can tell the difference in the way the two walk, and I'm glad she's up before Violet. I need to have a talk to her and set her straight once and for all. I was going to wait to tell her I'm not going to be forced into marriage with a girl of her choice because I'm in love with another woman. I wanted to wait until after I talked to Violet, but does it really matter? Even if she doesn't want me, nothing is going to change the way I feel about her.

Before I jump up, I check my phone again, hoping the email I've been waiting for is in my inbox. It's Monday, and it's still early, but I threw enough money at the problem to get answers sooner rather than later.

I toss my legs over the bed, and tug on a pair of sweatpants. I chuckle to myself. Before Violet, I wouldn't be caught dead walking around in sweats. They were reserved for running on cold, damp days. Now I'm in them and completely okay with it.

I step into the hall as Mum comes out of the loo, looking as fresh as a morning daisy, and dressed in her designer clothes. "Colin," she says, and sneers at my sweats. "Are you up for an early morning jog?"

"No, I wanted to talk to you."

"What is it?"

"Let's go downstairs, I don't want to wake Violet."

"Meow."

Mum steps back as Lucky presses up against my leg, and her lips pinch in disgust. "Can you please get that thing away from me." Lucky hisses at her, and I pick him up. He purrs against my neck and I bite back a laugh. But I'm happy we're friends now.

"I've got him."

"Can you lock him in the loo or something? He's dreadful."

"No, I'm not going to do that, and he's not dreadful. He's a gorgeous sphynx, aren't you, Lucky? Aren't you a gorgeous sphynx?" Bollocks. I do have a cat voice, and it's rather annoying. Lucky seems to appreciate it though, judging by the way he's nuzzling me.

Mum arches her brow, but says nothing. She heads downstairs and I follow with Lucky in my arms. I set the cat down, and make Mum a tea and put the coffee on for Violet and me. I've sort of gotten used to drinking it and it tastes less and less like dishwater.

I set Mum's steaming cup of tea in front of her and give her a spot of milk. Once my coffee is done, I sit down across from her. "I'm not getting married."

Her body goes poker straight, and she opens her mouth, but I hold my hand up. "I'm sorry, Mum." There I go apologizing again. "I'm not saying I'm never going to get married, but I'm not marrying a woman of your choice."

Her skin stretches tight as she purses her lips in thought. A moment later she asks, "Does this have something to do with Violet?"

"It has everything to do with her. I think you know that."

"She's not the girl for you, Colin. I see things you don't. Believe me, she's nothing like these women. She doesn't even compare."

"I know, she's in a different league."

She goes quiet and sips her tea and I know her well enough to know she's taking a moment to strategize. She's a woman used to getting her way, and up until Violet, I might have just gone along, followed tradition and expectations. But since being here in Canada, I've changed. I'm not that obedient son anymore, afraid to rock the boat, or bring shame to the family name. Not that Violet would bring shame. She's an amazing woman, and our family would be lucky to have her as a part of it, and fuck yes, I am thinking about marriage for the first time in my life. I have what it takes to love a woman, and she's a woman who doesn't want anything from me.

Mother nods, sets her cup down, and reaches into her purse. "If Francesca is no longer to your liking, perhaps, you'd like Veronica."

Francesca was never to my liking, and I told her that numerous times. She presents me with a picture of Veronica, practically shoves it in my face, like that's suddenly going to change my mind.

Lucky stretches on the floor and walks to the archway. I take the picture from her and look at the pretty girl, in a gorgeous, jeweled dress, a dress Violet would likely never wear and that's okay. I like her for who she is, and she doesn't need to change a thing for me.

Mum glances at something behind me. I'm about to turn, but she grips my hand, keeping my attention on her. "Did you have a good look at her?"

I shake my head. "Yes, I've had a good look at her. I've been looking at her for days." I've been looking at all the girls for days, and I'm done. I set the picture down. "You're right, she is nothing like these women and doesn't even compare." I hear a noise behind me. "Did you hear that?"

"I didn't hear anything," Mum says, an almost winning grin on her face. Which is odd, considering I just told her I wasn't marrying a debutante.

I push from my chair and walk into the other room. I spot Lucky darting up the steps. I follow him, but my gut tells me that Violet might have been standing behind me, hearing parts of our conversation. I want her. Love her. She needs to know that I'm breaking all the rules, because it's her I want.

I hurry after Lucky, reach the top step, and lightly knock on her door. Maybe she wasn't downstairs, maybe it was just Lucky I heard. I quietly open the door, and my heart misses a beat when I see her in her bed, all covered up, her back to the door. I listen to her sleeping sounds, and decide not to wake her. It's possible she's having a relapse from the flu and maybe her headache wasn't from Mother's incessant chatter last night.

I quietly close the door, and head backdown stairs. "Is everything okay, Colin?"

"I'm going to go for a run."

"I think we should talk some more."

"No." I've heard all she has to say, and I've had my say, nothing she or anyone else says to me is going to change my mind about Violet. Since I'm in my sweats, I head to the front door, needing to go for a long hard run to work out my frustrations with Mum's expectations. If she really cared about me, she'd want me happy with someone I wanted, not someone with the right pedigree. If she'd give Violet a chance, she'd see just how amazing she was.

I run long and hard, for over a good long hour. I don't expect Violet to be up for a while, although I think she said she had a shift this morning. I pass by the café, town hall and reach the new roundabout. I take a few side roads, exploring the area and every now and then check my phone to see if I received any new messages. I hope answers come in before the town council convenes.

I finally turn back and as I pass by the café again, a man who looks familiar raises his arm and waves me over. I glance over my shoulder to see if anyone is behind me. I slow to a jog and make my way over to the man with the long, wild white hair. What was his name. Willy?

I slow to a walk as I greet him. "Good morning."

"Morning, Colin."

Of course, he knows me, everyone in this town knows me and hates me. I'm hoping to change that soon enough.

"Getting the papers signed today, I hear."

"Yup, sounds like everything is in order." It's not. Not yet.

He smirks, and tosses an unlit cigarette into his mouth. He glances around, looking at nothing in particular. "I guess she finally got what she wanted?"

"What's that now?"

He laughs, and it morphs into a coughing fit. I could tell him he might want to give up smoking, but I don't.

"Violet, she got you to do her dirty work."

"Dirty work? What are you talking about?"

He laughs and coughs again. "She's been wanting that park off her hands forever. Can't put it up for sale. Nope. Townsfolk would have her head over that. She wants something sustainable there, and a school sure sounds sustainable to me. She couldn't let the town think she was behind the sale. That's where you came in. You're the bearer of bad news, and she's letting you take the brunt of it while she comes out the other end all squeaky clean. She'd have gotten rid of it years ago if she could."

I shake my head as I try to wrap my brain around what he's saying. "The park is a part of Violet's heritage. She doesn't want to see it gone. You have your facts wrong."

"You think so. Why don't you ask her? Once the papers are signed and she gets what she wanted from you, it's adios to you, sir."

My mind instantly goes back to when I thought Violet was pushing for the sale. She never did answer me when I asked. But this guy can't be right. Violet isn't like that. She's not using me as the fall guy. She's not using me to get what she wants at all right?

Acid punches into my throat as old insecurities creep back in and I struggle to push them down. Was my mother right? Did she see something in Violet that I didn't because I was blinded by the things I was feeling for her? Does mother really have my best interests at heart? I don't know, but I need to talk to Violet right this very second.

I take off running, a new kind of desperation driving me. I burst through the front door, and right up the stairs. Her bedroom door is open and her bed is empty. I frown. Was her car even in the driveway?

"Mum," I call out and go down the stairs two at a time. "Where's Violet?"

"She left. She was in a huge hurry."

"Where did she go?"

"She mentioned something about signing the papers. She was rather quiet." Her brows knit together. "Are you okay?"

"No, I'm not. I need to find her."

"Why don't you stop all this foolishness, Colin? You're making a fool of yourself chasing after a girl like her."

"A girl like her?" My anger flares and it's all I can do not to pound something. "What the hell is that supposed to mean?"

"You belong at home. Not here with a woman who somehow managed to get you to do her dirty work."

"Dirty work?"

Willy's words ring in my ears.

Mum makes a tsking sound. "Gardening...cooking, who knows what else she's been getting you to do."

Take the fall...be the bad guy.

Fuck me twice.

"Are the papers signed?"

"I have to go." I head outside, pick up my pace and jog to the café. Inside I take a fast glance around, and all heads turn to me. "Is Violet here?"

"Never showed up," The woman behind the counter says. "Not like her at all."

No, it isn't like her at all. Then again, do I really know her? I don't know but I get the feeling that she's avoiding me which only worries me all the more.

I reach for my phone about to text her when one comes in from her and I breathe a sigh of relief—until I read it.

Papers are signed by Cameron and me. Cameron is waiting for you at town hall.

What the ever-loving fuck is going on?

I text back. *Where are you?*

. . .

She doesn't answer, so I bolt down the road and rush inside to find Cameron, Corporal Davis and Wanda waiting for me. Violet is nowhere to be found.

"Colin," Cameron says with a snarl, not at all pleased that he couldn't stall me longer, or stop the sale altogether. "If you'll just put your John Hancock right here. Everyone else has already signed."

I walk up to the table, and look over the papers, but before I sign, I check my messages one more time, and the answer I've been waiting for comes in. But I'm torn. Do I try to save her park or not?

"I'll get back to you on these." Three mouths drop open as I hurry outside. I glance around, my mind racing as panic grips my throat. Where the hell is Violet? I take a breath to calm myself, and that's when it hits me.

The treehouse.

I need a car, and fast. I run back inside town hall and glance at the constable. "Can you give me a ride to the park?" He hesitates. "It's urgent, and your meal is on me afterward."

Nodding, he pulls his keys from his pocket. "Is everything okay?"

"I don't know."

He follows me outside and I hop into the passenger side of his cruiser and I'm practically vibrating as he drives. I'd ask him to speed up, but it is the law around these parts. We finally reach the park, and the vehicle hasn't even come to a full stop before I'm jumping out and thanking him. I hurry into the open-air entranceway, and the manager is behind the counter.

"Have you seen Violet?"

She blinks up at me, her gaze going over the rough, disheveled state of me. Yeah, I'm a hot mess, I get it. "She's around here somewhere."

"Is she working?"

"No, she just showed up unannounced. Sometimes she does that when she needs to think."

"Thanks." I take off, and run the long path until I reach the treehouse. I'm breathless when I reach it, and I'm about to call up to her when I hear another voice...a man's voice.

Caleb?

I stand there for a moment, but their words are low and whispered, and every insecurity I've ever had grips me by the nut sack. Bile punches into my throat, and a noise I have no control over rolls off my tongue.

Violet's head appears, and she glances down at me, her cheeks are flushed, and I nearly lose my fucking mind. "Colin, what are you doing here? The papers were signed already. I figured you'd be halfway to the airport by now."

She turns when Caleb says something to her, and a second later he's standing next to her, smirking at me. Fucking wanker. I ought to go up there and pound his face in.

"I didn't mean to interrupt whatever it is you two are doing," I say, my voice venomous, accusation dripping from each word.

She blinks and her body stiffens. "Is that what you think of me?"

Caleb sidles closer to her, a united front. "What do you expect me to think?"

"I don't know, but maybe you should go discuss it with your new bride, Francesca, is it? I'm sure your mother must be anxious to get out of here now that you've gotten what you came here for."

"Was it me who'd gotten what they wanted or was it you, Violet?"

She stares at me like she doesn't understand, and one brain cell kicks in and tells me I might be making a big-ass mistake here. At least I want to believe that. Every ounce of my being wants to believe that.

"I'm sorry, Colin."

Hope fills me. She's a girl who apologizes when she's not even in the wrong. "What are you sorry for?"

"For everything?"

Does that mean she's sorry for using me? That she did use me? Or is she sorry that I jumped to conclusions about what she and Caleb are doing in the treehouse? I guess I'll never know because she sinks down, out of my sight, pulling Caleb down with her, her dismissive actions giving me the answer I never wanted to hear.

I leave the park in a flurry, my brain racing so fast, I can barely see as I bolt it back to Constable Davis's car.

"Are you okay?" he asks.

"Yeah, no."

He gives me an odd look and I glance out the passenger side window as he starts the car and drives me back to Violet's.

"Thanks for the lift. Everyone's breakfast is on me," I say and hand over a couple hundred-dollar bills. As his face lights up, I bid him farewell, pull my cell out to call for a cab, and step inside to find Mum in a face-off with Lucky.

"Get ready. We're leaving."

Her face lights up. "You've signed the papers."

"Something like that." I stomp upstairs, and narrow my vision. Everywhere I look, I see Violet and I need to make a clean break before I break. I pack quickly, and by the time I finish getting my things from the loo, the car is outside. Downstairs, I bend to say goodbye to Lucky, and if looks could kill, I'd be six feet under.

"It's time for me to go, mate."

He swipes me, leaving a big scratch on my arm. I guess that's his way of making sure I don't forget him in a hurry. I'm not going to forget any of this for...well, ever. Offering me his backside, he sidles off, and I stand. I take a deep breath, my throat tight, hurting to the point of pain.

I head outside, leaving the door unlocked the way Violet likes it and Mum and I climb into the backseat and give directions for the airport. My phone pings, and my heart jumps. Is it Violet telling me it's all been a huge mistake and that she doesn't want me to leave?

"Is everything okay?" Mum asks.

"Yeah." I lie. "It's Nate."

She makes a tsking sound. "What is that boy up to now?"

I shoot him off a text as Mum continues with. "I finally got you on the straight and narrow, now I can work on Nate."

My hackles rise at the way she worded that. "I'm a grown man, Mum. I don't need anyone to get me on the straight and narrow."

Her face pinches tight. "What has happened to you, anyway?"

Violet happened to me. Sweet Violet who'd give me the shirt off her back if I was cold, unless she was cold too. A chuckle rumbles in my throat, but it comes out sounding pained and tortured. My phone buzzes.

Nate: Hey mate, how's it going over there.

Me: On our way home.

Nate: Mum got to you, did she?

Me: What's that supposed to mean?

Nate: She said something about a girl named Violet.

Me: Why didn't you warm me she was coming?

. . .

Nate: Check your phone, bro. I messaged a dozen times. I guess you were too busy to check. What's it like shagging in an igloo?

I laugh inwardly as my mind goes back to getting dressed for sex, instead of getting undressed. Only in Canada.

Me: You're an arse.

Nate: Nicest thing you've ever called me. Seriously though, bro, tell me about Violet.

Me: Nothing to tell.

Nate: Come on, mate. There must be a story if Mum had to travel to the armpit of the world to collect you. I'm dying to know more.

Me: She's just a woman I met.

Nate: Fit?

Me: Yes, she's fit.

Nate: Barmy then?

· · ·

My entire body stiffens. Violet is anything but stupid or crazy. Okay, maybe she's a bit crazy, what Canadian isn't, but she's crazy and sweet and apologetic, and...she's the best woman I know. I swallow the lump pushing into my throat, and glance out the window as we leave the town behind. My stomach cramps, and I'm not sure why but I suddenly feel like I'm going to hurl. Although maybe I do know why.

Me: No.

Nate: Twat? Tosser? Lost the plot? Daft as a bush?

A wave of anger goes through me as my brother tosses out derogatory terms. Violet is none of those things and he has no right to suggest it. As possession and protectiveness race through me, my fingers fly over the phone.

Me: Don't talk about her like that. You don't know her.

Nate: You do?

Me: Damn right I do. She's sweet and kind and if you keep disrespecting her, I'll knock your teeth out when I get home.

· · ·

A growl crawls out of my throat and I lift my head to find Mum looking at me.

"Is Nate okay?" she asks.

I practically snarl when I say, "He won't be if he doesn't piss off." Mum's eyes go wide and my phone pings. I turn back to it.

Nate: That's not going to happen.

Me: Why not?

Nate: Because you're not coming home.

Me: What are you talking about?

Nate: You're in love with Violet.

I pinch the bridge of my nose. Is my little brother playing some sort of psychological game with me? I know he's wild and reckless, but he's also brilliant. He might be able to see right through me, but he doesn't know what happened, how things ended between Violet and me.

. . .

Me: It's not what you think.

Nate: It doesn't matter what I think. It only matters what YOU think.

I set my phone down, my brain buzzing. What do I think? Do I think Violet was shagging Caleb in the tree house?

Do you really think that, Colin?

Do I really think she's the kind of girl who would use me to take the fall and run off and have sex with her old boyfriend?

Fuck no. I don't.

I lay my head back, my heart pounding so hard I fear it's going to burst from my chest. I breathe but can't seem to get in air as the car closes in around me. As the vehicle grows hot, I press a button and the window goes down. Natural air conditioning. I grin because it reminds me of Violet. Everything reminds me of Violet, and how much I love her....how badly I screwed up. If I turned around now, would she even forgive me.

"I've made a huge mistake," I mutter to myself.

Mum pats my legs. "Yes, you have, son, and I'm so glad you finally came to your senses and we're on our way home."

30

VIOLET

It's been days since Colin and his mother, the lovely Mrs. Parker, packed up and left my bed and breakfast. I think it's been days, anyway. I totally lost count, and have been doing nothing but eating ice cream, drinking wine, and sulking. Heck, I haven't even changed out of my clothes and why bother? I'm not trying to impress anyone, not since I've locked the world out, and myself in. I stopped answering calls or emails, and I even went so far as to lock my door.

Shocking, I know.

I told everyone I was sick again, and they're only going to believe that for so long. I give it another day or two and then I expect Constable Davis to use one of those things...what are they called? You know, in the cop shows, where they use a big stick thing to break down a door. I think it's called a ram, or something like that. Not that it matters, and I'm only dwelling on it because it occupies my mind and gets it off Colin. Kidding. Nothing, not even a good book, or a good movie, or copious amounts of wine can help me forget him.

Lord, my body is still tingling everywhere he touched, and my lips ached to be kissed again.

Not going to happen, girlfriend.

From the coffee table, my phone pings again for the millionth time today, and once again I ignore it. Lucky comes sidling up to me—I'm not sure how he can stand the sight of me, or the smell—and lays his head on my lap. I pet him gently. "It's just me and you from here on out, buddy."

"Meow."

My chest grows so tight, it's difficult to fill my lungs. I take a gulping breath. "Yeah, I hear you. I miss him too." I groan, and hate myself. Honestly, this is all my fault. I knew better than to get involved with a guy from another country. Why couldn't I keep my stupid heart out of it? I knew right from the beginning why he was here and what his timeline was, but did that stop me from falling for him, even though I knew he'd eventually leave? Of course not. I'm dense like that, or as Colin would say daft.

Stop thinking about him already.

"Meow."

"I know, I know." I run my hand down Lucky's hairless back. "He was sweet and kind, taking care of me when I was sick, even going so far as to work for me." I shake my head, and lean it back on the sofa, as I try to wrap my brain around that. "Who does something like that, Lucky? I mean, how could I not think he wanted more, right? Oh, and did I mention he was handsome too. And that British accent. I was doomed to begin with."

"Meow."

"Oh no, Lucky. I didn't forget," I tell him. "He saved you. That's a big deal, and I love how you learned to trust him in the end and stopped trying to kill him."

"Meow."

"Yes, he did basically accuse me of sleeping with Caleb." My throat squeezes tight, to the point of pain. I try to swallow, but it hurts. "Did he really think that little of me?" I exhale a fluttery breath and try not to cry. If I shed any more tears, I'm going to dehydrate. I close my eyes, the image of Colin standing at the bottom of the treehouse dancing in my mind's eye. My God, the last look he gave me suggested the mere sight of me gave him moderate to severe diarrhea. Great, now I sound like the small print for a drug advertisement.

"No, you're right. I didn't correct him. I was mad and hurt after I heard him tell his mother I was nothing like those women, didn't even compare to *Francesca*." I draw out her name like it's poison on my tongue.

"Meow."

Lucky jumps from my lap and goes to the window, looking outside with longing and I expel an exaggerated sigh. "I'm sorry. I didn't mean to keep you prisoner in here with me. Want to go outside?"

"Meow."

"You're right." I glance down at the stains of my T-shirt and sweatpants. "I should change, but that requires effort so it's not happening."

"Meow."

"Lucky I don't care if my hair needs a comb. Stop being so damn judgmental." He licks his paw and I'm pretty sure he did a big mental eye roll. Yeah, I get it, he's so over all this. I should be over it all too.

Needing to get myself together, I push from my very comfy spot on the sofa and move the curtain back to see the outside view. Other than taking care of Waffles and Popcorn, who also seem to be out of sorts since Colin left, I haven't been outside. I unlock my door, and step out into the sunshine, letting the breeze blow the stench off me. The park has now officially closed and maybe I'll visit it one last time before the whole thing is torn down.

"What do you think, Lucky, want to go for a ride?"

He stretches, and circles my legs, and I take that as a yes. I grab my phone, purse and keys, and after I lock up, I walk slowly to my car. Maybe I should move. I'm sure the townsfolk are completely pissed off at me. They all expected me to stop the sale, but it was out of my hands.

Don't think about Colin's hands.

Too late, thought about them.

In the car, I buckle in and set Lucky on the seat beside me. "Sorry I don't have a proper seat belt for you, but I'll get one, okay?" I'm already on my way to crazy cat lady so I might as well get all the accessories to go with it.

"Meow."

I drive through town, and as I pass the townsfolk many of them are trying to flag me down, but I just wave and carry on my way. I'm sure everyone has something nasty to say to me. They can wait until the next town hall. I am not stopping so they can take their wrath out on me. Not today, folks.

At least the non-profit organization will be happy to be free of the park and all the headaches. I drive down the long country road, and pass the bridge, and start singing loudly to a song on the radio so my mind doesn't wander to Colin and the fun we had breaking rules and jumping into the water. I thought he was learning to live a little, have a little fun, see the happiness in living his own life, by his own rules. But no, tradition and doing what's expected of him is so deeply engrained, he had no choice but to go home and marry.

The parking lot is completely empty and I ease into a spot. A heavy lump sits in my gut as I step from my car, and tears threaten. Lucky comes up beside me and I scoop him up and hold him close.

He rubs his chin against me, obviously sensing my distress. "This will be the last time I walk on this land, Lucky."

He snuggles in and my heart is lodged in my throat as I move through the empty open-air lobby. I briefly close my eyes, and if I try really hard, I can remember the excitement I felt the first time I came to the park, and the laughter of all the children who visited over the years. This time the tears fall, and there's nothing I can do about it. A piece of my heritage, my history is going to be gone.

We walk through the park, and I'm not greeted with scents of popcorn, or candy apple or the fresh aroma of lumber for Mr. Barker to whittle. I gave this park my life, every cent in my bank account, but nothing I did could save it.

I sniff, and follow the paved path I've walked a million times. I would do it with my eyes closed if I could and in a way, I am. The whole place is blurry through my stupid tears. Another text comes in from Emily, and I message back that I'm still not feeling well, and then power my phone down.

She's pretty insistent that we talk, but I don't feel like it at the moment. I might need a few more days and a couple more pints of ice cream. Or twenty. That would require a trip to the store, and then everyone would want to talk to me. I could, of course, always go to the next town over.

I continue to walk through the park and take a moment to stop at the treehouse. I probably shouldn't have let Colin think I was up there having sex with Caleb. I wasn't. He saw the state I was in when I came here to think and he was just being a friend trying to help. But when Colin jumped to the conclusion that I was jumping Caleb's bones, it really told me a lot about what he thought of me. I'm still shocked and hurt by that, more than him running off to marry Francesca. Or maybe I'm not.

I'm about to climb up, to stand in it one more time, but nearly jump from my shoes as a loud sound reverberates through the park. What the heck? Lucky practically claws his way up my chest, the noise scaring him too.

"It's okay, Lucky. I'm not going to let anything happen to you." He nuzzles me and I turn around and head toward the sound. My steps are quick as I listen to the bangs and booms, and tears once again flood my eyes when I run through the front entrance and find demolition machinery.

Wow, Waltonstound Foundation aren't wasting any time. Why would they? The park means nothing to them, it holds no sentimental value, so tear it down and get that school up.

"Let's get out of here, Lucky. We don't belong here anymore."

I keep my head down and walk around the heavy equipment. In the car, I don't look back. Instead, I adjust my rearview mirror so I can't see out of it, can't see the tractor demolish my beloved park.

We drive aimlessly for many long hours, until darkness is upon us. I don't want anyone in town to see the redness in my face, or my eyes. I ease into my driveway, let myself in, and lock up behind me. God, Colin wasn't even here that long yet he's imprinted himself on my heart and in my house. Everywhere I look I see him. I pinch my eyes, hoping the image of him at the counter cooking for me, taking care of me, is gone when I open them.

My lids slowly open, and I glance around to find my kitchen empty. Wait, what's that? I bend and pick something up from under the table and the picture of Francesca in my hand hits like a punch to the gut.

"Way to hit a girl when she's down." Did Mrs. Parker leave that here on purpose, just to drive the point home. I toss it onto the table, and Lucky jumps on it. He scratches at it, and lifts his head to glare at me.

"What?"

"Meow." He swats the picture like he can't stand the sight of it, hisses at it, and looks back at me, his head angled, like he's waiting for me to puzzle something out. As I relive the conversation Colin was having with his mum, Lucky meows louder.

She doesn't compare...

"Obviously, he was comparing *me* to those women, it wasn't the other way around." I point to the scratched picture. "Just look at her."

He angles his head, and stares at me like I'm the idiot. I'm not though, right? Colin was talking about me, and it wasn't the other way around? As that spins around my brain, I sink into a chair and my pulse jumps in my throat. Lucky can't be right. If he is, and Colin was defending me...and I let him believe I was sleeping with Caleb...then I totally messed everything up, and there is no chance he doesn't hate me now.

My kitchen closes in on me, and I jump to my feet, my lungs seizing. I grab the back of the chair to keep myself vertical. Is it possible that I heard wrong, that my insecurities got the better of me, made me think the worst?

Oh my God, Violet. What if you totally misunderstood?

I gasp a few times, and work to settle my scattered brain. If I was wrong, does it even matter now? Everything is messed up and Colin is off to marry another woman. Honestly, I'm still not even sure what he meant when he accused me of getting what I wanted.

Lucky jumps onto the floor and darts upstairs. With the world shattering around me, I follow him up and fall into my bed. I'd washed the sheets after Colin left, but dammit, his scent is still all over them. I fall into a restless sleep, and the sounds of the heavy equipment from the park make their way into my dreams. Bang. Thump. Boom.

I groan awake, and steal a glance at the clock. It's barely morning. I'm about to roll back over, and that's when I realize the sounds weren't in my dreams at all, but instead coming from my backyard. Is there someone, or something out there?

I slowly sit up, and glance at Lucky who is completely still, staring at me. Okay, that's not weird at all. Unease creeps through my bones and I stare back. "You're not an alien, right?" He jumps from the bed, and disappears into the hall. "You're not a watch-cat, I'll give you that. Maybe I'll trade you in for an animal that will protect the property, and me!" I shout but he's gone.

Colin was protective of you.

The second my feet hit the floor, the banging stops, and the backyard goes eerily quiet. I pull on a robe over my disgusting clothes, and quietly tip-toe into Colin's room, or rather the other guest room, where I can get a good view of the back-yard. Lucky is sitting on the windowsill, staring intently at God knows what, and there's a bright light shining into the room. My God, please don't tell me Chester was right and that a UFO might be landing in my corn stalks.

My heart beats faster, and my blood drains as I step up to the window, to see a great big circle in the middle of my garden. Sweet mother of God, the triple G's were right.

There are aliens amongst us.

31

COLIN

The excavator stops but the light continues to shine on the back of Violet's house as she comes running around to the yard in her robe and slippers. Dammit, I hadn't meant to wake her and as I look at her now, my heart aches at the mere sight of her. All I want is to take her in my arms, and make everything between us okay again, and I pray to God she can forgive me for being such a foolish muppet.

Honestly, the last few days, without being close, living under the same roof as her, being able to touch her, kiss her, go to bed with her and more importantly wake up with her have been torturous, at best. But I needed to have everything in place, and all the paperwork filed, before I showed up at her door. I wanted to make sure I was doing right by her and not giving false promises. But staying away was beyond painful.

Christ, to think I thought she was in the treehouse having sex with Caleb, and to accuse her of it straight up. Daft. That's the only word to describe it. After she didn't correct me, let me believe it, blind rage and hurt ruled my actions, and I stormed back to her place, and packed up my belongings.

Mum wasn't too happy with me when we pulled up to the airport and I didn't fly home with her. She was actually furious when I told her who I wanted to spend the rest of my life with, and while she disagreed with me, adamantly, she can do one of two things, accept it or not. That's totally up to her. I, of course, hope she does. I want my kids to know their grandmother.

Okay, slow down, Colin, you're getting ahead of yourself here.

But in my heart, I know Violet isn't a woman to use anyone to get what she wanted. She's a hardworking, caring girl who spent a life taking care of others. I think Willy told me she was using me because he had an agenda of his own, and I know, without a shadow of a doubt that she was not shagging Caleb in that treehouse. That is not who she is, and I let my stupid past cloud my future. I'm never going to let that happen again.

I take a step toward Violet as she stands in her backyard, staring at the big circle in her corn field. She's mumbling under her breath, something about aliens and Lucky and the three G's. I walk toward her, just as the flatbed out on the street starts beeping as it backs up. She spins, and in the dim light I can see her eyes bulging in her head. She throws her arms out, completely flabbergasted. I hurry to her, desperate to calm her down.

"Violet."

She spins fast, and I reach out and grab her before she falls. Her lashes blink rapidly, like she can't quite figure out what is going on, like she might be hallucinating, and I can't blame her.

"Are you okay?" I ask.

"No...no, I'm not okay." She shakes her head, her mussed hair falling into her eyes. "What is going on? I thought there were aliens."

"Not aliens, just an excavator, and a flatbed truck."

"Why...what is going on?" She breaks from my arms, and steps back, putting physical and emotional distance between us, and my throat squeezes tight. *Don't mess this up, Colin.* "Why are you here?" She makes a choking sound, and I reach out to her again, desperate to make this right between us. But she jerks backward.

"I'm here because I screwed up," I say quickly, desperately.

"No, wait, what?" Her face scrunches up as she works to puzzle things out. "You left to get married. You said...you said, I didn't compare to...to those other women."

My chest tightens. "So you did hear me." She moves even farther away, sadness all over her face and I hurry to explain. "I was worried that you heard Mum and me. I ran to your room, but you were sleeping."

"I did hear you, Colin. I heard what you said. It hurt me. A lot. I was pretending to be asleep because...I just couldn't..."

"I'm sorry, Violet. I'm sorry you heard that." I shove my shaking hands into my pants pockets. "But you didn't hear the whole conversation. Can I tell you?"

She tightens her robe, vulnerability and hurt in her eyes. "I...I guess."

"When you heard me say she doesn't compare, I meant Francesca couldn't compare to you." I take one tiny step forward and she doesn't move. It gives me a measure of relief.

"You are everything those women aren't. You're kind, compassionate, so sweet and giving, putting everyone ahead of yourself, taking care of this entire town. I want to be the guy to take care of you." As she stands there, her body tight, I shake my head, hating what I said to her. "I never should have accused you of sleeping with Caleb. That was a mistake. I was angry and hurt, and confused. I...Willy told me you wanted the park sold, he said you were using me to get it done, letting me take the blame so the townsfolk didn't hate you." I swallow against a tight throat. "I'm...I'm..."

"Daft."

I let loose a long breath, and let my head fall forward. "Yes, daft. There's no other way to describe it."

"Willy is a troublemaker. There was a feud between Dad and him from a long time ago. Apparently, it didn't die with my father."

"After he told me that, I ran back here to talk to you, but you were already gone and you'd signed the papers, and then Caleb, and..." I stare at my shoes, my thoughts racing as fast as my heart. "I stupidly let myself believe the worst, that I wasn't worthy of your love, or anyone's love, and—"

"Colin, no."

My head jerks up. "What?"

She closes the distance between us. "Don't you ever say that. You are the best guy I know and totally loveable." She pokes my chest, and I grab her hand, hold it in my palm. She gulps. "Trust me," She adds, her voice a bit lower. "I, for a fact, know you're loveable."

My vision closes in on me, my pounding heart making it harder and harder to breathe. "Why, how do you know that?"

"Because...I fell in love with you, that's how."

My vision clears, the world full of color again as she places her free hand on my cheek. "You...love me."

"Of course, I love you, Colin." She frees her other hand and puts it on my other cheek, and when she goes up on her toes and presses a light kiss to my lips, happy tears pound behind my eyes. It's all I can do not to drop to the ground and sob like a baby.

"I love you too, Violet. I wanted to come straight back to you. I wanted to run here and tell you how I felt, but I needed to get the paperwork in order, because I wanted to be sure, before I told you..."

"You love me, too?" she asks, as my heart nearly explodes.

"I think I loved you since you first teased me about my beaver."

She chuckles, and it brings light and happiness to my darkest corners. "I'm sorry."

"Don't be sorry." I cup her face and kiss her. "You don't ever have to apologize to me. I'm the one who needs to be apologizing to you."

"Colin, what did you mean? You needed to be sure about what?"

I pull a piece of paper from my pocket. "I bought Annapolis Park."

She stares at the paper like it's a bucket of worms, then lifts her head, her eyes moving over me like I might have just come from outer space. "I know that. That's the whole reason you were here, remember?"

"I remember. I'm not...Wait, no, you don't understand. I bought the park."

This time her eyes go wide, real concern on her face. "Colin, I know. Did you bang your head or something?"

I take a fast breath. "I bought it. Me. Not the foundation."

Her eyes narrow, and her eyebrows pinch together. "I don't understand."

"I found a way to make everyone happy. You, the foundation, this entire town."

As the sun rises higher, warm morning light filling her backyard, she says, "Still in the dark."

"The zoo," I say quickly, trying to get my jumbled thoughts straight. "The school will be built where the zoo used to be. There's enough land. The park, though. It's in my name. I own the title. It can't be turned into a school."

She blinks rapidly, confusion all over her face as her breathing changes. Her gaze goes from me, to the paperwork, back to me. "What are you saying?"

"Read this."

She takes the paper from me but her eyes are watery. "I can't read anything."

"You remember the old stone building, the one my granddad would have wanted taken down?"

"Yes."

"I had it declared a heritage home. No one can touch it, which means the land around it can't be amended to include a private or independent school. It's not permitted. The bylaws can't be changed. Not now."

Her hands begin to shake and she buckles a little. I hold her to me as tears spill down her face. "How…"

"I went into the building when I took your shift, and when I found old maps and pictures, and realized just how old the place was, I reached out to the heritage society in the city."

"That's why you went…"

"I didn't want to say anything until I was sure. I didn't sign the papers that day in town hall, but even if I did, they wouldn't hold up."

"That park…" Blue eyes full of joy and wonderment blink up at me. "I can't believe you figured this all out."

"I'm daft, but not that daft."

"How come…no one told me?"

My gaze moves over her. "With the way news spreads, I thought you would have heard that I hadn't signed anything."

She tugs on her robe. "I haven't been out much. Haven't been answering the phone." A grin tugs at the corners of her mouth and it wraps around my heart. "You own the park," she says quietly like she's still trying to wrap her brain around it.

"The park was built by your grandfather and father. I don't ever want you to lose it, Violet. You can remove the rides and just keep the land, or we can invest in it and build a huge rollercoaster to bring in new customers, or…whatever you want. No decisions have to be made just yet."

Tears flood her face. "I can't believe this."

"Is this what you wanted?"

"I never wanted to sell, Colin. I just knew I had to. I resigned myself to the fact that the park was failing...I'd put so much time and money into it, and I couldn't save it, but...you did."

"Now you get to keep the park in your family forever."

"It's not...in my family, though. It's your park. You said it's in your name."

Taking that cue, I drop to my knees and pull out a velvet box. "I learned something Violet." She blinks at me. "I learned that home isn't where the crumpets are. Home is where you are and if you marry me, the land, the park, it all stays in the family." She gasps, and off in the distance I hear Waffles and Popcorn traipsing through the vegetation. "Wait, that came out wrong. I'm not trying to bribe you into marrying me."

She laughs. "I never thought you were." She sinks to her knees, and stares at the big diamond I can't wait to put on her hand.

"Colin..."

"Marry me, Violet. Make me the happiest man in the world."

In the distance, Lucky purrs his blessing, but it's quickly drowned out by a loud beeping sound. I turn to the left and realize we're very close to getting crushed by the flat bed.

"Bollocks." I stand, and pull Violet to her feet. We both back up as the flatbed invades her backyard.

"What is going on?" she shrieks. "Is...is that my treehouse, from the park?"

"Yes."

"Colin, what have you done?"

"I cleared a spot in the backyard for it. I wanted it here. Actually, I wanted to propose to you in it. I was hoping to have it up and in place before you woke up."

"I'm not that sound of a sleeper." I chuckle and she angles her head. "Wait, why did you want to do this in the treehouse?"

"I want to be the last guy you ever kissed in it."

Tears fall down her face, and I brush them away. "I like that idea," she says.

I hold the ring out again. "Does that mean you'll marry me?"

She goes quiet for a long time as she stares at the diamond. Her head finally lifts, and she says, "You always say you're no one's prince charming, but you're wrong. You're my prince charming."

"Still not an answer." My gaze rakes over her beautiful face, and there is nothing I want more than to spend the rest of my life putting a smile on it. "Is that a yes or no to marriage?"

"Yeah, no for sure."

I roll my eyes. "Canadians!"

"If you can't beat 'em, join 'em, eh?"

"Just to clarify that's a yes, right?"

She laughs and the sound is musical and happy and fills my soul with all the love I have for her. "That's a yes, Colon."

"Wait...did you just call me...

Violet

The air is crisp this October morning, the leaves on the trees bursting with gorgeous colors of yellows, oranges and reds. I glance around the beach where we have the annual lobster boil, and my heart is full of love as the entire town surrounds Colin and me as we stand before a minister to exchange vows. I haven't known him long, but I've known him long enough to know I want to spend the rest of my life with him, and when he insisted we get married as soon as possible, I agreed.

At first I was hesitant, though. I didn't want to do this without his parents. Family is important to both of us, and while his mother and I didn't get off on the right foot—neither did Colin and I—I held out hope that she'd come to her eldest son's wedding. I let my gaze roam over my soon to be husband, dressed in a suit, looking as handsome as ever. I opted for a gorgeous ball gown, despite the fact that we're on a beach, and while we're both looking our best, we're both standing in the sand with bare feet. It makes me smile.

When I met Colin, I could never imagine him running barefoot at a beach, and while he's changed, I've changed too.

First, I'm actually in a fancy dress. Secondly and more seri-ously, I've learned to trust, and to lean on him and believe in my heart he's here for the good times and the bad. He's not about to run away from the sleepy town we both call home. The townsfolk have accepted him into our town and family and I'm pretty sure Clara has finally talked him into Sunday bingo.

I face the crowd and fight off the tears. I don't want to ruin my makeup on this special day. Nate, Colin's brother grins at me. I'm so glad he came to stand as Colin's best man, and he's as funny and reckless as Colin mentioned. One of these days though, he'll find the right woman, despite what he claims, and I'm looking forward to seeing him fall head over heels. You just watch, one of these days he'll be out and about—yes, Colin was right. When we Canadians say it, it really does sound like oat and a-boat—and he'll for sure meet the right woman and think he's been run over by a Zamboni.

The minister opens his book, and I hand my flowers to Emily, my matron of honor. My heart is so full, marrying my best friend here on the beach. It's funny, his mother told me he wanted a big wedding in the basilica. It wasn't what he wanted at all, which is why we're here on this beach, one of the spots where we fell deeper in love.

Honestly, how could I not fall for a man like Colin? And I still can't believe he saved the park. We decided to update it and keep it running. Even if the new attractions don't bring in a crowd, it will bring in the regulars who hold memories close to their hearts. It will also be a great spot for the influx of new students to unwind and play, a great place for them to work and learn about real life, commerce, and running a business.

I'm excited, to say the least and now the townsfolk don't want to oust me or leave Colin to perish in a corn maze. His grandfather was quite happy with how things worked out. After Colin told him he could no longer have the park land, but came up with a stellar solution, he was quite pleased and liked the idea of the students gaining real life experiences. Colin also plans to keep his job and will travel back across the pond when he's needed. I plan to take a trip with him, but for our honeymoon, we're going to Paris. I love it when everyone wins.

The minister speaks and we all turn to him. The crowd goes quiet as Colin and I exchange vows. It's all I can do to get the words past the lump in my throat, but even if I falter, Colin is by my side giving me strength, comfort and love. Once the rings have been exchanged, the minister glances out at the crowd, a cheeky grin on his face.

"Does anyone here have any objections to this union? Speak now or forever hold your peace."

"I object."

The voice sends shockwaves through the crowd, as well as my body. Colin and I both spin and the second I set eyes on his mother, standing there objecting to our marriage, blood drains to my toes, and Colin puts his arm around me before I faceplant and eat a bucket of sand.

"Ohmigod," Emily whispers and shuffles a bit closer to me, to give me her support.

"Mum, what are you doing?" Colin mumbles through clenched teeth.

His mother comes closer, and murmurs go through the crowd. I lean into him, absorb his heat and support, hardly able to believe this is happening. Hating me is one thing, but showing up to stop her son's wedding, that's insane. And you know what? Enough is enough. Colin has been a great son, and I'm a good person who always tries to do the right thing. What is going on here is not right, and I'm not going to stand for it.

His mother stops and turns her attention to me. "Violet."

"Yes," I say, squaring my shoulders, and letting Colin know I've got this.

"You can't marry my son."

"Mum," Colin says, and Nate makes a move to intervene, but I hold my hand up to stop him. God love him for wanting to support us, though.

"Why can't I?" I ask. "I love him and he loves me. I am going to spend the rest of my life making him happy. What more could you want for your son or in a daughter-in-law?"

She exhales and her shoulders sag slightly, her demeanor softening. "I want her to wear this." She takes her ring off her finger and holds it out to me. The second I realize what's happening, tears flood my eyes.

I look at the glistening diamond, the afternoon sun glinting off it and nearly blinding me. I don't think I've ever seen such a gorgeous ring. "You...want me to wear your ring?"

"You can't marry my son without a proper ring that comes from the family. It's tradition."

"Mrs. Parker," I murmur, my voice as shaky as my body.

She looks a bit sheepish when she says, "Please, call me Isabella."

"Isabella..."

"It would mean the world to me, and Colin's father." She steps up to me, wraps her arms around my shoulders. I hug her back and in a soft, pleading voice, she whispers, "Please forgive me."

"I forgive you and I'm honored to wear this. Thank you."

"I see how happy you make my son, and in the end, that is all that matters." I lift my head and spot a man who can only be Colin's father smiling at me. We've yet to meet and I'm so looking forward to us being close.

She lets me go, and turns to Colin. "Thank you, Mum." She hands the ring to Colin and he puts it on my finger. It's a perfect fit, but I might need a wheelbarrow to carry it around.

"There will be grandkids, correct?"

We both laugh. "Yes, of course," I tell her and give her hand a squeeze. "We want a ton of kids and we want you to be a big part of their life."

"Very well," she says, with an efficient clap of her hands that reminds me of Clara. "Let's get on with it."

My heart overflows with love as Colin takes my hands in his. I have never been happier, but I know come tomorrow, I'll be happier than today.

The minister clears his throat to get things moving along again. "I now pronounce you husband and wife. You may kiss the bride."

Colin leans in to kiss me, and before his lips meet mine, something tickles my bare feet.

"Want to get lucky?" I say.

Lips inches from mine, he grins. "More than anything."

"Meow."

"Bollocks," Colin curses.

"Cock blocked by a bald pussy," Nate screams out, and while the crowd gasps Emily chuckles beside me.

I meet her gaze. "Sorry, not sorry."

I shake my head at her. Honest to God, my life is filled with the craziest of people and I wouldn't want it any other way.

Colin bends to scoop up Lucky and the movement is much easier for him now—you know, because he no longer has a stick wedged in his arse. Lucky purrs and rubs up against Colin. The two have become quite tight again, after Lucky forgave Colin for leaving, of course. There was a lot of groveling, but now well...it's a true bromance. As I watch them, I realize that while my cat is named Lucky, I'm truly the lucky one here, and that's why I chose a Cinderella ball gown for my wedding. Honestly, how many small time Canadian girls get to spend the rest of their life with their very own prince? I don't know, but what I do know is that we're—and when I say *we're*, I mean Colin—in for one hell of a crazy ride.

***

Thank you so much for reading Violet and Colin's story. I hope you enjoyed it as much as I loved writing it. If you like Romantic Comedy check out Hooked on You and The Burbs and the Bees, and I have a KILT series coming your way. Kilting Around, Kilt Trip and Off Kilt-er.

ALSO BY CATHRYN FOX

Kilt (coming soon)

Kilting Around

Kilt Trip

Off Kilt-er

Scotia Storms

Away Game (Rebels)

Warm Up (Rebels)

Crash Course (Rebels)

Home Advantage (Rebels)

Shut Out (Rebels)

End Zone

Fair Play

Enemy Down

Keeping Score

Trading Up

All In

Blue Bay Crew

Demolished

Leveled

Hammered

Single Dad

Single Dad Next Door

Single Dad on Tap

Single Dad Burning Up

Players on Ice

The Playmaker

The Stick Handler

The Body Checker

The Hard Hitter

The Risk Taker

The Wing Man

The Puck Charmer

The Troublemaker

The Rule Breaker

The Rookie

The Sweet Talker

The Heart Breaker

In the Line of Duty

His Obsession Next Door

His Strings to Pull

His Trouble in Talulah

His Taste of Temptation

His Moment to Steal

His Best Friend's Girl

His Reason to Stay

Confessions

Confessions of a Bad Boy Professor

Confessions of a Bad Boy Officer

Confessions of a Bad Boy Fighter

Confessions of a Bad Boy Doctor

Confessions of a Bad Boy Gamer

Confessions of a Bad Boy Millionaire

Confessions of a Bad Boy Santa

Confessions of a Bad Boy CEO

Hands On

Hands On

Body Contact

Full Exposure

Dossier

Private Reserve

House Rules

Under Pressure

Big Catch

Brazilian Fantasy

Improper Proposal

Boys of Beachville

Good at Being Bad

Igniting the Bad Boy

Bad Girl Therapy

Stone Cliff Series:

Crashing Down

Wasted Summer

Love Lessons

Wrapped Up

Eternal Pleasure Series
Instinctive
Impulsive
Indulgent

Sun Stroked Series
Seaside Seduction
Deep Desire
Private Pleasure

Captured and Claimed Series:
Yours to Take
Yours to Teach
Yours to Keep

Firefighter Heat Series
Fever
Siren
Flash Fire

Playing For Keeps Series
Slow Ride
Wild Ride
Sweet Ride

Breaking the Rules:
Hold Me Down Hard
Pin Me Up Proper
Tie Me Down Tight

Stand Alone Title:

Crazy Apologetic Canadians

Hands on with the CEO

Torn Between Two Brothers

Holiday Spirit

Unleashed

Knocking on Demon's Door

Web of Desire

New York Times and *USA today* Bestselling author, Cathryn is a wife, mom, sister, daughter, and friend. She loves dogs, sunny weather, anything chocolate (she never says no to a brownie) pizza and red wine. She has two teenagers who keep her busy with their never ending activities, and a husband who is convinced he can turn her into a mixed martial arts fan. Cathryn can never find balance in her life, is always trying to find time to go to the gym, can never keep up with emails, Facebook or Twitter and tries to write page-turning books that her readers will love.

Connect with Cathryn:

Tik Tok: @cathrynfoxwriter
Newsletter https://app.mailerlite.com/webforms/landing/c1f8n1
Twitter: https://twitter.com/writercatfox
Facebook: https://www.facebook.com/AuthorCathrynFox?ref=hl

Blog: http://cathrynfox.com/blog/
Goodreads: https://www.goodreads.com/author/show/91799.
Cathryn_Fox
Pinterest http://www.pinterest.com/catkalen/